# The Film Explainer

'A half glum, half funny story about the author's grandfather, an energetic crosspatch who starred as the man who pointed his stick at silent films and told the audience what to think . . . a curious evocation of a tense time, written in an introspective key that reveals the author's love of Kafka and Gogol . . . a ruminative description, told through the innocent yet knowing eyes of a child . . . Brilliant . . . magically evocative, yet determinedly unsentimental'

*Independent*

'In his translation of this child's-eye view of a flawed, exasperating patriarch, the son has captured perfectly the sardonic economy of his father's prose, the malign comedy of his troubled, troubling vision'

*The Times*

'An expertly written book, ironic as to its own irony.'
Penelope Fitzgerald
*London Review of Books*

## About the author

Gert Hofmann was born in Limbach/Saxony in 1931, and died in Erding, near Munich, in 1993. For many years he made a living lecturing on German literature at universities in Europe and America, and didn't become a writer fulltime until 1979, when his first prose work was published (having been, however, a prolific author of radio plays). Thereafter, he put out a book a year for the rest of his life. He is one of the very few German writers of his generation to have and deserve an international reputation. *The Film Explainer* is his sixth book to appear in English.

## About the translator

His son Michael Hofmann was born in Freiburg in 1957, went to Cambridge, and lives in London as a poet and translator. His 1986 volume *Acrimony* is in part a passionate and critical confrontation with his father.

# Gert Hofmann

# The Film Explainer

Translated from the German by

Michael Hofmann

Minerva

In memoriam Karl Hofmann, 1873–1944,
film explainer

The translator would like to thank
John Gillett and Eva Hofmann
for sharing their particular expertise.

**A Minerva Paperback**
THE FILM EXPLAINER

First published in Great Britain in 1995
by Martin Secker & Warburg Limited,
This Minerva edition published 1996
by Mandarin Paperbacks
an imprint of Reed International Books Ltd,
Michelin House, 81 Fulham Road, London SW3 6RB
and Auckland, Melbourne, Singapore and Toronto

A CIP catalogue record for this title
is available from the British Library
ISBN 0 7493 9640 7

Typeset by Deltatype Ltd, Ellesmere Port, Cheshire
Printed and bound in Great Britain
by Cox & Wyman Ltd, Reading, Berkshire

# One

My grandfather Karl Hofmann (1873–1944) worked for many years in the Apollo cinema on the Helenenstrasse in Limbach/ Saxony. I knew him towards the end of his life, with his artist's hat, his walking stick, his broad gold wedding ring that from time to time would go into pawn in Chemnitz but always came back safely. It was he who gave me the idea – long after he was dead – of walking with a stick. He had trouble with his teeth and used to say: These gnashers will be the death of me one day, if I ever die. In the end, though, it was something quite different, not that at all.

My grandfather was the film explainer and piano player in Limbach. They still had those, back then. A lot of them came from the fairgrounds, from the 'apish origins of art' (Grandfather). You could see that from the way they dressed. In the cinema they wore red or blue tailcoats with gold or silver buttons, a white bow tie, white trousers, sometimes top-boots. Others would wear smoking jackets.

Watch out, don't nod off, here comes a wonderful sequence, maybe the most wonderful in the whole film, cried Grandfather, reaching for his pointer. He liked to wave that around a lot. Straightaway, the handful of people in the audience were silent. You could, said Grandfather, have heard a mouse ... well, whatever it is a mouse does. The sighing and snoring all but stopped. I was tiny. I leaned back in my seat. I took it all in.

1

That's right, said Grandfather, I used to be a lion tamer, when he told us occasionally about his 'previous existence'. Only difference was that he now held a bamboo cane in his hand instead of a whip. It was part of the uniform he had to wear, his explainer's uniform, just as there was an infantry uniform for the infantryman, and a cavalry uniform for the cavalryman.

So you had . . .

My explainer's uniform, said Grandfather.

It's possible – to the memory, all things are possible! – that Grandfather explained a film better in that get-up than he would have done in an ordinary jacket and trousers. According to him, he did. The minute he was in his little tailcoat, the sentences started to come. He took more risks: more forceful expressions, more subclauses, outlandish comparisons, more surprising turns of phrase and imagery. Also, 'in uniform' his sentences were longer. What times! Which I suppose I must have lived through – and how! –though not much of them remains.

And down there, you must imagine it, said Grandfather, stick in hand. He used it to point at the world. First he stamped his foot on the floor to gain my attention. He pointed into the empty cinema and said: There in the darkness sits the audience, that's the place for it. It's staring at me out of that darkness. And what bit of me? Well, he said, my mouth, of course, my teeth. But that's not what I want. I want it to look at my uniform. If its eyes are on my uniform, it will have more faith in me.

That gave Grandfather more time to come up with sentences. 'Because each one of them has to be made up by me, they don't just grow on trees, you know'. The style of the other film explainers, even in big cities, was pompous, their articulation was flaccid, the connections between the images on the screen – and how they used to flicker! – and their words were often baffling to the audience. And they mispronounce long words, said Grand-father. They are either too prompt with their explanations –

before the picture – or too slow – after it's gone – so that between what you see and what you hear ... you can't find the connection. After half an hour the atmosphere is unbreathable. Indeed, said Grandfather, looking at me earnestly, there have been cases of suffocation.

You mean, people actually died?

They died.

And what do you do then?

I wait till no one's looking, then I carry the bodies out.

Aren't they too heavy?

I pull them by the feet, Grandfather said imperturbably.

You mustn't tell the boy such stuff, said Grandmother. He can't sleep afterwards.

He's giving the boy an education in horror, said Mother. No wonder he wakes up bathed in sweat.

A lot of sweating went on in the Apollo too. Other people, the elderly in particular, preferred to sleep. They would wake up during chase and murder sequences. Then they would snort back into life. And all the time that 'pernicious smoking which shouldn't be allowed' (Mother). When the smoke got to be too much for Grandfather he would hang up a sign 'No smoking – Danger to life!' Then he would go on smoking on his own. When his throat was dry, he reached for the beer bottle with the stone cap which he would keep next to the chest he sometimes mounted for narrating. It was easier to see him up there. The air! And the heat! Sometimes colleagues came. They wore tall hats and had earrings. They didn't stay with the cinema long. With the coming of Hitler and the sound-film, they slipped quietly back to the circus. Grandfather remained.

His description at this time: His sated appearance, after lunch, his black Sunday tails, tie and tie-pin, brushcut hair, as he strolled through Limbach. Now with a foaming beer glass and in the same hand – how did he do it! – a 'cigar with a cummerbund'. When the photographer Wilhelm had finished, Grandfather lit up and said: That's all right, isn't it? And he started on the beer too. Behind him on the wall, photographs of the actresses of his middle years: Pola Negri as *Carmen*, Henny Porten as *Luise Rohrbach*, Asta Nielsen as *Marie of the Streets*, Theda Bara as *Carmen* as well, but quite different from Negri. Grandfather is supposed to have said to Grandmother once: Without the cinema I would find life unendurable!

That's my impression too, Grandmother replied.

His absolute favourite was Asta Nielsen, for reasons he didn't want to divulge.

Those reasons, Grandmother said, are her small but shapely breasts.

Her slender neck stretching 'like a swan's, up to the stars', she was at the centre of his photographs. They made a kind of second frame around her, where she hung 'at the level of his man's heart, that's where he put her' (Grandmother). Grandfather, in his own photograph, was careful not to stand in front of Asta Nielsen's. You could see them both. By the way he held his head you could tell he was aware of her behind him.

Often he sat in his smoker's chair and talked about his life. I sat on a stool at his feet. So that you'll know in time to come, who I was, and will be able to tell people about me, and nothing will be lost, he said. Nineteen-ten was an important year for him, that was when the Apollo Cinematograph came to Limbach, with its twenty-three seats and standing-places, 'till the walls bulged'. With their cloth caps on their heads, hands buried in their pockets, the people of Limbach milled nosily round the door of the cinema 'and no one dared to go inside'. No one had ever been to a cinema. They kicked their heels for a while and then the cinema – the den of vice, Mother said – swallowed them up. After a while they emerged from it, and went to the war. After the war – Grandfather had been sent home half dead, 'he couldn't march

4

as fast as they wanted him to' (Grandmother) – with nothing else in prospect, he had 'slipped back into the Apollo'. (He never said he *worked* there, because Grandmother would laugh.) At first he had only helped out there, and 'earned a few pfennigs or, later, billions, pin money'. The rest 'his womenfolk' had had to magic up.

The box-seat was already there. During the performances, he said, I would keep leaping to my feet with my stick in my hand. When I was really excited by a scene, I stood up on my box-seat –an old tea chest from Ceylon – and stared at the audience.

In what way?

Severely, said Grandfather. Because he smoked such a lot, he had brown fingertips and bad eyesight. 'He only sees what he wants to see' (Grandmother). For a long time he was too vain to wear glasses. But he had a pair. He called for more quiet from the audience. I was unimaginably small – isn't he tiny, and getting tinier by the day, Grandfather would often exclaim – squatting on my fingertips in the front row, because there he could keep an eye on me. Here I saw my first film, *Secrets of a Soul* (1926, with Werner Krauss and Ruth Weyher). That's about a man who is obsessed with the idea of murdering his wife. Sometimes he wakes up in the morning, thinking he has already done the deed. But he hasn't, and it's just a dream. Then a good friend of his, who happens to be a famous doctor, cures him of his obsession. He even finds happiness with his wife, because suddenly she gets a baby. For *Secrets of a Soul*, Grandfather wore his explainer's uniform. He had his beer bottle beside him. He never took his eyes off the screen except to see if I was still there. Then he went on speaking. No one would have understood the film without him. Next to him, in case of fire, stood a full bucket of water. Sometimes, because he had so many things on his mind while narrating, he would knock it over. Then we were all deluged. He cried: Oh my giddy aunt!, and: Now for a little music! Before that, he got the woman in from next door, who always wiped the floor. Everyone pulled their feet up. Grandfather played *Cavalleria Rusticana*. People talked and smoked. Then on with the film.

Grandfather's shadow when he lifted his head and looked into a cinematic sky! The air thick with smoke! The pattering of the rain outside, behind the words 'Emergency Exit'! Often I fell asleep. But also, my consternation on seeing the artificial man Golem and listening to his story as told by Grandfather. (*The Golem*, 1914, with Paul Wegener, Lyda Salmonova and Adolf Steinrück, also *The Birth of the Golem*, 1920, with the same cast with the addition of Otto Gebühr). After the film he grasped my hand. We staggered out into the street. Night had fallen. We could barely find the way home. Grandfather shook his head: That such a thing should be!

I asked: Isn't there such a thing?

Oh yes, he said, but it's very rare!

If only there'd been a bigger audience to see it!

It's not worth Herr Theilhaber's while any more, said Mother when Grandfather came home once after narrating in the Apollo, he'll close it soon. We had a bite to eat. The women, health-conscious, ate a sandwich with curd cheese, I had a sandwich with liverwurst. Then Mother suddenly thought of all the many people of Limbach and Oberfrohna, who, instead of going to the Apollo, sat around at home all the time. And had thereby missed seeing and hearing Grandfather, and had missed out on an unforgettable experience. Who could say how much longer it would go on! Herr Theilhaber too, who sometimes minded the till, was surely discouraged by the tiny audiences.

The financial strain on him is unbearable, Grandfather said to his womenfolk. We all nodded. Herr Theilhaber had gone so far as to hint at shutting down the Apollo. Then what?

The best thing in such a case, said Grandfather, is not even think about it!

In the afternoon, to collect himself for the evening performance, Grandfather walked round and round the Apollo for hours. That way Herr Theilhaber, should he come early, couldn't help seeing what a punctual fellow he was. Grandfather could thus be of assistance to Herr Theilhaber in the afternoon as well. Let him see with his own eyes how indispensable Grandfather was to the enterprise. Sometimes Grandfather took me with him. I was in short socks, or long woollen stockings in wintertime. If Herr Theilhaber had entrusted him with the key to the cinema, we could have gone in even sooner, 'and seen the cinema in a state of nature'. (Shortly Herr Theilhaber would indeed give Grandfather a key, only we weren't to know that yet.) But it was beautiful outside the Apollo as well, especially the fresh breeze if there happened to be one. Grandfather would hold his artist's hat in his hands, to keep it from blowing away. His hair, what was left of it, would be blown about. And Grandfather would collect himself. He did this best when plenty of people greeted him. When he walked with me through Limbach and no one greeted him, he felt he might as well be dead. He liked to be greeted first on one side of the street, then on the other. He would smoke a cigar end, if he happened to have one on him. He had to hold it at arm's length away from me, 'or else the smoke from it will exterminate the poor little shrimp' (Grandmother). Grandfather didn't talk much, because now he had to think. He thought about the evening performance and his forthcoming appearance at it, six times a week. The programme was changed frequently, sometimes as often as three times a week. As he walked, Grandfather would talk to himself. He would say: Now, what about the great Heinrich George! How shall I introduce him? Or: Shall I tell them at this point that she loves him, or shall I keep it till later? Sometimes he would ponder in general terms, 'how to present the material, and see that the art gets to its destination'.

It's really no cakewalk among these philistines, he said, but I'll do it, I'll do it!

Usually Grandfather got Salzmann the projectionist to run through the film once in advance, so that he knew 'what he was in for'. Herr Salzmann was usually not there when we arrived. 'The fellow's taking his time!' We took another turn round the Apollo. 'He'll be here any minute!' But Herr Salzmann habitually turned up only at the last moment. He walked up and down. I had to keep my trap shut because, before telling the film to other people, Grandfather had to tell it to himself first. He had written down a few words he wanted to use on a piece of paper. He would put it away carefully, and then forget where he had put it. Or he couldn't remember in what context he was going to use the words he'd jotted down, were they for the film starring Emil Jannings, or the one with Greta Garbo? Grandfather held me by the hand. And so the afternoon went by.

There, exclaimed Grandfather, see?

What?

In the sky! It's almost gone now!

What?

The afternoon, he said. It left Grandfather's silhouette against the display case, when he 'studied the film posters as though he meant to learn them by heart'. His Italian looks, squat build, the hooked unGerman nose, the moustache he kept twiddling as though 'that would make it longer'.

And so it does, he said.

His frequent exclamation, emphasised by a jab with the walking stick: Why those Limbach people can't get along with me! And as far as I'm concerned, it's mutual! We don't belong here!

What about me?

You don't either.

So? Where do we belong?

In another world which has still to be created, said Grandfather.

And so where is it, asked his friend Cosimo.

And Grandfather, pointing to the distant horizon: There, over there somewhere!

After the Saturday evening showing, when he had turned off the cinema lights and after a swallow of beer gone home on his own, he was 'knackered, eyes, head, feet, the lot.' Even his hands would be shaking. Once, when we were all asleep, Grandfather is said to have removed Grandmother's roast from the oven and 'out of sheer greed polished the whole thing off with a crust of bread, the ungovernable man' (Grandmother). Her outrage when in the light of day she went to the oven and saw the 'pathetic remnants'! Was that her Sunday roast? The man should be ashamed of himself! Now Grandmother had to go knocking on butcher Hilsebein's back door – 'Hilsersch's' – and ask him to let her have something 'on tick', so that we'd have a bit of meat to put on the table for Sunday.

After Sunday lunch – stuffed cabbage or potato and gherkins – he took off his jacket and put his feet up for an hour or so. He took his shoes off as well. Unfortunately, the sofa was so short that even he, relatively small of stature – 'small, but what a handful!' (Grandmother) – was unable to stretch out his legs on it, 'Of course with the most horrendous consquences for my circulation'. Or he would get the cramp in his calf that he was always waiting for. With difficulty he would get up and hobble about a bit. He would have to be careful not to fall down and break something. 'He has such brittle bones' (Grandmother).

After that, too restless to remain on his sofa long, Grandfather would go with Herr Cosimo and me up to the Hoher Hain. We were a male trio, though we didn't burst into song. Such were our Sunday afternoons, 'as God decreed them'. Grandfather would talk a lot. Sometimes he would take off his artist's hat, at others

9

merely push it back off his brow. Sometimes he would pull out his handkerchief and roll it up tight. 'A sausage!' he said to me, and wiped his brow with it. Then he would look closely at the handkerchief, shake his head and say: How I'm sweating! Wonder what that's to do with! Not a good sign, I'm sure! Then he would talk about his unfulfilled hopes and desires 'so that at least you'll have heard about them, and when the time comes you'll be able to pass on to your children the kind of man I was'. To emigrate to America, oh, to emigrate to America, or further still, and finally leave all this behind! In life so much accumulates that you'd like to leave behind. Isn't that so, Cosimo?

Yes indeed, said Herr Cosimo, in my life as well!

Unfortunately Grandfather had missed the moment when he might have slipped everything off and emigrated. Now, 'wherever he looked, he saw moss and grasses sprouting on him'. And he wanted so much to have changed once more! For instance, he would have liked to 'put on a bit more height, even just a couple of inches!' He claimed: I used to be taller! After my own birth in 1931 and the disappearance of my natural – or as Grandfather said: unnatural – father 'to Berlin with the other criminals', his rage that someone had 'tricked' his daughter and 'got something from her without paying for it' had caused him to shrink further. 'I never used to be as small as this!' Also, he craved better teeth with which to chew his bacon, more hair to comb and some more reliable equipment to stick into Grandmother and Fräulein Fritsche who lived by the sewage works.

What sort of equipment, I asked.

The kind that some men have, said Grandfather. If you are a good boy, you might get some like that one day.

The rumour went around Limbach that 'since time immemorial, no, even longer than that' Grandfather had had a 'more than platonic' relationship with a young woman twenty-five years younger than himself. Sometimes, when Grandmother was still sleeping the sleep of the just, he would go round and visit her 'in her little house and in her little bed' (Grandmother). Nights too, it was said, they had assignations in the Amselgrund and the Hoher Hain.

Even in winter you were seen holding hands with her, said Grandmother, you should be ashamed of yourself!

Grandfather merely shook his head and said: That, like so much else, is purely a figment of your imagination.

When we went for our walks, Herr Cosimo would be half a pace behind Grandfather as a sign of his own lesser importance. When they both spoke out at once, Herr Cosimo said: No, after you, Hofmann! and let Grandfather have his say first. In return, Grandfather allowed Herr Cosimo to cross the rickety wooden bridge first, to see whether it would hold. When it did hold, and Herr Cosimo was on the other side, he set foot on it himself. I went last. On the other side, Herr Cosimo walked more slowly and talked about himself. First of all, he said, everyone wants to know why I haven't starved to death yet. I live, he said, off welfare, I'm a pensioner on Father State. That didn't bother Herr Cosimo, though. He knew that in his case welfare money was well invested. I can't lose dignity through scrounging off the state, I've been undignified for decades, said Herr Cosimo, and he quoted: Whoever works and doesn't shirk must be berserk!

The man should be ashamed of himself, said Mother, and moved across to the bread cupboard, because that was where she could best think about our supper. Once again she didn't know what she was going to give us. How could Grandfather always go out for walks with such a specimen! Well, she said, I'm not surprised!

What are we having for supper, I asked.

God will provide, said Mother.

Salad of rats' tails, then?

Garnished with mouse teeth!

Herr Cosimo didn't have an artist's hat. He wore a cloth cap. He claimed to be descended from knackers. A long line of them, he said. But that, like most of what he says, is made up, said Grandfather, I don't believe him at any rate. They had also served as hangmen. From them he had learned that it was always the wrong ones who got it in the neck.

And then, I asked.

The three of us, 'Three Musketeers – "Musky Tears", you used to say,' said Grandfather, tramped through woods and fields. The weather was always fine. Sometimes I wore Grandfather's artist's hat, sometimes I carried his stick. Then it would happen. Grandfather would suddenly become restless. His breathing grew louder. Sometimes there was something in his throat, or he said there was. Then he would take a deep breath and squeeze, there was something to get out. He slowed down, stopped, pulled a notebook from his jacket pocket and wrote something in it.

There, he said, that was it!

And now? I asked.

Much better.

Then he put his notebook back in his jacket pocket. Herr Cosimo nodded and said: Yes, that's the way it's done! Something new there, eh Hofmann? Well, let's hope it was worth the wait! I'll keep my fingers crossed anyway! That's the most we mortals can do. Ah, the work, the work! No one knew whether Herr Cosimo was being serious or not. When Grandfather had recomposed himself and I asked him: What did you write just then? he replied: Sentences! or: Word-salad. Now, he said, I just add salt and pepper, a little oil and vinegar and give it a good stir!

And then?

Then it's sit down and tuck in.

And when I asked: What kind of sentences are we having

today? he replied: The ones that were just going through my head. Maybe they'll come in handy one day.

For what?

For a poem.

And a poem? What's that good for?

That's enough, cried Grandfather, if you don't know what a poem's good for, I can't talk to you. He at any rate had to have poems. Herr Cosimo was no poet. That's all I need, he cried and shuddered. But he did have some rope in his pocket that someone had been hanged with. Or at any rate Herr Cosimo sometimes pulled out a bit and said: This is the rope that hanged—. It was a while ago. Even when we were talking about something completely different, he would suddenly produce the rope and hold it under my nose. He said: There, feel that! and I had to feel the rope. Then I had to smell it too, but it just smelled of rope. When we were home again, Grandfather would beckon me over to him: What are you going to do now? he asked.

Now I'm going to wash my hands.

Why?

Because I've touched the rope.

Go and wash them then, said Grandfather, and use soap!

Anyway, said Herr Cosimo on our walk, this is the rope that hanged a man of my acquaintance.

You knew him, I asked.

Very well!

And he was hanged with this rope?

Till he was well and truly dead.

Herr Cosimo knew a great many people. Many of them were now emigrating. In the morning, I would get out of my bed, and another dozen would have gone. Who would be left for Grandfather and Herr Cosimo to talk about, if that trend continued?

From our 'walks and talks' Grandfather knew Herr Cosimo's

life as well as his own, just as Herr Cosimo knew Grandfather's life inside out, 'warts and all or not'. Generally they talked about films they had both seen or that one of them hadn't. Of their two wives, only one was alive, and only Grandfather knew her at all well. Herr Cosimo was 'not her cup of tea', but he always sent her his regards anyway. As conversational partners Grandfather and Herr Cosimo were attuned to one another. If one of them was stuck for a word, the other would supply it. They would both stop and rack their brains for the missing word. One of them would look for it up in the sky, the other lower down. They always managed to come up with something. Then they would cry: Yes, that's it! and congratulate one another. If ever anything should happen to one of them, and he lost his memory or his speech, the other would surely leap in and help him out. And say what had happened or been said in such and such a year in Limbach/Saxony. Everyone said how well suited they were, and how well they complemented one another.

I just wish he would wash a little more often, said Grandmother.

Are you saying he doesn't wash, asked Grandfather.

I am indeed!

You could be right, he said pensively, he probably doesn't wash very often.

In step, their well-worn elbows rubbing against each other, we walked through the Hoher Hain. Everywhere the birds were singing. After a good half hour we emerged on the other side.

Where now, asked Grandfather, stopping.

Now, said Herr Cosimo, we have no option but to retrace our steps. Unless we are to go on and on for ever, and gradually become lost to the world.

No, I cried, I want to go home!

On the way home, more talk, more talk! At first about unsolved crimes, mysterious natural phenomena, the possibility of changing the world, unemployment. There were now two thousand in Limbach alone, Herr Cosimo had counted them. Then about Herr Cosimo's heart, which was no longer in the best condition. Then about the hearts of Grandfather and Grandmother, how long till they pegged out. Grandfather's would go on for ever, Grandmother's probably not quite as long, she got cross about so many things. And then my own little heart, which would surely go on for ever too. Grandfather's friendship – 'I put the word in quotations marks, even as I speak, because there is no such thing!' – with the knacker was so close, because in his youth Grandfather had once worked in the circus, and had known many people like him. The circus was called the Orfeo. In that circus Grandfather had appeared in a uniform, first to announce the individual acts. Later on he had led the artistes into the arena by the hand, and introduced them to the public. He had also been stable lad, odd-job man, ticket seller and nightwatchman. When he announced the acts, he stood between the director and the clown, they had the whole of the circus in front of them. Grandfather took so much pleasure from it that instead of sticking to his task, he sometimes tried to add little stories 'and other little extras' (Grandmother). 'His imagination ran away with him.' In the process, he made the show unnecessarily long, and had to be replaced.

The circus is just like life, said Grandfather to Herr Cosimo, sooner or later everything goes wrong and you're replaced.

What goes wrong, I asked.

What you say there, said Herr Cosimo to Grandfather, is a bit obscure, the little chap's right. Still, I will think on it.

The circus was now behind him. Grandfather had travelled the neighbouring countries with it, all except for Switzerland, where he hadn't been admitted.

Enough of that rigmarole, said Herr Cosimo, and we walked on. The sun went down. A wind got up. We were going home.

And now consider a man such as myself, said Grandfather, walking on ahead again. What can such a man do to make life bearable, if he's already tried everything, and nothing has worked?

That's a tough question, almost philosophical, said Herr Cosimo, but I don't know the answer either. Go for more walks?

No!

Let your hair down occasionally? Sniff a few flowers?

A few what, said Grandfather incredulously.

Flowers!

As the son and grandson of knackers, and the scion of a family rooted in nature, Herr Cosimo felt himself powerfully drawn to nature, where he could identify with birds and insects. Not so Grandfather. He had no use for nature. When Herr Cosimo asked: Why not?, he replied: Because it's not sufficiently artificial for me!

Are you sure you mean *artificial* and not *artistic*, asked Herr Cosimo, who was still not on 'Du' terms with Grandfather. He didn't want to be the one to suggest it, but nor did Grandfather. You're not thinking of another word by chance? There are so many.

Not that many, said Grandfather.

Well, said Herr Cosimo, quite a number anyway.

Whatever, said Grandfather, *artificial* is the word I want!

Really?

No question!

Then we walked a bit. Sitting, lying or walking was how Grandfather had his thoughts. He 'pondered'. For instance he was looking for 'another world' beyond the natural world, which bored him. When I jumped out of bed in the morning, he would already be standing by the kitchen window, searching. And in the day, when he made notes on films 'and wasted whole reams of paper' (Grandmother), Grandfather would be searching. He

16

would often stop while walking, put his hands across his eyes, and want to say something. Only he had forgotten quite what, and had to search for it. Then he said: Oh, it was nothing, and we walked on. That indicated that Grandfather hadn't found his second world yet. Even after supper, when he was off to the Apollo and I had to 'hit the hay', he would still be looking. It wasn't that easy. Apart from the one world which we had, there was no other. 'Perhaps we don't even have that one!' Therefore Grandfather was jealous of anyone who had a second world, and was able, for example, to paint it, the way the painter Böcklin (1827–1901) had his *Isle of the Dead*. But Grandfather wasn't able to paint because of his hands, which he had ruined by tanning work. Nor yet was he musical enough to develop his voice. Worse: he had none! He had had to shout too much in his circus days. And as for the bit of piano playing he did . . . . Grandfather had never had a piano of his own. He was never able to practise enough. If only he'd been able to practise more! But instead, he now wrote, sometimes for four hours a day. He wrote 'fantasies, perspectives and inspections for a head and two hands', things like: Happiness and sadness both have a negative side and a positive side, a top and a bottom! (Actually Grandfather had meant to say something else at this point, but had forgotten it while writing. So I just put that down, no one will know the difference!) Or: The only reason we like nature so much is because she can't tell us what she really thinks of us! Or: The cinema has come just in time. If it hadn't come, we would have had to throw ourselves into the Big Pond, hand in hand! His hope was to put these sentences together and make a philosophy out of them. He felt he was only at the beginning. I, at any rate, said Grandfather, when we stood at the door of our flat having brushed off Herr Cosimo, put on my artist's hat every morning and view the future with excitement! In any case, he said, and looked at his fob watch, just two more hours. Then the misery will be over.

17

What misery, I asked.

What misery do you think, he said, life, of course.

And then what?

The Apollo, said Grandfather, what else?

# Two

Grandfather was now in his sixty-third year, and he had a brown beard. The beard was dyed. The children in the street would shout: Good morning, Mr Film explainer! to him. Grandfather would then always act surprised, and say: Well, well! and raise his artist's hat, but only a little bit. If a grown-up greeted him, he raised it a little more, and said: And to you a fine day with no unpleasantnesses! And he held me tightly by the hand. He would have liked everyone to call him 'Mr Film explainer', only it didn't occur to them. He liked to spend his mornings alone. He sat around at home, and sent Grandmother off to our landlord Lange in the Pestalozzistrasse for the latest newspaper. That always meant yesterday's, when Herr Lange had finished with it. Grandmother asked: Do you really have to stick your nose in the newspaper at this ungodly hour? There's nothing but murder and mayhem in it anyway.

Grandfather replied: Yes!

Then Grandmother put on her woolly cardigan, went round the corner with me, knocked on Herr Lange's kitchen window, and said: I'm sorry to trouble you, but would you have yesterday's paper for my Karl? He's so avid.

Herr Lange asked: Can't he come and get it himself?

Not today, I'm afraid, said Grandmother, he had a bad night of it yesterday. There was a feature with Adele Sandrock, so he's having a bit of a rest now.

All right then, said Herr Lange, and handed Grandmother the old newspaper. Grandmother folded it up neatly to make it look like new. Then she said: Thank you very much, Herr Lange! and we went home again. Here's something for you to immerse yourself in, said Grandmother when we arrived, and held out the newspaper to Grandfather. Now he was once more *au courant*, albeit with a day's delay. On Mondays it was two days, and then he had a lot of catching up to do.

After our return from the Hoher Hain, the weather wasn't that good any more. We went out into the yard. A strip of Sunday's sun still lay on our garden. I had quickly got changed. I had on my gardener's apron. I had a spade in my hand, but I didn't feel like playing. The women were talking about Grandfather, who had disappeared into the bedroom. He liked to put his feet up before going 'on the job'.

He's not just an artist without any bread, he's an artist without any art, said Grandmother heartlessly. She meant: An art like his can never come to anything. He had the expressive urge of an artist, but no particular gift. Or, as Grandmother said, so that everyone could understand: It seems something wants to get out of him, but there's nothing inside! If only there was something! But the urge is all there is. Nor, sadly, did Grandfather possess the tenacity and industry of an artist! He was eager to impress. But what with? Do you know, Grandmother asked Mother, while Grandfather had put his feet up next door.

Nobody knows, said Mother, who was topping and tailing beans. She had her apron on. The beans were young and tender. One after another they flew into the enamel cooking pot. Grandmother, sitting by, looked as though she might be counting them. But she wasn't counting them. She said she didn't know what Grandfather wanted to impress everyone with either. Now he was off to the Apollo to see a film.

Can I go, I asked Mother.

No.

Why not?

You're too small still. Grandfather needs quiet for his storytelling.

This is what storytelling meant for him: Finally, finally, a chance to impress, no matter with what, to be heard, finally, finally! In order to be *even better* at telling stories, and make a still deeper impression in the darkness of the Apollo cinema, he worked on expanding his vocabulary. 'There's more I can do.' Hence, work on vocabulary and syntax, with the aid of old newspapers and a school encyclopaedia that later came into my possession. He was forever leafing in that. Now it would be on his bed, now in the lav. 'Day and night he's turning pages' (Grandmother). When we had important visitors, he would sit on the encyclopaedia to make himself appear bigger. The words he wanted to use in the evening in the Apollo he would jot down on pieces of paper in the morning. Grandmother trimmed them for him. Before he set off with me into town, I had to ask him: Did you remember your pieces of paper?

Just a minute, he said, and reached into his pocket. Here they are! he said. Or he exclaimed: Well I never! I almost left them behind! The time that would have cost us! Just as well I've got you. Then he would put them in his jacket pocket and walk them up the Helenenstrasse and then back down again on the other side. He studied them until he had 'inwardly digested' all of them. Sometimes he took the papers up to the Hoher Hain. There we would take a couple of lungfuls of air, and turn back again. His jacket was always full of them, there were some in every pocket. When Grandmother went into the wardrobe to give his jacket a brush, she could only shake her head at so many pieces of paper. 'What does he need that many for, it's only a small cinema!' Grandfather never saw them again.

As a 'master of short-lived impulses' (Grandmother), he was full of plans which came to nothing. Instead, the next plan! He wanted to produce a new type of book and 'have it printed from back to front' (this was around 1936), only he wasn't sure what he wanted to write in it. Or else he wanted to have voice training, 'especially in the lower register'. Or collect butterflies and exhibit them 'in order of beauty' under glass in the museum in Chemnitz.

If I can succeed, he said, in bringing the ten most powerful men in the world to my exhibition, and showing it to them, in good lighting, of course, it will bring us closer to lasting peace.

You see, said Grandmother, he has the drive, but what form should it take?

Grandfather had 'all-round talents, but they're no use for anything'. Unshakeable his conviction that he towered above all other people of Limbach and Chemnitz, because he was 'able to receive more signals'. Not only was he a master of the art of living, like the barber Erblich, he was an artist like the Nobel Laureate Paul Heyse (1830–1914) who lived in a castle outside Munich, and whom Grandfather once almost walked smack into in Schwabing as a young man. He recognised him right away.

Every evening around six – 'Except for Mondays, when we play *Closed*' – Grandfather went to the Apollo. The moment he entered it, he whipped off his artist's hat and said good evening, if there was already someone there. Sometimes he said good evening when there was no one there at all, perhaps someone would come along in a minute. Then he would hang his hat on a nail, 'but not his personality'. He kept his boots on night and day, 'getting them nicely sweated through' (Grandmother). Then he went into the projection room, and hoped there would be a good house tonight. He stood by the door marked 'No Admission' and closed his eyes. That way he could hear better. He pressed one ear to the door, and stood on one leg. Sometimes he put his eye to the keyhole too. He listened long and desperately. Not enough, once again not nearly enough! Once again not a decent audience! So Grandfather preferred to wait a little longer, in case another one or two people might come along. As he was waiting like that, and no one came along, he suddenly looked very small to me. He had made up his face, his lips and his eyebrows, and he had his little tailcoat on. In one hand he held the box he would mount any minute – it smelled strongly of tea – and 'get his mouth moving'. No one could tell that he was already over sixty, at least not in the dark. If he'd been a little taller, it would have been an improvement. Sometimes he would say: Too old, too old! He was punctual at his work. 'I couldn't survive without it.' He took another look through the keyhole with his good eye – 'it's not really good, just better than the other one'. He wanted to see 'the public pouring in'. If he pressed his ear to it, he could hear an immense rushing sound, like the sea. It was because it was so empty.

Funny, said Grandfather to Herr Salzmann, I can't see anyone! What about you?

Herr Salzmann, who had younger eyes, said: Six.

Just six, exclaimed Grandfather sadly.

All right, said Herr Salzmann, let's get going then, shall we?

Grandfather cleared his throat and said: The fewer the people, the louder the roaring. Can you hear it?

No, said Herr Salzmann, but I can imagine it.

It was the dimensions and the emptiness and the strange acoustics that produced the roaring in the Apollo. Grandfather put his hands over his ears so as not to hear it. He worried a lot. For instance, that he might lose his voice in the middle of a show. Or that he might be inaudible in the back rows. Grandfather would be standing up by the screen, talking away, and no one would hear him. Sometimes he scratched himself behind the ear and said: Perhaps my hearing is too old? Then he would grab me by the shoulder and, even as Herr Salzmann

23

looked at his watch and shouted: What's the matter now, aren't we going to start today? put me next to the screen. Then, while Grandfather stood at the back, I had to shout something like: I'm standing here shouting, and I wish the film would start soon!

You mustn't be so impatient, said Grandfather, before I begin I have to make sure I can still hear.

But I'm not impatient, I shouted back through the empty Apollo, I like waiting! And then I shouted: I'm still standing here shouting something, and I'm not impatient, but isn't it time to start the film.

Then Grandfather found to his delight that he could hear everything, not a syllable missing. On the contrary, the words grew to fill the whole of the Apollo.

The way it sounds, it's as though the place was full, said Grandfather.

Then in came Herr Lange, whom Herr Theilhaber had to admit for nothing because they'd known each other for so long, Herr Cosimo, and a couple of old cinema biddies. They were allowed in for half price, they didn't have much money. Last of all came Fräulein Fritsche who waved to Grandfather, but only with one finger, no one was supposed to see it. Then Grandfather went to the lav one last time, so he wouldn't have to go during the show. He had a final look around, in case more people might have come. And he asked Herr Salzmann too: Are there any more now?

Hardly.

Well, perhaps there will be more, said Grandfather.

I'll just say that would come as a pleasant surprise, said Herr Salzmann, and Grandfather said: Well, one thing's for sure, it won't be a full house. And he hoped there would be more than eight people at least, bcause then Herr Theilhaber couldn't cancel the show and send everyone home. He didn't like to do that, unlike Herr Salzmann. Herr Salzmann would even send them home when there were seven and they didn't even want to go, he just pushed them out. He didn't need to worry about the box office, he was a regular employee. If there were eight or nine there, and Herr Salzmann couldn't send them home, Grandfather took one last deep breath and said: All right, Salzmann, here we go. Wish me luck.

And how do you like your luck, asked Herr Salzmann, who knew it was easy to put Grandfather's nose out of joint.

Say: Break a leg, said Grandfather.

Herr Salzmann stood beside his projector and said: Break a leg!

Grandfather took a deep breath and entered the auditorium. Then he made his way towards the screen, for now he had to 'earn his crust'. The hall being so empty made it a terribly long way. Some of the time Grandfather looked at the floor, some of the time up in the air. Well, it wasn't completely empty! Herr Lange, Herr Cosimo and Fräulein Fritsche were sitting there waiting for him. Sometimes someone else would wave to him. Of course Grandfather knew them all, if not by name. Those he didn't know by name, he had a nodding acquaintance with. He knew roughly where they lived and whether they had a job or not. Many didn't. And of course everyone knew Grandfather. Now, holding his tea chest in his right hand, he walked – pattered, said Grandmother –with short firm steps down the aisle. With the hand that wasn't holding anything he brushed the backs of the seats. Empty, all of them empty! And what was worse: They wouldn't be filled now either! When Grandfather reached the screen, he had touched each row. Now he felt at home. A flickering appeared on the screen. Let's hope the film doesn't catch fire today! At that moment, Grandfather was always very excited. You couldn't tell though, he kept such control of himself. He put the tea chest down on the floor. Then he turned up the piano stool, because he wanted to be able to reach all the keys with his short arms. 'They can't do without my music! I'll keep them waiting.' He liked to dawdle.

And what if you don't turn up at all one day, I asked.

Why would I do that?

If you're dead?

There'll be no more cinema then.

Grandfather sat down. He began. First his piano. The music he played was beautiful. It was much needed too, because it drowned out the clattering of the projector. Or at least it offered a distraction from it. Also it served to while away the time for the audience in case the film tore again and Herr Salzmann had to patch it up.

Sorry, it needs sticking, he would call down to Grandfather, I'll be ten minutes!

Right you are, Grandfather called back from the piano, I'll hold the fort.

His pointer lay on top of the piano. He didn't need a score, he couldn't read music in any case. Energetically he brushed back his coat tails and flounced onto the stool. He stretched out his arms so that his cuffs shot up to the elbows. Then he began to play – *to tinkle*, Grandmother said. A march, a march first! The Hohenfriedberger or the Imperial or the Radetzky March, so that no one dropped off while the film was being repaired. Grandfather filled the hall, which took about seventy people, to its corners with the march. Then the march went out the door. It turned right, down the Helenenstrasse and came back up the other side. Then the film resumed. Grandfather was a self-taught pianist. Very gifted, but idle, said Grandmother when she talked about him. Grandfather said: Playing the piano isn't hard. In his youth, in the house of a 'rich friend' who had a piano, he had heard a few bars and simply stolen them. Later, in his circus period, on mornings off he went to the caravan of the musical director, who had a little piano, and 'made up melodies'. And lo, he could play the piano! In his early days as cinema narrator – I only witnessed Grandfather in his late days, but of course he had a beginning and a middle as well – he was said to have worn a cast-off wedding coat, which gradually became worn to a shine. Then he wore other tailcoats. They were no more than rags by the time he was finished with them. Because of his 'financial impotence' he was only once able to afford a new set of working clothes. Later still, his artist's sweat soaked into a 'pig-coloured' cardigan. In another, mud-coloured set of tails, he showed *The Hands of Orlac* (1924, with Conrad Veidt and Fritz Kortner).

There goes Orlac crawling along on his belly, cried Grandfather from his chest, note his wonderful pallor! The cause of which, he cried, is the accident he has just had. It was a Sunday afternoon, we had had tripe for lunch. To keep out the light, the cracks in the cinema door were stuffed with old furniture covers from the removal firm of Hartmann which had gone bankrupt. At first I wasn't allowed to see the film on account of the woman's bare breast that flashed up – a seduction scene, tsk, tsk, said Grandmother – but then I was allowed to after all. In this car accident, Grandfather explained, the brilliant virtuoso pianist Orlac (Conrad Veidt) loses both his hands. But a surgeon hurries along, and deftly replaces them with the hands of a freshly executed murderer, said Grandfather, and pointed with his stick at the old severed hands and the freshly attached new ones. And there, the shadows of his old hands, and here, of the new ones! The speed with which they managed to cover the greatest distances on the keyboard! But think of it: A piano virtuoso with the wrong hands! With the hands of a killer! Every single finger is wrong! And such a one is in our midst, only for a long time no one realises it! Only the blackmailer Eusebio (Fritz Kortner) realises, and he tries to blackmail the virtuoso. He persuades him that his new hands want to go on killing, as they have been used to doing. And here – Grandfather gets up, and takes a step back, the better to survey his audience of seven – here already is the murder, that of the rich concert-goer Hermione.

Here she is dancing with Armando the Gigolo, but she's about to be swiftly strangled. Here is the virtuoso Orlac, naturally convinced that he has committed the murder, rushing through the streets at night in his despair. Before that, cries Grandfather, the quick glimpse of breasts! But then the chance arrest of the true murderer, and Orlac's innocence is proved! Orlac never killed the rich Hermione, and even the supposed murderer whose hands he has, was the innocent victim of a miscarriage of justice! The actual murderer was a third party, who can't be shown in the film because he has already done away with himself. So the virtuoso's hands are clean, and that's what in America they call a *happy ending*, Grandfather said more or less. And wiped the sweat from his brow.

After his performance, when Herr Salzmann had switched on the house lights and 'abruptly killed off all the cinema spirits', everyone rushed past us and out 'as though they'd been given a boot up the backside' (Grandfather), whether it was raining or not. Some groaned, some yawned, others sighed with relief. Some went very slowly, they didn't want to go home. Fräulein Fritsche was the last to leave. She blinked at Grandfather. He was still sitting on a seat in the stalls. He had one hand across his brow.

Strange how cold it always feels when Salzmann turns the lights on, and they tear you away from the film, said Grandfather. Do you know what that coldness is?

No.

It's reality, said Grandfather, which we have every reason to fear! And to shiver at too, he said.

When reality came back, Herr Salzmann stood in the projection room, rubbing his eyes. They were very itchy. He looked to see that everything was the way it had been before: the walls, the floor, the air. He had torn open the door to the street, to let in some oxygen. Then he wound *Orlac's Hands* back with his long fingers. You're a dreamer, aren't you, he asked me, am I right?

Yes.

Can you remember what you've just seen?

Yes, he didn't have any hands.

And then?

He gets some new ones.

That's right, said Herr Salzmann. And how he gets his new hands, it's all on this, he said, pointing to his reel. He had his celluloid visor on. He was smoking a cigarette. That was forbidden in the projection room, but he did it anyway. There were more cigarettes in his breast pocket. Sometimes he would offer me one. I said: No thank you! Grandfather, who by now had changed out of his clothes, was standing beside us again. He said nothing at all. He had gone into the 'dark corner' of the room, where he was less visible. In the Apollo, he was often shy once the lights came on. No one told him what a good film he had shown them, and how beautifully he had told it. They were all in a hurry to get home. Easy does it, said Grandfather, allowing himself to be barged aside. He stood by the piano again and held on to the lid. He had the feeling the Apollo was 'full to the rafters', but that was an illusion. The Apollo was quite empty. Grandfather smoothed the strip of green felt over the piano keys. Some of them sounded. The ones that needed repairing didn't. He shut the lid. Now the dust could do its worst! And where to put the bamboo pointer? At first Grandfather stuck it in his jacket pocket, whence it protruded for a long time. Now he could no longer stay in the cinema, but he didn't want to go home either. When he had taken off his make-up, he went up to the coathook. There was his artist's hat. Grandfather stepped up to the blind mirror and put his hat on. He put it on at a slight angle, he looked jauntier that way. The way he felt.

It takes a hat, he said, to make a man feel complete!

You too? I asked.

With me, he said, it's like nailing a pudding to the wall. Come on, he said, let's go home!

29

Then the hall was empty and the 'aroma of the public' had gone – an audience, he said, never stinks, it has a fragrance! We stepped out onto the street. Grandfather was still not himself. What I need now, he said, is air. And time too, to find his way back into the ordinary person he had been before the film. Deeply immersed, up to nose and ears, in the world of Orlac, or, shall we say Dr Caligari (*The Cabinet of Dr Caligari*, 1920, with Werner Krauss), Grandfather took me home groaning and blinking his eyes.

What's the use, he said. Wherever you are transported, in the end all you do is crawl back into your own four walls and collapse on your bed.

The Helenenstrasse was deserted. Only very occasionally did someone come the other way, and tip their hat or cap. Grandfather said: I wish you a fine, happy evening with no unpleasant surprises!

Thank you, Karl, the other said, and the same to you!

The houses had grey fronts and were shrivelled up. Grand-father had to stop frequently for breath. Then, after a few steps, he would yawn. He needed more air than there was. He started going through his jacket pockets. He was looking for his pipe. Surprise, surprise, he found it! Grandfather, hands trembling, quickly filled it and lit it. Impossible to address him now, he would just have replied: What's that? or: What are you burbling on about now? or: Grant me a moment's peace! After every film, before he was once more capable of thought, he needed 'to be reassembled', and you couldn't disturb him during that. I walked at his side, to be sure he didn't suddenly collapse. I waited for him to surface. It could take a while. How I sympathised with Grandfather, who always got so exhausted in the cinema and found so little recognition, and earned so little money!

The screen on which the film took place, for those who were there to see it! It looked different from the first two rows –

'children's seats' – than from further back. Getting into its world was difficult or easy, depending. The screen consisted of eight bedsheets. Fräulein Müller, before she married, had stitched them together one rainy evening in March on her Singer sewing machine. The old screen had disintegrated. It had been too small as well. What Grandfather had wanted to show hadn't fitted on it. In the top right-hand corner, if you looked closely, there was a piece missing. The film had a hole there, where 'reality peeped in' (Grandmother). Reality was a piece of the back wall. Fräulein Müller, sewing the sheets, had made lots of mistakes. Herr Theilhaber, because it was typical of his swanky style, had had gilt doorknobs fitted to make the Apollo look like a theatre. He had put a blood-red curtain in front of the screen. It ran on a rail. When it was drawn, it revealed the screen. Could that skimpy piece of cloth, slightly skew-whiff at the top, really contain so many different places and so many deeps in it? Another show tomorrow.

We sat in our seats in the Apollo. We were waiting for Herr Salzmann. He had just gone out into the yard, he had an evil-smelling cigar in his mouth, and was taking his time about it. He leaned against the 'No Entry' door in his grey twill trousers. It was left ajar to let in the air so that no one was asphyxiated. Herr Salzmann, underneath his beard, was really still quite young. He had his cigar cupped in his hand, now you saw it, now you didn't. Over his forehead he wore his green celluloid visor, so that the flickering lights didn't make him blind. That was a regular occurrence. In Berlin there were dozens of film projectors who hadn't put on their green celluloid visors and who were now all blind as a result. That would never happen to Herr Salzmann. He wore his all the time, even in bed. Safety first! was his watchword.

On that day I was leaning against the wall. Grandfather disappeared. Then he emerged from his cubbyhole, having changed. The cubbyhole was just big enough for him to change his jacket in, but not his trousers. For the trousers, Grandfather had to stand with his belly to the wall, so you couldn't see his front. You could see his behind, but that didn't matter so much. Today we were even earlier than usual. We were impatient for the film. Grandfather had made himself pretty already. Like a true artist he had powdered his face and painted his lips. In his hand he held the bamboo pointer. Herr Salzmann came along. Sleep well? he asked.

Grandfather, who always slept beautifully, incredulously: Me? What makes you think so?

Well, let's get the show on the road then, replied Salzmann. Nothing else for it.

And what are we in for today?

*The Strong Man* (1926, with Harry Langdon and Gertrude Astor) replied Grandfather, who juggled the programme in his head months in advance. In that one, he said, the American soldier Harry in the war in France gets letters from an unknown but obviously beautiful woman as the handwriting tells him. Later Harry is captured by his whiskered enemy Fritz. Later still, the two of them travel about in the world, appearing together in circuses. In America Harry falls in love with the blind daughter of a vicar who lives in a village controlled by a gang of criminals. It's this band that . . . . On one occasion, said Grandfather, he has to fill in for Fritz, who is drunk again, but . . . . Everything comes out right, said Grandfather, he marries the vicar's daughter, she recovers her sight, and . . .

Any saucy bits? asked Salzmann.

No.

Then they talked for a bit about the fire in the Capitol in Halle. Three dead, so Grandfather had heard.

According to my information, it was seven, said Salzmann, and put in the film.

*The Strong Man* is a delight, said Grandfather, and 'kissed his fingertips' (Grandmother). The audience began to arrive. Herr Lange, Herr Cosimo and Fräulein Fritsche nodded to Grandfather, one after the other. He stood there, almost happy.

In the morning, immediately after getting up, we went out onto the balcony in our shirts. You could hear the birds already. Grandfather shielded his eyes because of all the light. His eyelids didn't close properly. The women were brewing malt coffee. The street was empty as always.

If we had a proper balcony, we could see much further, said Grandfather. He had a pot of water in his hand, 'to drown the geraniums'. Grandmother laid out the plates. And the cups. She had a scar on her forehead. I kept asking her to show it to me.

She asked: Have you seen it now? Can I move my head again? The scar came from her 'wild period', when they had 'lived and loved'. Grandfather had thrown a saucepan at her.

You meant to kill me, didn't you, she asked.

Yes, said Grandfather.

But you missed.

Yes, he said.

Her hair was grey at the temples, and kept getting thinner. On account of 'those worries you don't reckon with, and that only come with old age.' Earlier, she used to pin a curl over her scar, now there was no curl to pin any more.

Breakfast anyone, she called.

The sun climbed higher still. It even shone down on the balcony, narrow as it was. Grandfather, in whose eyes it shone, was the first to go inside.

Giving in, he said, is always a sign of strength.

On Sundays, if it wasn't raining, he took me round the block. He wore the same clothes as on weekdays, but ironed. We strolled

33

along the Helenenstrasse. He held my hand. Because we were walking side by side, we had the same thoughts too.

Strange how well they all know him, though his cinema's always empty, said Mother over supper, when he was off in the Apollo again. Even his silhouette.

What's a silhouette, I asked.

Grandfather's silhouette is Grandfather's silhouette, said Herr Lange, who hadn't only come for the rent. He came on account of Mother too. He needed to examine her shoulders. He felt twenty years younger when she was sitting beside him.

Yes, I said, but why does his silhouette matter?

Anyone who's ever seen Grandfather's silhouette against the screen in the Apollo will always remember it, said Mother. When we're all dead and buried and forgotten, there will still be people who will remember his silhouette.

Why?

Because Grandfather is an artist, said Mother, he just needs to discover in what field. Let's hope he does it soon, so he can achieve something, because he hasn't got all that much time left.

And then?

Then he'll shut up shop. But people will still remember the things he says in front of the screen!

What things does he say?

Oh, said Mother, whatever comes into his head. If you're so keen to know, listen to him yourself!

Very well, I thought, and resolved to attend even more closely the next time, but I forgot again. This is what Grandfather now looked like. Still the tails and waistcoat that Grandmother had got him as work clothes at Hagen's Gentlemen's Outfitters, in the Helenenstrasse, reduced to 39 billion marks. Under the waistcoat his little potbelly. In summer he didn't wear the waistcoat, 'otherwise he would drop dead in mid-sentence' (Grandmother). With that the pearl-grey collarless shirt – 'pearl-grey is elegant,

34

and it doesn't show the dirt' – which Grandmother quickly ironed for him with the 'hot stone' in the kitchen. Then he was off 'to the office'. For a long time, he had only one presentable shirt. Every year he'd be given a new one for Christmas, lying among the gingerbread men. Luckily Grandfather had two collars, one of which went well with the shirt, the other less well. But you couldn't see that because it was always so dark in the Apollo. Instead of changing his shirt every day, he often used to change just his collar. Sometimes he changed his shirt for the performance and kept the same collar on, whatever Grandmother decreed. With unimportant things you do what I say, but never with anything else, she said and pushed him over to the window. There she could examine him better. She turned him so she could see, and said: It's high time. This very day (for *The Indian Tomb*, 1921, with Conrad Veidt and Mia May) we're changing your collar! or else it was: No, we'll wait awhile! Today (for *The Honeymoon*, 1928, with Erich von Stroheim) you're not changing! The collar stays! It was secured by a horn button at the front, and there should have been a stud at the back but it was lost one day in May in the Apollo. All summer we hunted for it, even under the seats. But it never appeared. One of those criminals – the casual public – must have picked it up and quietly slunk off with it. Every May Grandfather would remember the collar stud. My God, he would exclaim, how could I have forgotten that! And he would shout through the whole flat: I want to buy a new collar stud today, don't let me forget! Or tomorrow, he said. Then he'd forget it again. From behind, in the darkness of the cinema, Grandfather looked quite ordinary. But once he opened his mouth . . .

Through practice and repetition, he had acquired a store of set phrases in his bristle-haired skull. There got to be more and more of them. New ones kept appearing. One would emerge in our flat, then disappear again, phrases like '*the Führer's birthday*' or '*the*

*Röhm Putsch*'. Now now, said Grandmother, on hearing them, let's not get political! Sometimes Grandfather would tap the side of his head where words and phrases were allegedly located, and say: Here, yes here! At his appearances less and less would come to him. He would fall silent, stare into the audience and say: My, my! or: That was all I wanted to tell you for now. Perhaps more will come to me later! Or else he drove himself on and said: On, on, old man, forward, forward! And he would get up and rock on the balls of his feet.

At about this time Grandfather started getting little red veins on his cheekbones, like crows' feet, because his skin was forced to breathe the poor cinema air, and that made the blood vessels burst. 'Yes, that's how bad things have got with me. My blood has started to explode.' He waited till his womenfolk were out of the house, and went to the medicine cupboard and started digging around. There were plenty of things there that might help. Every two or three days he would alight on some new preparation and try that. But nothing seemed to help against the veins, all he got was diarrhoea.

No, he said to me, none of it can help me, the causes lie deeper.

One Saturday he took me by the hand and we went to the head teacher Herr Ernst Willibald Zauner. He rang the doorbell himself and asked if we could consult his medical encyclopaedia, he promised to be careful turning the pages. Herr Zauner, who for professional reasons sometimes came to the Apollo, gave us the encyclopaedia and took us into the front room. We spent a long time looking for Grandfather's illness. He kept thinking he had found it, but then it turned out not to be the one after all. However much we leafed around in it and left our fingerprints, we simply couldn't find his rash. We said thank you nicely and went home.

Isn't he ugly, Mother asked me when we got home and had had another look at Grandfather's face.

And it's only just beginning, said Grandmother happily.

You mean it'll get worse, I asked.

Much worse, said Grandmother.

Heartless creatures these women are, said Grandfather and retreated to the bedroom. The door slammed shut behind him.

He's going for a lie-down now, said Mother.

Why, I asked.

To reflect on his fate, said Grandmother, and maybe to have a little cry as well.

Every morning now, as soon as I was awake, I went into his bedroom. I didn't even knock any more. Grandfather had two pillows under his head and looked at me. He was already waiting for me. Quickly I turned his head towards the light to look at the broken veins. Sometimes he wouldn't want me to see them, and covered them up with his hands. 'He's embarrassed by his condition' (Grandmother). When he did let me see them, he said: Just quickly! and took his hands away. I examined the 'bloody mess' his veins were making first on one side, then the other. Sometimes I was even allowed to touch them. Finally he would say: Well, what do you think?

I said: They won't go away now.

Grandfather in his vanity tried everything to be rid of the veins. But neither a damp cloth, nor soap and a stiff brush were any use against them. They're there for good, said Grandmother chirpily, not even bothering to look any more. For her, 'Nature had nailed them down'. They were caused either by (1) Grandfather's money worries, or (2) by smoking cigars or (3) poor diet – potatoes, nothing but potatoes! – or (4) his exhausting occupation as cinema narrator and piano player in the sweaty atmosphere, full of people's thoughtless exhalations, of the Apollo. A fifth cause for the veins had slipped Grandfather's mind just for the moment, but it would come to him soon. With so many causes, the little blood vessels had no option but to burst! And that led to the appearance of the 'birds' feet'. Grandfather's hair – 'my crowning glory' – he was losing not over his forehead like the majority of men, but at the back of his head. How long he had been trying to cultivate a bald spot there! For years! Grandmother said. But soon he'll have done it! Yes, she said, a strange fellow he's getting to be, inside and out!

In the Apollo, Grandfather was now no longer speaking just with his 'speaking gear', but with his hands and feet as well. He wants to conduct his words, said Herr Cosimo. He had popped in again and gave us a demonstration. He laughed.

It's not much of a laughing matter any more, said Grandmother, I think it's rather sad.

As Grandfather had already had so many jobs, and not a proper one among them, no one in Limbach knew what it was he actually 'did' or where to 'place' him. And that at his age!

He's a one-off, said Grandmother, and we'd better learn how to live with him. She was still proud of him, she just didn't let it show. The Limbachers, seeing him standing feet apart outside the doors of the Apollo, or beside the screen, for instance in *Joyless Street* (1925, with Asta Nielsen) had learned how to live with him.

There is a bit of the artist about him really, said Mother to me, I just hope you're not going to turn out like that! And I had to swear that I had nothing of the artist in myself, and didn't want to become one either. More something practical, like Erblich the barber, who was an artist as well, but just a hair artist. And who one balmy spring night in his barber's saloon had been seen dancing in the nude with his friend Sybille, with flowers in their hair, two neighbours had witnessed it.

Didn't he have anything on at all, I asked.

No.

What about her?

She didn't either.

Why not?

Because it was so warm, said Mother.

As an artist, Grandfather stood above Herr Erblich, yes, higher than any of us. He could look down on us. And it wasn't just that Grandfather *was* an artist, he also walked like one. Everywhere, even on the road to Mittweida, his artist's walk caught the eye. Farmers in their fields stopped to watch him. With the piano music he devised every evening, he felt his way into the plot, for instance in the Alpine drama, *The Blue Light* (1932, with Leni Riefenstahl and Matthias Wiemann). In that one, Junta is a young girl living in a village in the Dolomites as an outsider. (Grandfather does some girlish trills on the piano.) She (Leni Riefenstahl) is feared by everyone, like the blue light. It always shines when there is a full moon up in the mountains. (Grandfather suggests the blue light in the meantime with a couple of high notes.) The villagers – great confusion in the lower notes – accuse Junta each time a lad falls to his death looking for the blue light. They believe she has bewitched him. One day, the painter Vigo (Matthias Wiemann) – Grandfather suggests his firm, manly strides on the piano – comes to the village in order to paint. He immediately falls in love with her. Then the next man falls to his death. They are on the point of stoning Junta, but she manages to get away and flees up to the mountain to a shepherd boy. (Grandfather climbs into the upper range and performs her flight to the shepherd boy.) Vigo follows her and by the light of the full moon he discovers the secret of the blue light. He finds Junta in a crystal cave which colours and enchants the moonlight, and . . . . In the end, there's an earthquake which kills Junta and Vigo and everyone else.

At the piano Grandfather created the appropriate mood for each scene, be it joy, fear, suspense or horror. He created everything, everything! If someone asked him: How do you do it, Herr Hofmann? he merely tapped his brow and said: It's all in there, you just have to get it out! Herr Theilhaber didn't have to tell him what to play for a particular film, on the contrary it was Grandfather who told Herr Theilhaber what the film required. And him the owner of the cinema! Shame it didn't belong to Grandfather instead! A lot of effects didn't come from the pictures at all. They were evoked by his piano music and his explanations, especially in the dramatic bits. Then the Apollo would go quiet, no more whispering. Grandfather's music would slow down, and finally stop completely. No one so much as rustled a sweet paper. Grandfather stood up. He turned his back to the piano and confronted the audience. That way he could talk more freely. Then he picked up his bamboo pointer. He stood, so as not to get in the way of the film, beside the screen, and started to talk about the scene in question. For instance, with a cracked voice how Anne Boleyn is condemned to death for adultery by her own uncle (in *Anne Boleyn*, 1920, with Henny Porten and Emil Jannings). Or how the daughter of the rich oyster king has another fit of epilepsy and insists on marrying a nobleman (in *The Oyster Princess*, 1919, with Ossi Oswalda and Curt Bois.) Or how in *Tragedy of the Street* (1927, with Asta Nielsen and Oskar Homolka) the ageing prostitute Augusta is on the point of embarking on a new life with the student Felix, and wants to put her savings into a down payment for a sweetshop, but Felix in the meantime has fallen for her younger colleague, Clarissa . . . . Grandfather, with his bamboo stick, showed it on the screen. That way the scene was there twice over: To hear and to look at. When Grandfather spoke, he spoke clearly, but in Saxon dialect. Sometimes an audience made him nervous, especially when there were children who wanted to talk as well. Then Grandfather would shout at them, that was his artistic temperament showing itself. Sometimes, in the darkness, he would suddenly feel afraid, of himself usually. He thought he couldn't go on, that he wouldn't be able to think of what to say next. Then he would call right across the whole cinema to Salzmann: Help me, Salzmann, I don't know what to say next!

Yes, it's warm tonight, Salzmann would shout back through the empty cinema. Once again, he hadn't been listening.

Grandfather, talking in the Apollo, rumpled his brow. 'That's where the thoughts are, in the wrinkles' (Grandmother). His neck and shoulders were tense. 'The man will become a hunchback if he carries on that way.' If he came home after ten o'clock that meant: I've had a hard day! Please give me peace! Sometimes it was the film that was so long, or it had torn lots of times. Then Grandfather would tear open the bedroom door and shout: Is there no one here who will stand by me in my hour of need? Are you all asleep? Then Grandmother would have to get up, put on her dressing gown and rub Grandfather's neck with brandy. After that he became a human being again.

Ah, that feels good, he said, go on, go on!

Here, asked Grandmother, or higher up?

No, deeper, cried Grandfather, much deeper!

When he told stories, something came over him, from his shoulders down to his calves. When he got to a big moment, he stood up on tiptoe and his belly swelled. His nose was apt to sweat, his knees even more apt to shake. The film *Spies* (1926, with Willi Fritsch and Gerda Maurus) he would like to have put over better than anyone else, as if it was *his*. He was often perplexed, not knowing 'what was happening' to him. Going for a walk round the Big Pond he stopped and asked: What's going to become of me?

I said: I don't know either!

# Three

At that time, Grandfather would often take me by the hand and say: Well, what now?

I have an idea, I would say.

Because now he would sometimes take me along on his 'tours of inspection' as he called them. They took place – so long as Grandfather didn't have to lie down and rest ('The spirit is willing, but the bedclothes are warm!') – on Mondays, which were his days off, and he went out into the countryside with me. One Monday morning, when it was still dark, we clambered out of our beds. Next door Grandfather groaned as he crept out of his, I crept quietly out of mine. Then we dressed – it was wintertime – in warm clothes. Grandfather wore his long johns, I wore my long woollen stockings. Grandmother was already up. She stood in the kitchen with a bread knife making up a stack of bread and butter. Then she made each of us a soft-boiled egg, and a hard-boiled one for the road. (To save gas, she cooked them all in the same saucepan, leaving the hard ones in longer.) She put two apples on the table and two pickled cucumbers and said: There, now you shouldn't starve. I had my child's rucksack. In that we put a twist of real rock salt for Grandfather – 'eggs are bad for you if you eat them without salt' – and a map of the Kingdom of Saxony, and a flask of hot or cold linden tea. I got the rucksack to carry, because Grandfather had to carry his walking stick. The rucksack wouldn't have looked well with the artist's hat either.

Are you quite sure you have to go to the cinema again this week, Grandmother asked Grandfather.

Quite sure, he growled.

Well then, be sure to come back again in one piece. If you can, before it gets dark. That is, if you mean to come back at all, and don't decide to stay away for good.

So far they've always come back, said Mother.

What else are a poor old man and a child supposed to do with themselves, said Grandfather, and we set off. Our bus left at seven o'clock. It went into the country.

And how, asked Grandfather, to pass the time, and so that I might learn something, can you say that in other ways?

I said: Up hill and down dale.

What else?

To the wild blue yonder.

What else?

Wherever the fancy takes us.

Thank you, said Grandfather, that'll do.

Sometimes we went to the station and got into the early morning train. But because we weren't going to Chemnitz like the factory workers, but 'the wrong way', we often had a whole compartment to ourselves. As I hadn't yet seen anything of the world, I was given the window seat. Grandfather sat opposite me, he already knew the world. My rucksack lay on top of us, in the luggage net, so we could keep an eye on it and it couldn't run off. There was a smell of cold cigar smoke and of our pickled gherkins.

And where are we heading this time, I asked.

To Wittgenstein.

Is there a cinema there?

Yes, the Tivoli, said Grandfather. There are cinemas wherever we go, otherwise we shouldn't be going to those places.

So we sat in the train to Wittgenstein, or maybe Rochlitz. Or to Flöha, change twice. In Flöha each of us ate a piece of bread and butter and a pickled gherkin, and in the afternoon, instead of the church or the craft museum, we had a look at the cinema, the Regina. Where we stayed to take in *The Student of Prague* (1913, with Paul Wegener, Grete Berger and Lyda Salmonova). In that film, the student Baldwin sells the adventurer Scapinelli his reflection for 100,000 guilders. But Scapinelli is the Devil, and Baldwin never sees himself in the mirror again. After that we ate the last of our bread and butter and our apples, and went home. Grandfather told me about the Devil, but I fell asleep. The next time, we went to Borstendorf, where we took off our jackets because it was spring, and we saw *The Street* (1923, with Eugen Klöpfer and Lucie Höflich). In that, a man rushes out of his house, because otherwise he would suffocate. (Grandfather: How I know the feeling! How I sympathise!) He runs off, in order finally to experience something, and chases a woman into her flat. But by chance her husband is there in the other room, just murdering another gallant who had also been pursuing her. Everyone runs off, but the man who wanted to experience something is apprehended, and almost hanged. Then he's able to say who the real murderer is, and goes back to his wife. He buys her a bunch of carnations. I hope you liked that, said Grandfather, and learned something from it. You have to be patient if you want freedom in your life, he said enigmatically, and we went home. The sun had already gone down. My knees were cold. Grandfather took off his jacket and laid it over my knees. I must have fallen asleep soon after.

If we couldn't find a train or bus to take us, we stood by the side of the road to Oberfrohna and stopped a lorry. Grandfather said we wanted to get to Lichtenau, and would they give us a lift. If the lorry driver said he wasn't going to Lichtenau but to Zschopau, Grandfather asked: Does Zschopau have a cinema?

And if the driver said: I think so! he said: Fine, then let's go to Zschopau! On the way, Grandfather explained that we came from Limbach, but did a lot of travelling. For professional reasons, he said. Then he told the story of the last film he had seen and explained and accompanied in Limbach, and the lorry driver said he wouldn't mind seeing that one if he had more time, it sounded good.

Grandfather beamed, and said: Yes, I am fortunate in my profession. Not everyone is as fortunate as I am.

The driver took us right up to the Palace bioscope in Zschopau. He let us out, and said: Well, I hope it delights your hearts, if it's something in that line! And your eyes and ears!

Grandfather said: It's a silent film!

Well, just your eyes and your hearts then, said the driver, and he drove off without us. We were in Zschopau early, and because we'd saved on the fare, we could each afford a large ice-cream and a rock cake. Then, because we still had time on our hands, we took in the sights of Zschopau, and after that because it just happened to be running, *The Doll* (1919, with Ossi Oswalda and Hermann Thimig). In that one, a shy young man afraid of marriage flees to a cloister. There, in order to find some peace at last, he marries a doll. But then it turns out to be a pretty young lady instead, and he has to lie down in a bed with the young lady and be happy. But sometimes the car that was taking us to a place that had a cinema broke down in the middle of the road, and we had to get out.

Oh my giddy aunt, Grandfather would say on such occasions, and push his artist's hat back off his forehead. We stood and watched as the driver took his motor apart and cursed his vehicle. Grandfather explained to him how he had accelerated wrongly.

The driver asked: Do you think that's what it was?

Grandfather said: What else? Well, what now, he asked later, and looked at his watch, has your racer given up the ghost? We've got a long day ahead of us. We have to be getting on.

I don't know what the matter with it is, said the driver, who had wanted to take us to Chursdorf.

Well, goodbye then, if you don't know either, said Grandfather, and hailed another car. He didn't want to waste time standing around. The other car took us along for a while, and again Grandfather told the driver the story of a film, but a different one. In Chursdorf, where there was a cinema, we got out, and hoped it would be playing. But it had gone on, 'just as all of us, for the most divers reasons, will some day go on', said Grandfather. For a time we stood in front of the orphaned and locked-up Crystal Palace in Chursdorf, me carrying the rucksack on my back. Grandfather shook his fist at the 'padlocked amusement palace' and exclaimed: 'A dead cinema! It had to happen! Well, let it rot!' Then we each ate a roll with liverwurst, and stood on the roadside again. We took a lift from a milk lorry to Penig, where it happened to be going. In Penig there was the Central Cinema. That wasn't shut. We knocked on the door, and said who we were. The cashier was just about to open up anyway. He hadn't heard of Grandfather, but even so he offered us each a glass of seltzer water. The programme started in an hour. We sat down in a corner and looked around. All the cinemas we inspected had already seen their best days. Many were teetering on the point of collapse.

Some of them, said Grandfather, are a danger to life and limb. I'm the best judge of that, because I have to keep going to them. But that's art for you. It's always associated with danger, often mortal danger. Regardless of that, we keep going in and looking.

Yes, I said, we do.

In some cinemas, before we went in, Grandfather gave a courteous knock on the door marked 'Private', and had himself shown around by the proprietor. Sometimes he would take notes. He would steal ideas and copy them in Limbach, if Herr Theilhaber allowed him to. In Grüna he had stolen air freshener 'so that it doesn't smell so bad in our place', in Lungwitz an icebox for beer, in case someone was thirsty and had fifty pfennigs to spare. To date Grandfather had inspected thirty-two cinemas in his life, another eighteen were still ahead of him. 'Then I will have seen what there is to see in this world, and can leave contentedly, no one can fit more into a human life.' Once he said: Not only is film itself an art, so is the way you narrate one. Through the many cinemas he had seen, he had come to the conclusion that Herr Theilhaber should close his cinema. 'That man does everything wrong. He's bankrupting himself.' But Grandfather never told him that, he only told me. A week later, we knocked on the next cinema door, explained who we were, and asked if we could go in and see a film for free.

Why for free, asked the man in the box office.

Because, Grandfather said, and acting as though Herr Theilhaber's cinema belonged to him, I have a cinema myself, and admit colleagues for free. It's only a little one, he added.

I see, said the man at the till, and let us in for nothing.

But you don't have a cinema at all, I whispered. It belongs to Herr Theilhaber!

The man isn't concerned with the details of ownership. He's just standing there doing his duty, nothing more, said Grandfather, and as there was still time, we began to make an inspection of the premises. With a foot rule that Grandfather carried around with him, we measured the height of the cinema's ceiling, we tested the seats, and asked for programmes, preferably a whole stack of them so that we might have something to browse in on the way home. Now and again a cinema proprietor would treat us to a piece of potato cake. Then, after he had stepped into the light and tasted it, Grandfather would say: I pronounce this the best potato cake I have ever tasted in my life! and gave me the bigger part of it. I tasted it and said: And I in my life too! In none of the cinemas was there a film explainer, Limbach was unique in that. Nor did anyone play the piano either.

Well, said Grandfather, that may be the way you do it. We in Limbach do it differently.

Then we would watch the film, say we'd liked it, but we had to dash, otherwise we'd see the last bus – or train – just pulling away from under our noses. In the train – or bus – Grandfather would tell the film to me once more, the way *he* had understood it. Often he had understood it quite differently from me. I thought: Why does everyone understand every film differently? and, so thinking, fell asleep.

That spring, our streets were dry and rackety. Later on, they started to empty. We looked up at the heavens and shook our heads. 'Something is brewing!' (Grandmother.) Then the rain began. The Apollo was always empty. If few people had come so far, there were even less now, for 'climatic reasons'. Herr Theilhaber still went around in sandals. He held a newspaper over his business hat when he was caught in the rain. That way he was doubly protected. Grandfather, who never carried a newspaper around with him, was quite drenched. I was as well, but it didn't bother me, I was an Aquarian. Herr Theilhaber pushed Grandfather into the cubbyhole. He wanted a word with him.

The way you waffle on to people is all very well, Hofmann, but it won't be required any more, he said. I'm going to have to close the Apollo. It isn't worth my while.

What are you saying, cried Grandfather.

It was early evening, warm but overcast. I was wearing my round cap which made my face look like a pancake, 'as appetising as one, I mean' (Mother). Grandfather had his artist's hat on, which was dripping steadily. Because it was supposed to be summer, I was in my knee socks. Everyone could see part of my legs. Grandfather, who didn't offer so much seasonal variety, looked as he always did. Herr Theilhaber, with his business hat, was dripping as well. His feet, in their health sandals, had a subtle smell if you got too close to him. But the sandals were good for him, they helped his feet to breathe. On top, wide and mighty, he wore his black robe. Mother said: That's not a robe, it's a kaftan! Can you say kaftan?

Kaftan, I said.

Yesterday, Grandfather said to Herr Theilhaber, I showed *The Fire* (1914, with Asta Nielsen). A wonder of a film.

There were seventeen there to see it, said Herr Theilhaber.

If you think people would have understood it without me, you're mistaken, said Grandfather, to the rustle of the rain. They would, he said, have understood nothing! And the music I played was original too, particularly for Limbach, but elsewhere as well. *The Fire* hit home like a bomb.

Herr Theilhaber shook his head. Film culture, he said, mopping his brow, is changing. Films are now going to be made in such a way that all this palaver about them will be superfluous. Including yours, Hofmann! There are certain truths that may have a bitter taste, but we have to look them in the eye. If I've gone on showing silent films, it was purely on your account. But you know that, don't you?

Not a bit superfluous, said Grandfather, and he began to change for work. He took off his jacket and trousers, and got into his explaining suit. You could tell it wasn't new. He had put a flower in the buttonhole, a white carnation, 'as though another person from his year had gone on' (Grandmother). In his explaining gear, Grandfather immediately made a far more determined impression. He didn't put on the waistcoat today, in the 'procession of the seasons', it was already too warm for it.

Yes it is, said Herr Theilhaber, whatever you say in those talks of yours, it's superfluous!

As we're on the subject: Next week we're showing *Sumurun* (1920, with Pola Negri and Paul Wegener), said Grandfather, and did up his little trousers. What do you say to that?

Showing what, asked Herr Theilhaber.

*Sumurun*, said Grandfather, a wonderful movie. With Pola. You must have heard of it?

I don't recall.

*Sumurun*, said Grandfather, will give us our breakthrough. And it will come, it will come.

Yes, when I'm dead and in my grave.

Later, said Grandfather, powdering his nose a bit and painting his lips, so that everyone could see the artist in him, we will have the surprise of the season: *The Birth of the Golem* (1920, with Albert Steinrück, Paul Wegener and Otto Gebühr). It's been on here before, but you can't show that sort of quality too often. *The Birth of the Golem* is shot in the old town of Prague with its crooked lanes. There isn't a straight line to be seen, everything's crooked, do you understand? But you'll be able to judge that for yourself. All in all, said Grandfather, finishing his make-up, I'm anything but superfluous.

Of course you are, said Herr Theilhaber rudely. He had sat down, although his trousers were a little damp as well. He was worried about his business. When he saw how few people came to the Apollo, he turned pale, and covered his eyes. He didn't want to look. He was pale now.

Would you like a drink of water, asked Grandfather.

What?

Or beer?

I've been asking myself for some time, said Herr Theilhaber, whether your incessant chattering doesn't actually irritate the public, Hofmann. After all, there are the subtitles, if there's anything they don't understand. So everyone can read what he's seeing and what's going on. There's no need for you to put in your twopennyworth as well. It's superfluous.

No, said Grandfather firmly, it's not superfluous. Quite the opposite.

Superfluous, cried Herr Theilhaber. Then he stood up and went over to the door marked 'No Admission'. He was dripping badly. He took off his business hat, and poked his head into the auditorium. We have another tiny audience for your chitchat. Look at that, you can count them on the fingers of both hands.

Eleven, actually, said Grandfather, who was standing behind him, and had long since counted them up. He didn't know why so few people came either. But compared to Mittweida, he said, it's not at all bad.

You mean even fewer people go in Mittweida?

Compared to Mittweida, we have large audiences. And they are growing bigger all the time. You just need to give people a taste for it. Last week, when I was showing *The Fire*, I met with sceptical faces to begin with. Then I drew the attention of the public to Asta Nielsen . . .

To what?

. . . to Asta Nielsen, who plays the heroine. In particular the scene where she's leaning against the door of a large salon, about to say something.

And what does she say?

What could she ever say, it's a silent film, said Grandfather. He was now ready for his appearance, only the little stick and his tea chest were missing. You have to picture Nielsen standing next to her witch-like mother, who's crept into a black shawl. Asta Nielsen is wearing a luminous nightgown trimmed with lace, and holding a candelabra in her hand. Three white candles are burning on it. If you consider that barely a couple of years ago Nielsen so hated herself that she wouldn't allow herself to be photographed! What a transformation! To either side, her astonishing sleeves hang down to the floor. She has a page boy haircut. She's tilting her head as though she's listening. Who knows? *Perhaps* she is listening. Perhaps, said Grandfather, to the fire of the title, which is raging in the distance and is inexorably coming closer. Well, I won't tell you what she was really listening to, because I know it would spoil the whole thing for you, in case you decided later to see the film yourself. I know you haven't seen it, but I'm sure you already wish you had. Anyway, we haven't seen such beautiful photography here for a long time. If someone doesn't know what art is and would like to know, he just has to come to the Apollo and study the shot with Asta Nielsen and the candles, then he'll understand!

And meanwhile no one who doesn't have a cinema can have any idea what financial losses are, said Herr Theilhaber.

Anyway, said Grandfather, I have always made a point of providing elucidation of this sequence to the public. For instance, the fact that in real life Asta Nielsen is engaged in a fight to the death with the actress Pola Negri. The reason is that the two are deadly rivals for the crown of their art. In real life Negri is called Apollonia Chavulez. But she was quickly given a different name, because no one could be expected to pronounce that. She comes from a village in Poland, which is something she doesn't want to have generally known. So now she calls herself Pola Negri. The two ladies are in the most ferocious competition possible for the favour of the audience. They must have killed one another a hundred times by poison or knife in their thoughts. They would have done so in real life, if they hadn't been bodily restrained by their respective directors. Because written in gigantic letters in the sky above their heads is the question: Who ranks higher? I don't know your opinion, said Grandfather to Herr Theilhaber, but, after long pondering, I have taken the part of Nielsen. I have been to see *The Fire* twelve times, and not once regretted it. Now her film *Sumurun* is coming our way.

There there, Hofmann, said Herr Theilhaber. He was still dripping. I know, he said, that you do everything possible to get films here, but that aside . . .

That aside, everything goes its old joyless trot, said Grandfather to Herr Theilhaber. Herr Teichert in Erdmannsdorf has hanged himself. Frau Jassing from Crimmitschau drowned herself in the pond. And the company of Liebscher in Burgstadt is facing bankruptcy, which will throw dozens more people out of work. No wonder everyone is waiting impatiently for *Sumurun*. In that, Paul Wegener will play a sultan who catches his mistress in the arms of his own son. They are betrayed by a gambler, who appears to be a hunchback. Of course we're all dying to see what Paul Wegener will look like as the sultan. I hope the film doesn't tear too often. *The Fire* kept tearing. I was forced to break off my explanations time after time. Thank God I had so much to say. I didn't allow the house lights to be turned on, so that no one was torn out of his dream. No art can stand that. All art is based on the precondition that reality is interrupted and kept at bay, and isn't allowed to butt in. So I sat down at the piano, and filled in the repair-time with a waltz of my own devising. Many people were whistling it as they left the Apollo at the end of the evening. That's why I call upon you, Grandfather suddenly said, to reconsider the pay cut you said you were forced to impose with all the small houses . . .

No, said Herr Theilhaber, I can't reconsider your pay cut. For me a film explainer is superfluous.

Superfluous?

A third nostril.

Grandfather shook his head sorrowfully. Oh, Herr Theilhaber, he said, I'm not superfluous. An audience needs someone to explain a film to them, at least its finer points. They have no idea what is contained in a film if you look at it closely, in every single shot. No no, said Grandfather, that must be explained. Otherwise, it would be lost.

Well, you can go on explaining it all to them a little longer, but not much, said Herr Theilhaber. You should realise yourself that your profession is finished. In the cities it's extinct. From the business point of view it makes no sense at all. People like to have young ladies singing to them, not you chattering. And in God's name not in such detail! No one today wants to be told things in such detail, said Herr Theilhaber, who was afraid that Grandfather was driving away the last of his audience. For the moment, Hofmann, it's still all right, but I can give you no guarantee as to the future. Technical progress continues to be made, whatever the interests of any particular individual. Well, you've been warned! One day I'll have to take you to one side and say: That's it, Hofmann, either you start looking for another job, or you live on your pension . . .

My pension, said Grandfather, haha!

. . . however small. Your profession no longer exists. It has withered away as entertainment has advanced, it is no longer required. However much I have always appreciated your services, you must look for something else.

And where am I to find something at my age, asked Grandfather.

You'll just have to look!

And when do I have to start looking?

In half a year or so.

Ah, there's plenty of time till then, said Grandfather, relieved. Film explainers, he said, have always existed. They will continue to exist in future as well.

Well, said Herr Theilhaber, I've warned you. He put his business hat on again. Then he picked up his pages of newspaper and draped them over the hat. People, he said, want to see film actors who do their own talking.

Oh, they don't mind it if I chat away to them a bit, said Grandfather. Then he picked up his tea chest and me. Right, and now it's off to work, he said to Herr Theilhaber, and we went into the auditorium. There he put me down on the 'seat for non-paying customers'. Then Salzmann turned off the house lights.

Only the little bulb by the exit was left on. Grandfather muttered: Into battle, old man! and gritted his teeth. All by himself, he walked through the rows of those 'poor addicts who can't live without their Greta Garbo' (Grandmother). There was no one else there anyway. Grandfather went up to the piano. He bowed to the front, and then to right and left. Apart from Herr Cosimo and Fräulein Fritsche, no one applauded. People were too familiar with him to feel like clapping him. Swiftly he opened the piano and played a little 'for the general public and to get my fingers warmed up'. Then came the first pictures, and Grandfather, one eye on the audience, and one on the screen, explained the new film, especially its dramatic moments. For instance in *The Salvation Hunters* (1925, with George K. Arthur and Georgia Hale), how the young man and woman, being unemployed, have to live on a dredger in San Francisco harbour. After a quarrel with the owner of the dredger, they put their heads together and look despairingly straight at the camera, 'and so straight into our hearts' (Grandfather). Or how the young Mongol, cheated over the sale of a valuable fur, stabs a white man in the market with his dagger, then after his bungled execution discovers a document that identifies him as a descendant of Genghis Khan, so that he comes into an extraordinary inheritance (*Storm Over Asia*, 1928). Or how the old stationmaster's wife learns that the inspector has seduced her only daughter. She throws herself down on her knees to pray before a crucifix at the edge of the forest. There she is caught in a snowstorm, and dies a painless death (*Shattered*, 1921, with Werner Krauss). Then it would happen. Something went through Grandfather that he couldn't describe, but that made him grow 'beyond that charade we call life'. 'You can see him grow, even if he's sitting down' (Grandmother). He got up, took a step towards his public – which made him still taller – opened mouth and eyes wide, and with his right hand stroked his war wound, which wasn't far from his heart, on his ribs, though no one knew it.

There, he cried, when the snow started falling on the crossing-master's widow, there, see that!

Then he stretched out his hand in the air, and let us study the fingers. With our poorer imaginations we could not feel as he did, but at least he was able to show us the greatness of his emotion. Later on, he leaned against the wall, and he looked calmer. On the way home, instead of asking: Well, was I good, he asked: Well, and how did you like the film?

I said: Very much.

Man, he said, is the only creature that knows his own grandfather. Then he put his right hand in his trouser pocket, and played with his key. With it he could get into the cinema at all times, even in the middle of the night. In the other pocket was his handkerchief. He would crush it into a ball when the dramatic bits came. Grandmother had to wash and iron it over the weekend. A solid and convincing figure, his stick in his hand, he walked me home through the darkness, his head full of pictures. Little wonder he slept badly! And then the next day, all over again. We saw *The Waxworks* (1924, with Emil Jannings and Werner Krauss). I sat a long way away from him. I was embarrassed by how loudly he spoke. I pinched my thigh and silently implored Grandfather to speak more quietly. It was as though he himself was the owner of the cabinet where the waxworks were on display. Why did he show off so? Today, because it was raining, he had put on his vulcanised rubber raincoat. He gave it to me to hold. I had draped it over my head so that no one would recognise me. Only my eyes peeped out, the left one especially. The whole of the Apollo was already talking about the raincoat and the peculiar smell it gave off. All were asking themselves: Why does this child smell so? Grandfather had handed me the rubber coat with the words: Here you are, but don't let it trail in the dirt. Then he left me alone with it. So what could I do with the coat? I always did as follows. I rolled it up, so that as little of it as possible could be seen or *smelt*. Still, it seemed to me, from the way my neighbours kept looking across at me . . . The comedy *The Parson's Wife* (1921, Hildur Carlberg and Einar Rod) was lost on me because of the rubber coat. In that, the young vicar, who had had to marry the widow of his old predecessor, introduces his young lover as his sister to his parish. Each time they're alone together, they quickly give each other a kiss. I thought: What nonsense! When will the old baggage finally realise? When Grandfather had shut the piano, I held the coat out to him, so he could take it back right away.

Hold on, he said exhaustedly, what's the rush, you'll end up breaking a leg. Then he pushed me and the rubber coat aside, and stepped up with arms outspread – I thought, this is how he would have announced the lions at the circus – in front of the screen, which by now had come to rest. He announced future attractions. 'Dear public, I trust *The Parson's Wife* has been a pleasant distraction to you these past two hours, and that you will be able to patronise our next screening . . . . The next film was made just thirteen years ago, and is called *Shadow*. Fritz Kortner, Gustav von Wangenheim and Alexander Granach appear in it. It is about a young husband who is consumed by jealousy. His wife, you see, has a lover. And three further admirers are also seeking her favours. Then a galanty show comes to town, in which the puppets . . .' But by then, the audience, who knew long ago what film was coming next, already had their hats and caps on, and had already surged out onto the street. What with the distance and the wind – my, isn't it blowing, Grandfather would exclaim in a moment – they could no longer hear him.

When we went out into the street in the morning, Grandfather, like every artist, was convinced that life is not real. Mind, you mustn't say that ever, he said, or they'll pack you off to Wermsdorf. If you play things the way they really are, he said, they'll wrap your fiddle round your head.

57

When I asked: So what is life really, he replied: An imitation!

How do you mean?

It's all happened before.

Grandmother?

Yes.

Mother?

Yes.

And me?

You too, probably, you just haven't realised it yet.

Only Grandfather knew what a life that wasn't an imitation looked like. Maybe he would tell me one day. Not now, he had other worries now! For instance, with Grandmother out buying pork belly, and himself in the kitchen unsupervised, he had to have a little something to eat. Fry up an egg, or a piece of smoked bacon without the rind. Would you like a bit, he asked me.

No.

Grandfather sat down. He sat in such a way that he could keep the whole street in view, and could quickly clear everything away, in case Grandmother came back. Then he cut the bacon into little strips, and started eating. He said: We are connected to the earth.

How do you mean?

Through posts, he said enigmatically, to the centre of the earth. Every word we say has already been spoken. We just repeat them.

I see that, I said, but what about the posts?

Just posts, Grandfather said. He ate one strip of bacon after another. Then he stretched out his legs and stroked his ribs. That was where he had his war wound, which he liked to show me. Sometimes, when Grandmother was about to go out, and Mother was sitting sewing in the next room, he gave me a little wink. That meant: If you like, I'll show you something!

I asked: What? and he said: My war wound. Then we waited till Grandmother was out of the house. Grandfather waved her off. Then he said: Now come over here!

I went up to him. Here?

No, closer!

Grandfather had stood up, and was standing beside the window. That way we had more light. He pulled the curtain across a little, so that no one could see him from outside. Then he pulled me even closer – I was afraid of getting too close, and smelling him as well – and he whispered: The French!

How do you mean?

He said: The ancestral enemy did that to me!

Then, while Grandmother was at the baker's, and Mother was in the next room sewing, he stepped into the corner of the room, to be quite sure no one could see him from the street. He untucked his shirt from his trousers. He had a sleeveless vest under his shirt. He untucked that as well. Then the white and shrivelled old body – the man's withering away, his women said – with a handful of loose skin and his old man's pot belly. But Grandfather wasn't ashamed. He looked steadily down his body. Then he stood up erect with his arms out and a finger in the air, and proclaimed: My marytr's body! A martyr, he said, is what I always wanted to be. Even as a child, when someone asked me: What do you want to be when you grow up, I replied: A martyr! And now I am one.

How do you mean?

Think of my life and you'll understand, said Grandfather.

His war wound was on the left side of his ribs as I stood facing him. A piece of shrapnel came along one day and hit him there. Half an inch higher, and I wouldn't be here talking to you now.

Why not?

Because I wouldn't be here.

Where would you be instead?

Well, there's a question, said Grandfather, but it wouldn't have been much of a loss. It's never that much of a loss, he said.

Grandfather got his war wound when he was forty-one, at

Ypres. Having just a second earlier called to his comrades: Now all charge at once, and we'll take the next trench! – Grandmother said: *Run away* is what he'll have said, not *charge*! – he was hurled backwards into the trench with incredible force by a piece of shrapnel. He thought, that's it, and remained lying in the trench. For a long time no one knew: Is he dead now, or will he just get up again? No one moved him or tugged at him. He was laid on a stretcher, with his arms dangling down. Grandfather tried to look down his body to where the splinter might have hit him. Once inside him, the orderly said, it would roam about his body. Into his arms, his legs, his neck the shrapnel might roam. Perhaps it already had! But if the shrapnel touched his heart, then it would be all up with him.

And then?

Then your Grandfather wouldn't have been there any more.

So where? Go on! Say!

The orderly felt Grandfather all over, to check that all of him was still there. Then he asked: Can you feel the shrapnel here, Hofmann? Or here? Or here? Quick, think about it! Or had the shrapnel not stopped in his body, but gone flying on its way? Grandfather was dizzy for much of the time. He let his arms droop and wondered about whether he could feel the shrapnel. First he wondered low down, then higher up, first one side, then the other. When after a while he couldn't feel anything any more, he said: Hey, orderly, I can't feel the shrapnel any more. Has it flown away? From that time on, the orderly didn't come so often, although each time he asked where the shrapnel was, Grandfather pointed to a different spot and said: I think he's there now! Or: I think he's over here! Grandfather had no idea whether the shrapnel was still in his body or not, the wound had long since healed over. Only the scar from it was still there, but that remained.

The odd thing is that the pains are still there too, said

Grandfather, when he showed me the wound. He looked to see that Grandmother wasn't coming up the street to catch us with the wound. Grandmother was always cross when he showed it to me. She said: Do you have to. But when she was out of the house, he would show it to me anyway. There it is, Grandfather would say, but don't tell her I showed it to you. Nor your Mother either.

Then we went nearer to the window again. His shirt billowed out in the morning light. He took my finger in his cold hand, and said: Straighten it! But quickly, before she comes back! Then he ran my finger along his scar. It was red and looked fresh. Up and down and up again. This is the place where they tried to kill your Grandfather. Many years ago, he said, maybe five hundred. That's how long I've been carrying it around with me for.

Does it hurt?

Sometimes.

And how long will it stay there?

Till I'm dead, then they'll bury it along with the rest of me, said Grandfather, and he chuckled at the idea of the scar being buried with him. Then he tucked his vest and shirt back into his trousers, and forgot about the scar again, at least for the moment. He had other worries.

He had to go to the *k*inema, as he said now. He was playing the piano. It cost seventy pfennigs to see a film, the music was free. Grandfather was a little worn by now, but at least the bird's feet had lightened a bit. He turned to the audience, and said whatever came into his head. He told them how to interpret the film. He had forgotten about the scar. At any rate he didn't mention it. Occasionally, he would think about it again, especially at the weekends. Then he would get restless, put down his little pointer, and with his now-empty hand covertly feel for *the spot*. Sometimes he gave me a little nod as he did so. Yes, it was still there! Sometimes he even put his hand under the shirt, and scratched the naked skin, although Grandmother had prohibited

61

that because of the risk of infection. Slowly, so that everyone could follow him, he would recount *Backstairs* (1921, with Fritz Kortner and Henny Porten), in which the servant girl H. Porten is impatiently waiting for a letter from her lover. The letter simply will not arrive. Finally, when she's quite beside herself, it does come. But it turns out not to be from her lover at all, but from the lame postman F. Kortner, who, having delivered so many letters to the girl, has ended up falling in love with her himself. The servant girl in turn grows fond of this simple man, but then, when he's least expected, her original lover shows up. He hadn't been able to come sooner because he'd been in hospital. Nor had he forgotten her either, every day he had written her a letter. Only she hadn't been able to answer them, because the lame postman had burned them all. When the lover hears that, he murders the postman out of jealousy, and the servant girl gets the sack, and commits . . . . As Grandfather was telling the story of *Backstairs*, he was looking for his war wound. Then he found it. Gently, with the tips of one or two fingers he stroked it.

By taking long walks in the Hoher Hain and around the Big Pond, Grandfather tried to forget about the advance of the sound film. 'Each time he goes for a walk, he has company, which is to say his worries' (Grandmother to me). Sometimes he stopped in the middle of the Hoher Hain, and said: If ever you need a friend, buy yourself a dog!

I said: What will happen now?

He said: What will be will be. And when I said: I mean, when you're out of work, he said: I've stopped thinking about it!

Oh. So what do you think about?

Of a splendid film in which a little boy keeps going for walks with his grandfather, without incessantly bombarding him with unanswerable questions.

Fewer and fewer people now went to the Apollo, so that Herr

Theilhaber had to cancel more and more performances, and Grandfather often found he had changed and prepared himself in vain. Sadly he stood by the door of the cubbyhole and said: At least help me out of my trousers! Then, wheezingly, without having earned his bread and water, he crept back into his everyday trousers, and, once back in our flat, went to bed in broad daylight out of sheer despair.

Or he took me for a walk outside the town, 'to put all that behind me'. And in the dusk began to tell me the story of the film he would so much like to have shown. 'The poor man is getting a little eccentric' (Grandmother).

Many an afternoon we wouldn't know: Was there anything happening in the evening or not? I carried his artist's hat for him, sometimes his stick as well. In the Amselgrund, lest we forget that brilliant film, he pulled me close to him and told me about *Tired Death* (1921, with Lil Dagover). The length of the little birch wood, a little muddy underfoot, there was *The Street* (1923, with Eugen Klöpfer and Lucie Höflich); in the mixed wood – almost as far as Wüstenbrand – *The Fiddler of Florence* (1913, with Paul Wegener and Lyda Salmonova); and round the Big Pond, among frogs and dragonflies and for the umpteenth time, *Secrets of a Soul*.

In that, a man, no, said Grandfather, a gentleman, becomes obsessed with an idea, these things happen. It's the idea of having to murder his wife, for which he, like every man, of course has his reasons. He takes . . .

I know it, I said, I've already seen it.

Never mind that, said Grandfather, do you want to hear it or don't you?

I do.

Then stand up straight and listen. It's about an emotional confusion, because when a man feels the urge to kill . . . . We circled round the Big Pond. I was happiest walking in the puddles, Grandfather not. Sometimes I pulled him through one all the same. Then he exclaimed: What are you doing, unhappy boy? And we were back on the dry. It was because she didn't have any children, but then at the last moment she does get one, and they're saved.

And then?

What do you mean: And then? That's the end, said Grandfather, and got onto the next film. Sometimes I was walking behind him, sometimes at his side.

Do you know why I'm telling you all this, he asked me once.

No.

Because, Grandfather said enigmatically, I have to prepare for a life and death confrontation that will decide everything. And, after a pause: God, this boy's slow-witted! With Herr Theilhaber, of course! A confrontation the like of which you can't imagine. No one can.

And why with Herr Theilhaber?

We may have the same sort of shoes on, but we're marching in different directions, said Grandfather, who had long since joined the ranks of the most prominent personalities of 'Greater Limbach' (Grandmother). He was hailed from all directions and often from afar. Grandfather replied to every greeting that came his way, one after another. In January, he had got a new hat. This hat, because 'the poor man will soon be out of a job', had if anything an even broader brim than its predecessor. 'You could use it to sweep the streets with' (Grandmother). Once we had passed people in the street, they started whispering about us.

Listen to the wagging tongues, Grandfather said to me quietly. Yes, he said, the hat suits me!

Many people had now at least once in their lives experienced Grandfather in the Apollo. Others had seen him standing by the box office and beckoning people in when they probably just wanted to look at the stills in the foyer. If someone asked him: What are you doing out here, Hofmann? Isn't your place beside the screen? he said: I'm barking at them. Others again watched as he scraped yesterday's poster off the wall with a trowel. Or as, new hat and all, he queued his legs off in the line for cheap meat. The provider of his daily bread, so as not to remind him of his own existence, Grandfather now preferred to steer clear of. When he saw him approaching on the other side of the street, we would quickly turn away. If it was too late for that, Grandfather would give me a nudge and say: All right, pay attention! Then we quickly shut our eyes, so maybe he wouldn't see us. Grandfather no longer left little notes on Herr Theilhaber's desk with the titles of films he wanted to explain one day. He was relieved if Herr Theilhaber didn't leave little notes in his cubbyhole, asking how many people had come to the last screening. Or suddenly materialise in the doorway in the middle of a film, and start counting the audience, out loud. And withal Grandfather was such an outstanding cinema pianist and storyteller that no cinema proprietor could have wished for anyone better, and yet he was treated like *that*!

Not that he tells me what to do, it's worse, Grandfather said to me as we left the cut-price butcher's shop. As always he led me by the hand. He doesn't interfere in the way I do my work. What he does is worse. He blames me for the attendances. With looks that say: It can't go on like this! I can't keep the Apollo going any more, it's too often empty! It's dragging me into an economic abyss, on whose slippery floors I can see my ruination glittering.

And what is . . .

Ruination, said Grandfather, is something that hangs over a man all his life, and when the time comes falls on top of him. Ruination, he said, is our destiny.

But then what was Grandfather to do? He was just a hired artist, albeit a very important one. Should he stand on the pavement and pluck at the sleeves of passersby and say: Come to the Apollo, and I'll show you something! He was obsessed with the cinema anyway, and told everyone what he was missing if he let a film like *Hamlet* (1920, with Asta Nielsen in the title role) pass him by. In that, Hamlet's father is just off to war as his wife is having their child. When she's given birth to a daughter, she gets news of the king's death. In order to save the kingdom, the queen announces the birth of a son. So the little girl grows up as Prince Hamlet. He is a woman, with woman's breasts, which are concealed, said Grandfather up front in the Apollo, and everyone believed him. Everyone, except for Grandmother, always believed everything he said! Herr Theilhaber could have combed the whole of Saxony and not found another film explainer like Grandfather! But instead of keeping quiet and being happy to have him, he had to keep whingeing. And then his habit of never knocking, but simply sticking his head round the door marked 'No Admission', when Grandfather was just collecting himself, and calling out: Only ten today, Hofmann! or: Eight! or: Five! As if that helped Grandfather with his performance! As an artist he knew that the size of an audience isn't the point. The main thing is to have anyone there at all, even just one person. Then the art could take place, and it would affect him all the more deeply. Or Herr Theilhaber's habit, when Grandfather was standing at the front and explaining a comedy film – *Two Tars*, for instance (1928, with Stan Laurel and Oliver Hardy) – of shouting from right at the back over everyone's heads: Herr Hofmann, you're mumbling! Speak up a bit please! Can't hear you at the back! That never failed to throw Grandfather off his stride. He started to stammer and then repeat himself. Whatever thoughts he might have had were blown away, and his pronunciation, his style of delivery. . . . They were gone. Or looking reproachfully at Grandfather and lisping out: Six, Hofmann, six! if that happened to be the number. The sound-film is our only hope, Herr Theilhaber would then exclaim. After all, as well as eyes to see, we have ears to hear. Is that my fault?

Oh, as if the sound-film would help, cried Grandmother, and

brought Grandfather another beer. People are just losing interest in the cinema.

The cinematic bog is being drained, said Herr Cosimo, who was also present, but on account of his heart wasn't drinking.

A lot of people, said Mother, have misunderstood the cinema. They will persist in believing it's an invention they just need to see once, and that's it, they need never go again. They have no idea that the content of a film can be interesting, and it's possible to go again and again.

That's right, said Grandfather, who, as Grandmother said, would do better to walk quietly through the town, and stop hopping about. No wonder everyone stares at him, said Mother, when, at the beginning of our sound-film period, Grandfather went out looking for mushrooms with us. It was really embarrassing. But we needed him, he knew all the best places. He just had to crawl under a bush, and there would be a lovely boletus, just waiting for him.

Herr Theilhaber stood by the door of the Apollo and scratched his chin. He had a Jewish beard. His version of things now was that it was only on Grandfather's account that he had waited so long before introducing the sound-film. 'I don't want to stop anyone's livelihood'. Granted, he paid Grandfather punctually, but so little, so little! At Christmas he gave us four white candles, and gave us each three free admissions to the cinema. Sometimes he had cream bonbons in his pocket. He asked me: Do you want one?

I said: No thank you!

And why can't I have one, I asked Grandfather when Herr Theilhaber had gone.

Then came our sound-film period.

# Four

Our sound-film period came one spring, on a Friday. Things were beginning to bloom outside. Mother said: Those are forsythia, those are lilacs, and if I'm not mistaken those are Japanese quince. She was wearing her short-sleeved blouse and had finished with her warm stockings. 'To turn men's heads, you have to show your legs' (Grandmother). Grandfather sat around a lot, with newspaper and without. That was because, for want of an audience, he was now often sent home from the Apollo. There were times he didn't even feel up to changing out of his little tails. It made him too sad. He went home in his work clothes, without having explained a film. When people stopped and called out: What's that, no flimmery-flammery today, he made a tired gesture and said: It's been cancelled. Then he turned round and called after them: But we've a screening tomorrow if more people turn up than today, so if you feel like coming along. We're showing *Gang in die Nacht* (1920, with Conrad Veidt and Erna Morena), a wonderful film, don't miss it. And he went on home. And settled down on the sofa at home in his little explainer's jacket, flashing his buttons. He had made himself all smart 'insofar as that's possible' (Grandmother) just for the Apollo. Sometimes he would be on the point of nodding off in his chair, but Grandmother would give him a nudge and say: Don't go to sleep!

All right, said Grandfather, I know you can't bear to see me relax even for a second. It's all right, I'm going.

68

It was still terribly early, people were still strolling outside. Mother, not yet tired, had pushed her sewing-machine, at which she 'spent her sad existence', up to the window, and stared out into the dusk. She sighed and said: Are things always going to be like this? Are there no more good times ahead? Then she went on sewing.

Ah yes, the sound-film era!

It started in the afternoon, some time between four and five. Sparrows fluttered around it. I wanted to throw stones at them, but Grandfather wouldn't let me. Bound up with a piece of string so tight that it couldn't move – twine, Grandmother said – the sound-film era sat in two boxes in the handcart of the cinema proprietor S. Theilhaber, who was always on the side of progress.

That's his mistake, said Grandfather, all this novelty and newfangledness! Chasing after it with his tongue hanging out. He's too fashionable for me.

Herr Theilhaber, at the end of the Willibald Gluck Strasse, was already clad for spring. Because of the harmful solar rays, he had coated his face with beef fat, in particular his big nose. He wanted to look tanned and fit, because he was a vain man. That's why he was glistening like that. Herr Theilhaber was pleased with himself today. He was backing the sound-film era. He had asked his brother Isidor, in Potsdam, the owner of the Citizen cinema there, all about its prospects. He had gone so far as to take notes which he carried on his person, 'next to his heart'. He was forever saying: My life is piebald with worries, I just don't look at them. Sometimes he made veiled remarks that no one understood. They were always gloomy-sounding. For example, he said: Not much longer, then everything will collapse. And who will it collapse on top of? Your obedient servant, none other! Or: What's coming now won't be pretty. So let's not talk about it. Even his business was only 'middling to poor'. But the blue-painted delicatessen on the Weidmannsdorfer Strasse still belonged to him, where you could buy sweet pickled gherkins and Hungarian salami. Even the inn at the sign of The Long Ear belonged to Herr Theilhaber, only no one knew that. Now the whole of Limbach knew it. And of course the Apollo, 'which is crumbling away, and will soon be on its knees and finished' (Grandmother).

Herr Theilhaber, who 'had many plans, but few friends' (Grandmother) wore his black coat that went down to his ankles.

And that's called a . . . ? Mother asked me.

Kaftan, I said.

In summer, if no breeze blew, Herr Theilhaber took off his kaftan and draped it over his arm. That way it went right down to the ground. If someone important was approaching, he quickly slipped it on, took off his hat and said hello. Once the person had gone, he pulled it off again, 'hypocrite that he is' (Grandfather). The coat was somewhere between black and grey. And the business hat has been on his head ever since I've known him, said Grandmother.

Has it really grown on to his head, I asked.

I wouldn't go so far as that.

And does he keep it on in bed?

That, thank God, I wouldn't know.

His hair was still long, but no longer black. He had too many worries for that. He had curls he would allegedly wind up before going to sleep.

He's even proud of them, the fop, said Grandmother, who should have been thinking about our supper, but had once again forgotten about it. There are more things in life than chewing and swallowing, she said. Plus she'd cut her finger, lucky she hadn't cut it off altogether! Now she couldn't peel potatoes, so we had to eat noodles. But we liked noodles anyway. Grandmother had on her flowered pinafore apron, and was standing by the window. She put down the jar of noodles and said: When the Apollo was doing good business, which is a long, long time ago!, Herr Theilhaber carried all his mark coins home in an old sugar sack.

Illusions, sang Mother, illusions, there's no sack of money in the kind of houses the Apollo gets.

People, Grandmother said, have other things on their minds than to crowd in front of Marlene Dietrich and listen to her singing 'Falling in Love Again' when they should be tucked up in their beds.

Marlene Dietrich, said Mother, is gone anyway.

Is she, I asked.

She's emigrated, said Grandmother.

These are poor times for love, said Mother.

As I know Theilhaber, and I've known him for ever, said our landlord Herr Lange, who had just popped by, and who couldn't stand Herr Theilhaber, he wouldn't carry the bags of money himself. He'd get someone else to carry them for him. He'd promise him a tip, and then conveniently forget all about it. Not that I've anything against him, mind you, said Herr Lange, I just can't stand him.

Grandfather was hunched on the upright chair in the smoking corner. Normally he sat in the smoking-chair, but Herr Lange was sitting there today, he took precedence. Grandfather wasn't smoking either, he needed to economise. Besides, Grandmother didn't want him to get smoker's leg, then there'd be no more walking for him. Now he looked up at the ceiling. He was worried again. Mainly about his 'occupation', because God knows it's hardly work, goggling at one film after another, and chatting about it a bit, and tinkling away on the piano, but it's impossible to talk to you about that, said Grandmother.

Yes, he's a great one for banging on about films, said Mother. The one drawback is it provides no income, the way a job usually does.

That's enough of that, cried Grandfather, and despite Herr

Lange's presence, he banged the table, for land's sake leave me alone! and we were silent again on that Friday afternoon when the sound-film era began, and we wanted to see Herr Theilhaber hauling it into the Apollo. He had his round hat on his head, and his spring scarf round his neck. His motto was: Best be on your guard, especially in spring! When he walked a bit faster, his scarf fluttered beside him. On his feet he wore sandals, 'because he wants to show everyone what an apostle of health from the Levant he is' (Grandmother). And indeed, his heart and lungs and liver and everything were all in good order, because for all his melancholy, he looked after himself. Each time he felt like getting agitated, he remembered his health, and he decided against it. Grandfather said: He's in good shape. It would take some powerful blows to finish him off, or a long period of hunger and thirst. Or holding under water.

Yes, said Herr Lange, those people are tough. They live for ever, you can see that from the shape of their noses. He laughed.

Herr Theilhaber pulled his handcart right through our town. We stood on the corner of Bismarckstrasse and watched his approach. When he was quite close to us, we saw the boxes. Inside them was the sound-film era. It consisted of two enormous loudspeakers, loaned to Herr Theilhaber by the firm of Türmer and Co. for a trial period, and they were hollow. Over the coming weeks, Grandfather often climbed up onto his tea chest to sound them out. Now he knocked on one of them, now the other. Listen to that, he said. Grandmother, on hearing that Grandfather was climbing onto tea chests to knock on loudspeakers, said: He'll end up doing himself a mischief! Apart from them, the sound-film era consisted of two rolls of wire, which Herr Theilhaber had picked up at the same time, and was also towing up to the Apollo. It was slightly uphill. By now Herr Theilhaber had pulled the sound-film era through most of our leading streets.

Can you imagine why, Grandfather asked me.

No.

For publicity, of course. So that everyone sees him, that's how calculating he is. Free publicity, said Grandfather contemptuously.

As he approached, Herr Theilhaber often doffed his business hat. He greeted everyone. He sent greetings up to people's windows, when he saw someone there. With people who were important for his business, he even stopped to exchange a few words, usually about the weather and the sound-film era. Asked or unasked, he explained to them what was in his waggon, and where he was taking it, and that he didn't have the time to stop and chat.

I am a driven man in this world, particularly these days, but so much I am able to say now: The possibilities of entertainment will grow into infinity, and will be unrecognisable, Herr Theilhaber shouted across the Bismarckstrasse, and everyone shouted back: How wonderful! How splendid! How excellent! So we won't be bored in Limbach any more, or?

No, this machine will change all our lives, cried Herr Theilhaber, and everyone nodded, though they didn't believe him. He talks the hind legs off a donkey, they thought, unfortunately life for us will remain the same. Just as well, they thought. Then Herr Theilhaber put his business hat back on, and went on his way, directly towards us. Grandfather reached for his artist's hat. He took it off too.

Hello, Herr Theilhaber, Grandfather called out across the street.

Hello, Hofmann, called Herr Theilhaber.

Look at him, he won't even stop, Grandfather whispered to me, he won't even take the time. We're not important enough.

Herr Theilhaber pulled his handcart right up to our feet. And then he did stop, so that Grandfather wouldn't be able to say later that he had been rude to him. He even touched his business hat,

73

though just a little bit. He didn't have the time to take it off altogether. Then we all stood around in the mild afternoon light. Grandfather stared at his toes, Herr Theilhaber more up in the air. I looked now at my fingers, now at the sound-film era. Herr Theilhaber was embarrassed by the meeting, because he knew what impact the sound-film era would have on Grandfather. He had often said: The sound-film will be my death-knell!

Grandfather stood in front of the tobacconist's. He wasn't smoking, though. He was fiddling with his tie. It was the spotted one, not the striped one. 'Apart from that, it's best not to say anything, just: it's different' (Grandmother). Grandfather was silent. He guessed what was coming. When a little time had passed, he took a deep breath and said something quite different. He said: Strange that, in spite of the way the day began, it's turned out so pleasant.

What sort of beginning are you referring to, asked Herr Theilhaber.

This one, said Grandfather, and scratched the ground with his stick.

The beginning wasn't so bad, said Herr Theilhaber.

Didn't it look like rain?

No, said Herr Theilhaber, that was yesterday. Do you know, he asked, pointing to the sound-film era, what I've got in my boxes?

I'd sooner not, said Grandfather.

You set your face against progress, you stubborn man?

I'll wait and see before taking any measures, said Grandfather.

Just you go ahead and take them, Hofmann! I'm going on, said Herr Theilhaber and on he went. Silently Grandfather touched his artist's hat. But he didn't take it off again, because Herr Theilhaber was no longer looking. He was looking up the Bismarckstrasse, to see who else he might speak to. Grandfather sent another greeting after him. But instead of saying: Goodbye, Herr Theilhaber! he said: Drop dead, you gravedigger of cinematographic art! And after a pause for thought: Yah, cannibal! And because Herr Theilhaber's back view looked so exotic, more even than Grandfather himself: Mousetraps, rat-traps, anysing you vant to haff! Herr Theilhaber went on his way, with the appearance of a nod. Grandfather said: That men like that should even exist! We watched him until he was out of our sight.

So there he goes, the assassin of art, said Grandfather.

And what are we going to do, I asked.

We're going to buy ourselves a large ice-cream.

And what about the sound-film?

The sound-film, said Grandfather on the way to the ice-cream parlour, he might as well throw away. As long as I'm there, it won't be needed, it will never catch on. And rightly so, because it isn't artistic. We walked on a bit. But I know Theilhaber's game, said Grandfather. He wants to economise on my wages, but I won't be that easily got rid of. As far as the cinematographic art is concerned, everything in this hole stands or falls with me, he said, when the following evening – a Saturday – I was allowed to accompany him to the Gala Opening of the Sound-Film. It was the first film in the Apollo at which he wasn't allowed to talk. I had on my new suit, 'green as a canary bird' (Grandmother). My haircut was as good as a new head. Grandfather came along to spectate at his indispensability. With his freshly laundered collar and pressed trousers he looked spick and span, 'as if we'd run him through the dry-cleaners a couple of times' (Grandmother). Unfortunately he was getting smaller all the time. As we passed the window where the stills from Limbach's first sound-film were on display, he holding an unlit cigar in his fingers, greeted from all sides and greeting back, and I looking at my reflection . . .

The square in front of the Apollo was black with people, as though there'd been an accident. Grandfather was wearing his dark jacket but without the waistcoat, it was already too warm for that. In my green one, I looked supposedly 'like a smart hunter' (Mother). Herr Theilhaber, 'in whose place I wouldn't try and seek the limelight quite so much' (Grandfather), had on a frilly shirt with gold cufflinks, 'but all that glitters is not gold'. Not only was his face clean shaven, it gave the appearance of having been licked clean. He stood at the entrance, supervising everything. Our womenfolk had stayed at home. They wanted to wait and see if 'that sound-film business' amounted to anything.

If it does, we can always go and see it next week, said Grandmother, it's not going to run away. And if it doesn't, that's no matter, we'll have saved ourselves time and money.

On the Helenenstrasse, Grandfather held me tighter, so I didn't get lost. We turned the corner. Fröhlich the baker stood outside his shop, all white, and exclaimed: All these people! I haven't seen this big a crowd since Frau Höflich killed herself! How about you, Hofmann?

Me neither, said Grandfather, but I don't get around that much these days!

People were lining the street in both directions. The lines met in front of the Apollo. It was completely blocked. Herr Salzmann stood by the 'No Admission' door in his celluloid visor. He motioned to everyone to go home. We're full up, he cried. Why hadn't we set out earlier? Now we were so deep in the crowd that no one could see my suit.

Don't worry, they won't start a film in the Apollo without me, said Grandfather, they wouldn't dare, and he banged the ground with his stick. Never has a film here begun without me, he said, and pushed me in front of him through the crowd. Of course they've come from all over, from as far away as the Erzgebirge. Everyone wants to see the sound-film.

And hear it, I said.

That, said Grandfather, is of less importance in films.

So what is important?

The man who stands in front of the screen, holding everything together by the force of his personality.

It was ten minutes to go till the Gala Opening. 'It had been chock-a-block for hours' (Mother). Some people were in uniform, green, grey or brown. A foreigner – a Czech? – advised us to go home. He was going back to Czechoslovakia himself.

Nonsense, said Grandfather, this is my cinema, we're staying, and he pulled me along in his wake. The crush was entirely Herr Theilhaber's fault. He had over-publicised the event. Very well, if it's beneath your dignity to put up a few posters, I'll put them up myself, he had told Grandfather, and had stuck up dozens all over town. He had never done that for any film of Grandfather's, not even *Joyless Street* (1925, with Werner Krauss, Asta Nielsen and Greta Garbo), which had been showing the previous week. The subject of that one is the luxury and misery of the inflation period in the beautiful city of Vienna. A Court Councillor loses his entire fortune including his pension by speculating, and becomes just as poor as everyone else. Meanwhile, the butcher (Werner Krauss) is thriving. Whole rows of desperate wives and mothers offer themselves to him in exchange for a piece of lean pork. The shadowy Frau Greifer loans money to young girls, and drives them into prostitution. Then an American lieutenant, who can pay in dollars, moves in as a subtenant of the Court Councillor. He falls in love with his daughter (Greta Garbo), but the Court Councillor sees in him only a former foe, and throws him out. Greta Garbo is just about to give herself to the butcher, but the love of the American saves her at the last moment. The prostitute Marie, however, (Asta Nielsen) is past rescuing, she has killed someone. The butcher is killed as well, in fact by Frau Greifer. . . . And Frau Müller, the usherette, seeing Grandfather and me in the crowd, shouted over everyone's heads: But Herr Hofmann, what are you doing in this throng? You are insatiable! Do you want to go to the cinema yet again? Have you at least got a seat?

No, shouted Grandfather, not really.

And the lad?

Him neither.

Well then, the pair of you, come along with me.

Then she took us out of the queue and through the entrance. There we had to wait while Frau Müller found a couple of empty seats for us. I leaned against the wall of the Apollo, scraping my heels.

Mind you don't scratch Herr Theilhaber's floor, I'll only have to pay for it, said Grandfather. He looked out of the Apollo door. Up the Helenenstrasse. It was called the Adolf Hitler Strasse now. Grandfather was nervous, as always when he was kept waiting. 'A hole is being worn in the world'. He would rather talk, and so he said what he thought and what he saw. Here comes the barber Erblich with his Dulcinea, seeing how many are already here. There are too many of us anyway. Good, he's going again.

Grandfather embarrassed me with his loud voice. I wondered: Why do you talk so loud? He liked to say what he saw or smelled or thought to persuade himself that it was true. Otherwise, he might not have believed it. And now, he said, we'll keep our traps shut until we're called.

With so much waiting, Grandfather was getting tight and then hot under the collar. No wonder he sweated so much! I helped him out of his artist's jacket. He trembled, his lips especially. When Frau Müller returned and ushered us in, he trailed his jacket behind him in the dirt.

Grandfather, I called, careful!

What am I doing now?

Your jacket's trailing.

No wonder, he said, I'm about to collapse.

I saw other children being led along by their grown-ups, just as Grandfather was leading me. They didn't want anyone to get lost.

Well really, Frau Müller plonks us in the next to back row, said

Grandfather, who knew his Apollo, and knew where we should be sitting. Not even in the middle either, but in the rowdy corner, he said. Then again she's let us in without paying, which is nice of her. Wonder if Theilhaber knows? At any rate, we're lucky to have seats at all, he said, they are already standing at the back.

The film chosen for the opening of the Apollo Sound-Film Theatre was *The Jazz Singer* (1927, with Al Jolson). Grandfather said: It's not exactly hot off the press, but it will do for Limbach. The film had music. But that wasn't provided by Grandfather at the piano, it came out of the two loudspeakers that Herr Theilhaber had towed from the station. Unfortunately the film was half an hour late in starting, because without Grandfather's participation things inevitably went wrong. For example, the people who hadn't managed to get in because it was sold out were banging on the doors. Herr Theilhaber had to keep bustling out to calm them down. He had to promise them that the new sound-film would run for at least another week, that way they would all get to see it, and it would still be just as good.

On the contrary, it'll get better and better, the people shouted, and refused to disperse. Then Grandfather suddenly sprang up from his seat and shouted: Everyone without tickets leave the cinema immediately! Clear off, or do you want me to chase you?

No no, the people shouted, we're going! Calm yourself, Hindenburg!

When we had got rid of the people without tickets, Herr Salzmann realised *The Jazz Singer* was wrongly wound. I'm not the least bit surprised, when there's no one to take charge, Grandfather whispered contentedly to me. He had laid his artist's hat on his knees, and was stroking it. That's the consequence of not asking me, he said. And they think they can get by without me. If they'd asked for my opinion . . .

Herr Theilhaber had to have the first sound-film to be screened at the Apollo rewound by Herr Salzmann. That took a further ten minutes. Grandfather called across the whole cinema to Herr Theilhaber whether he shouldn't in the meantime play a little something on the piano, but he shouted back: That won't be necessary, Hofmann! Then the loudspeaker fell off its bracket on the wall, and had to be re-attached. Herr Theilhaber did that himself as well. Then he wanted to step out in front of the curtain in person to say a few words, but at that the people of Limbach, who wanted to see *The Jazz Singer* and not hear Herr Theilhaber, got a little impatient and started to whistle. So Herr Theilhaber just wished everyone some first-rate entertainment! and disappeared. The performance began.

As soon as it began, silence descended. There was no more craning around. All eyes looked ahead. Then Grandfather, because of the now prevailing silence, suddenly grew restless. His jacket off, in his explainer's shirtsleeves, he sat beside me and couldn't keep still. He kept fidgeting and scratching. Then he leaned across to me. I could hear his breathing.

I think, said Grandfather, there's something the matter with me. I can't seem to breathe, at least not properly. Can you breathe, he whispered.

I can, yes.

Funny, he said. Then we were both sitting, watching the film again. We breathed, him on the right, me on the left. And everyone else in front of us and behind us was breathing as well. Funny, said Grandfather, is there not enough air here? Or is it me?

It's you.

Yes, I should try to breathe more regularly, absolutely regularly, said Grandfather. He put his hand on his heart and breathed regularly. I began to think he was over it, but then Grandfather suddenly couldn't see any more.

How do you mean, I asked.

Damnfool question, he said, just what I said.

Well, of course he was exaggerating, but in truth Grandfather was suddenly seeing much less than he had always managed to see before. Funny, he said, can you see everything?

I think so, I said.

Quiet, shouted someone behind us, and we both shut up.

What's that on the screen now, whispered Grandfather, in your opinion?

People.

Funny, he whispered, I don't see any! Why are they so blurred? He waited a moment, then craned his neck and called out: Salzmann, focus please!

Ssh, called the audience, we can't hear the sound-film!

Can't get it any clearer, Karl, the focus is as sharp as possible, Salzmann shouted through the projection opening in the wall. We could see his teeth gleaming.

Then why is everything so blurred, Grandfather shouted towards the projection room. Perhaps it's me, something the matter with my eyes, he whispered to me, and was quiet for a moment. But then he was too quiet, and wasn't even watching any more. I thought, has he gone to sleep? Or could he be dead? I said: Grandfather, what are you doing?

I'm not even watching any more, he said, I can't see anything anyway. I don't want to see anything either, it's not worth it. Then, when the sound broke down again for a while, he wanted to get up and run down to the screen, and explain the film to everyone. They wouldn't let him through, though, and said: You stay put, Hindenburg, and pipe down! and pushed him back into his place. After a while, the film started talking again. It explained itself. The actors opened their mouths and sang, individually or in groups. Or they explained what film characters they were portraying, what was going on in their heads, and what they meant by the many movements they performed with their heads and feet and hands. When someone clutched his forehead, he said: I'm thinking, when someone

81

scratched his shoulder: I've got an itch! and when he rubbed his eyes: Am I really seeing this!

Ridiculous, all that talking! Who does that in real life, whispered Grandfather, I certainly don't, and everyone shouted: Quiet! You're being a nuisance, Hindenburg!

Grandfather had to be quiet, and sat, shaking his head. When he had got used to all the talking and singing, he looked around for a long time. He wanted to see what impression the sound-film was making on the general public. We're here to conduct research, he said to me, but what are *they* all doing? For my part, he said, I find this film ridiculous! It's unnatural. The lip movements don't fit with what they're saying. There, just look!

The jazz singer's name in real life was Al Jolson. He was a Negro who had a musical gift. That's why he sang such a lot. After seeming to be dumb for a time, he started talking as well. To his old mother he said: Hey, Mama, just listen to this! And all of a sudden he burst into song. On hearing him singing, Grandfather covered his ears.

No, I can't bear it! How unnatural! Can you bear it, he asked.
Yes.
It doesn't make you feel ill?
Not really.

On seeing everyone listening, Grandfather said: I don't get it. He interrupted aloud, shouting: Stupidity, thy name is flimflam! Then he put on his artist's hat. 'After all, we're not in church here!' The people sitting behind complained that they couldn't see.

That doesn't matter, shouted Grandfather, you're not missing anything! Or he closed his eyes so that everyone could see he wasn't looking, and still wasn't missing anything. I'd rather go to sleep, he said. Then he even began to snore. I was embarrassed. I moved away from him. Grandfather disrupted the performance in every way he could. Finally, Herr Theilhaber came out of the corner where he was standing – he's even sold his own seat to make more money, said Grandfather – and shouted through the whole Apollo: Herr Hofmann, I must ask you not to spoil the public's enjoyment of this little masterpiece! That shut Grandfather up for a while, and Herr Theilhaber returned to his corner. Anyway, instead of sitting and listening quietly, Grandfather talked and commented his way through the first sound-film ever shown at the Apollo in Limbach. In the most touching moments, when many were reaching for their handkerchiefs, he laughed aloud. For instance, in the place where the jazz singer turns down a wonderful career opportunity by going to sing on one particular evening, not on stage, but in church, for no money, a chorale for his dying father. Grandfather repeatedly asked the people behind us and in front of us whether 'such stuff really had an appeal' to them, and whether they would kindly tell him 'the point of all this nonsense'. For me, Grandfather said to me aloud, there is no point. That's not the way people talk in real life at all. Out of Saxon politeness and because they guessed how much Grandfather feared the sound-film era and how worried he was, everyone said after the show: You're right, Hofmann, there is no point to it. It isn't art any more. We're disappointed. We don't want to see that sort of thing. It's you we want, Karl, you!

Did you hear what they said, Grandfather exclaimed when *The Jazz Singer* was over, and the Apollo was emptying. With difficulty I dragged myself at his side out of the sound-film era. The jazz singer had made it onto the stage after all. Up in the box sat his mother, a widow by now, under a fetching hat, smiling tearfully but happily in his direction.

If you want my opinion, said Grandfather, brandishing his stick, this kind of thing will never catch on. It's not artistic enough.

We stood by the cinema door. The whole of Limbach was going past. Grandfather scrutinised people's faces, to see what they were really thinking. Some of them he even spoke to. Whether they wanted to hear it or not, he explained to them that 'these efforts to conjure up illusions by means of light and air and spittle are as old as mankind'. And what came of it? Nothing came of it, he cried. As if a natural human voice, like my own for example, could ever be replaced by a recording! Absurd, cried Grandfather, talking now with one person, now with another. Instead of having one man – Grandfather! – talking, they all talked at once, even trying to explain the action and ideally what was going on inside them as well 'and all their inner workings'. 'But Nature won't play along with that, she says No.' Only one person could hold the whole thing in his hand and take the long view of it, and that was himself! Listen to what I'm going to tell you now, said Grandfather to me. That Theilhaber will take things so far that everyone in the Apollo will fall asleep from sheer boredom. And then, when they're all asleep, he'll remember me, and he'll send for me to wake them all up again and put everything to rights, but by then it'll be too late. I'll say no.

And what shall we do now, I asked.

I'll shut up for a while, he said, and you talk. Never, even if they covered the walls with loudspeakers, would they be able to replace Grandfather and his 'living word', never! It's not just me that says so either, it's other people too, for whose judgment I have the greatest respect.

You mean Herr Lange?

Others besides him.

Fräulein Fritsche?

Grandfather gesticulated. In my performances, he said untruthfully, no one has ever slept, no one. And the new sound was so artificial, and . . .

Don't excite yourself! People nowadays will try anything once, said Herr Cosimo, who had looked in to ask what Grandfather had made of the first sound-film in Limbach. He hadn't managed to get a ticket for himself. When that fashion, he said, is over. . . . And then he wanted to know what it had been like.

# Five

By the time the blossoms were gone from our two apple trees, the sound-film had established itself in Limbach, wasn't that right?, and Grandfather had lost weight. We stood outside the tobacconist's, he was counting his money. He said: My life is finished! We looked at all the cigars he couldn't smoke. Instead, with the last of his money, he bought himself some dark glasses made of celluloid. That way you couldn't see his eyes, while he could still see everything in a dark sort of way. Because of the popularity of the sound-film, Grandfather was now permitted to explain a film only twice a week, Tuesdays and Thursdays. Herr Theilhaber was running everything himself.

Do you notice anything, Grandfather asked me in his dark glasses on the way home.

No.

How boring life has become.

Now, instead of Grandfather, you could see Herr Theilhaber at the door counting the audience, but that didn't make them any more numerous. After 'a few weeks of sound', the Apollo was as empty as before.

Grandfather said: Serves him right!

He had a lot of free time now, and he spent much of it staring into space. Grandmother said: He's counting the flies. When he gets to a hundred, he goes out in the garden, and starts all over again. Often he shut his eyes, so as not to see anything at all.

He talked less and 'was eaten up by something'. When I asked him a question, he said: Don't talk! It's improper! Am I talking? Or: Keep your eyes open and your mouth shut! Or else an elephant'll walk in there! Often he would be yawning by lunchtime. 'My day's over.' He now had far more time 'than a man ought to have!' and far less money. I would never have believed it was possible to have so much time and so little money, he said, putting on his celluloid glasses. That way, you couldn't tell if he was laughing or crying or even already dead.

And why should he cry, I asked Grandmother.

For joy at having so much free time now, she said.

Grandfather looked at me through his glasses. The 'birds' feet' were gone now. We almost missed them. The mornings dragged. The afternoons were even longer. 'Never-ending really!' He wondered whether he was still entitled to put on his artist's hat, 'Seeing as I'm not one any more.' He often stopped in the street, lost in his thoughts. He was certain to be run over one day. Now do you notice, he asked me sometimes, be truthful!

What, I asked.

That life is never-ending. And now it's even more never-ending. Well, you still need to grow a bit. But eventually they'll steal your job too and leave you sitting there with all the time in the world. What do you want to be when you grow up?

A film explainer.

Save us, Grandfather said.

Hitting the sack in the evening instead of going to work, holding his pillow over his face so that he couldn't see any of the misery, he missed 'the commotion, the toing and froing', even though it was only on the cinema screen. 'I'm dead now, nothing will happen any more, I can shut up shop.' Because he always fell asleep right away, he was awake again by one o'clock. For a long time he wouldn't know where he was and what he should do, he

86

had dreamed all his dreams already. He lay on his back and stared at the ceiling. Grandmother lay beside him, 'buried in sleep'. For hours he looked at the walls, waiting 'for light, if it should ever come'. Because he was now allowed to 'join the other madmen' only twice a week, he had less 'homework' to do. Instead of thinking about his talk, he lay there thinking about nothing at all. As soon as it was practicable, he would get up and go for a walk. The people of Limbach greeted him rather less frequently now, because he was no longer important. No one asked him what film was coming next, and who was appearing in it. 'I'm slipping out of their lives.' Nobody knew what to talk about with him, standing beside him on the pavement. Many avoided him altogether.

Some time between eleven and twelve, just as Grandmother was thinking of 'maybe a spot of soup', Grandfather began to wait. As if he was just about to leave for work, he had his good shirt on and his trousers with the crease and looked 'like a nice root vegetable' (Grandmother). He liked running his finger up and down the creases. He had distributed his hair evenly over his scalp, so that his 'bald patch' wasn't visible. 'It makes him ten years younger, unfortunately only from the back' (Grandmother). Then he picked up his artist's hat and said: Where shall I go today? Then he called for me.

Come on, let's go into town and stare at the idiots, called Grandfather. The ones who thought what I had to offer them day in day out wasn't good enough. No, they wanted a film with sound. Well, now they've got it! Then he took me by the hand, and we set off. In step – Grandfather took especially little ones, I had to take very big ones – we trudged twice through Limbach, once up and once back. Once I had to pull him, the other time he pulled me.

What now, I asked him, when we were back at our front door and it still wasn't lunchtime.

He looked at his fob watch. What do you think, he asked, did you notice anything?

87

No.

Nor did I.

After that, if it hadn't started raining, we sat down outside the Apollo on the bench Herr Theilhaber had endowed. It was almost always empty. Nor did anyone come to join us, because Grandfather didn't like to talk any more. If he did talk, it would be about people who themselves hadn't talked for a long time, and had then suddenly dropped dead. Or about films, which because of the 'fuss about sound-films' weren't shown any more. And had been forgotten by everybody except Grandfather. He never forgot a film. Occasionally someone did sit down beside us after all, for instance Herr Lange, who even crossed the street specially. For a long time we all looked up at the sky, and no one spoke.

Do you remember, Grandfather suddenly asked, the wonderful film *l'Âge d'Or* (1930, with Gaston Modot and Lya Lys)?

No, said Herr Lange, should I?

Most certainly, said Grandfather. It shows the road taken by a pure man . . .

What poor man, cried Herr Lange, who by now had not only poor eyesight, but was also hard of hearing.

A pure man's road to the ideal, cutting straight through reality, shouted Grandfather, that's what it said in the programme. It's about a couple who are prevented by the powers that be from consummating their love.

How did that happen, asked Herr Lange.

That was in the programme as well. So do you remember the film?

I, said Herr Lange, have other worries.

So you don't remember?

No.

Well, said Grandfather, if your memory's gone, and you've even forgotten that wonderful film, it's simply not possible to

88

have a conversation with you. It would be a waste of time on my part and on yours. Come along, sonny-my-lad, that's enough sitting around, he said to me. Better go stretch our legs a bit. With that we got up, and walked up the Helenenstrasse a way, where there were some more benches. There we didn't have to talk, and just sat. Then Grandfather called out: Look who's coming now! and waved to Herr Cosimo who happened to be passing. Here we are, Grandfather called out, over here! Then he said: Come and join us, Cosimo, and you'll have some company, I could only wish it were better. When Herr Cosimo had sat down and taken off his peaked cap, Grandfather asked him whether he too had been unable to sleep the previous night.

Well, said Herr Cosimo, you know I never sleep particularly well.

Quite, said Grandfather. I expect you were thinking about *Cimarron* (1930, with Irene Dunn and Richard Dix) as well. As Grandfather had been.

I see, said Herr Cosimo, and what was it like?

Very good, said Grandfather contentedly. He was sitting in the middle. He had taken my hand so that I would feel secure. The state of Oklahoma, he said, has just been opened to settlers, and Yancey Cravat wants to start a newspaper, but so does the lovely Dixie Lee, and she beats him to it. So Yancey Cravat moves on to another place, where his predecessor has just been murdered . . . am I boring you, Grandfather asked.

No, no, said Herr Cosimo, go on, please.

Are you sure you want me to go on?

Absolutely, said Herr Cosimo.

At any rate, after many misunderstandings, explained Grandfather, Yancey Cravat ends up leaving his wife and child, and stays all alone in the boundless prairie. And he finally goes missing there. Now do you remember?

I'm afraid, said Herr Cosimo, I must have missed that one.

Well, if you've forgotten it, and haven't any memory, and prefer to go through life like an unthinking beast, then I can't help you, cried Grandfather. The only question then is: What's a man supposed to talk about with you? Come on, lad, Grandfather said to me, we're going home! Maybe lunch will be ready. No wonder no one joined us and everyone preferred to pass by, even if they did all wish us a good morning, because whatever else, they are always polite in Saxony.

You notice how they're letting him stew in his artist's juice, but he's only got himself to blame, Mother said to Grandmother after lunch as Grandfather leaned on his cushion in the window, staring out over the empty street. He didn't hear us. There was no one coming up the street for him to watch. Grandfather lit up his half-cigar and went outside. No one now stopped for a chat. If someone did happen to stop, either Grandfather said nothing at all, or he would talk about his own case, which everyone already knew about. Grandfather would look at his case now from one angle, now from another. He couldn't get away from the great injustice Herr Theilhaber had done him. He put me out on the street, this one here, he said, pointing up the Helenenstrasse. After I'd built up the Apollo and kept things going for him for years, no, for decades, he doesn't need me any more. He suddenly doesn't need my eyes, my voice, my whole head any more. I'm superfluous. Instead he has machines to drone on to people. Do you suppose that sort of injustice is allowed, what do you think, he asked me.

Is it not allowed?

It probably is, said Grandfather.

It's so sad, but with his job at the cinema he's lost all his courage, said Mother quietly, and was once again laying the table for supper. Grandfather turned his back on us. He blew smoke out of the window.

All his sense too, if he ever had any, said Grandmother. She had boiled an egg for each of us, mine was a nice white one.

And what will you do when you've no more work at all, I asked Grandfather. But he didn't answer.

He'll think about the good old days when he did, said Mother.

Won't he find any other work?

He doesn't want any other, because there's none that will let him blather on so, said Grandmother. Grandfather had come to table, but didn't say anything. He had one hand shielding his eyes, so that he couldn't see anything either. Then we sat down round the table, ready to start eating. I had my napkin on.

Now you can make as much mess as you want, said Mother.

What about salt, I said, don't I get any salt?

Suddenly Grandfather smacked his hand down on the table, took a deep breath and said: I had three brothers!

Mother said, What?

It was a while ago, said Grandfather.

You had three brothers, exclaimed Grandmother. She smiled. She shook her head.

Grandfather looked at his feet. Then he nodded and said: That's right. Willy, Emanuel and Franz. Dead, dead, all three of them dead!

Grandmother was still smiling. She said: You and your stories! Why don't you let the boy eat in peace? We all know you didn't have any brothers.

I had my egg in front of me. I had opened the shell. Grandfather took some bread and butter. He didn't eat it, though, he didn't even so much as sniff at it. He said: There are photographs of two of them. I can show them to you.

Our family photographs were kept together with Grandfather's medals in the bottom drawer in my grandparents' room. They weren't really photographs of his brothers, who didn't exist.

They were of Grandfather himself in his younger days. He went off to get them.

Oh Lord, said Mother, now he's starting that again!

Grandmother said: Now he'll talk about all the falsehood in the world. And about death, said Mother, and took another piece of bread, but only a little one, because she didn't want to get fat.

Here, cried Grandfather in triumph, back already. He held up two photographs for me to see. Don't you want to know who that is, he asked me.

Who is it then, I asked.

Your Great Uncle Willy. And that's your Great Uncle Emanuel.

But you didn't have any brothers, I said.

There wasn't time to get a photograph taken of your Great Uncle Franz, said Grandfather. There are no photographs of him, it's all in here, he said, tapping his brow. He was so small, you couldn't have got him onto any plate.

And then what?

He disappeared again.

Where to?

Let the child alone with your stories, said Grandmother, let him eat his egg in peace.

Most of those who knew him, said Grandfather, are by now either dead themselves, or will shortly die, like myself. There are only a few, a very few who are able to say what he looked like, what he said and thought and dreamed. Without leaving any trace, he whisked over the earth and cacked in his pants.

Grandfather, cried Mother, not at table please!

But it's the truth, said Grandfather.

Well, said Grandmother to me, but with your Grandfather it will be different. There won't be too little left of him when he goes, too much more like.

What sort of things, I asked.

Grandmother said: Clothes, like the embroidered waistcoat from the Sauerland. Or his old felt slippers we should have thrown in the fire, and other such sweet secrets.

You have secrets, Grandfather, I asked. What secrets? Tell me! Some!

Grandfather shook his head. He didn't want to tell me his secrets. He turned away from me. Only Grandmother went on looking at me. She said: His application for membership of that little Party which the earth swallowed up again right away. The amber cigarette holder he found in the Apollo and kept quiet about.

He kept quiet about it?

Yes.

And what else?

His three poems about the little hillock near Mittweida, said Grandmother. And of course his 'Confession of One Who was Cold-Shouldered'. And the note that once came in the post: 'Drop everything, fill in the accompanying form, and take ship to Australia! Make a new start in life!' He wrote on it: Too late!

Too late?

Yes, too late!

And then?

At that time, Grandfather was still speaking, even though it was less often and less loud than before. If not about the betrayal of Theilhaber whose business he had carried 'Atlas-like' on his shoulders, then about 'his performances, his triumphs'. He could say 'my triumphs' three times in a single sentence without it sounding odd. It was really embarrassing to his womenfolk.

They were packed in there, said Grandfather, stepping outside the house with me in the fine season after supper, and gesturing in the direction of the Apollo, quiet as mice, listening to me, dozens of them, no, more! They didn't miss a word, he said, and reached into his jacket pocket where the key to the Apollo had been kept until lately, but now Herr Theilhaber had asked for it back, so that Grandfather couldn't even go into his own cinema any more. On the two days he still had, he had to walk up and down outside the locked cinema as in his early days, waiting for Herr Theilhaber or Herr Salzmann to come and let him in. Of course they both had keys. Whereas all Grandfather had was the key to the piano. But Herr Theilhaber didn't know that. He thought it had been lost.

We walked out of town and into the woods. It was getting dark. On the right were the evergreen trees, on the left the deciduous ones. Over all of them hung the sky with the moon that the Lord God had hung up there and then forgotten. Grandfather now had so much time that it was 'dribbling out of his nose, his ears, his mouth' (Grandmother). Sometimes we walked to Hartmanns-dorf, yes, as far as Mittweida, 'if our calves would carry us'. Grandfather told me how everything had been in his life, or might have been.

It was like this, he said, and gestured sweepingly with one hand, I sat on my chest, and everyone . . .

Were there really that many there?

Yes, said Grandfather, so many! They all looked at me, straight at my mouth. Here, he said, pointing at it. There's where the words came from and the thoughts I'd pondered over whole nights. I had my bamboo cane in my hand, and explained everything to them: the kings and queens, the tragic destinies, great happinesses on small islands with the most beautiful women in the world. Their mouths watered, I could hear them drooling. They wouldn't have understood a thing without me, not a thing. And now, because one Theilhaber has fixed a pair of loudspeakers on the wall, they've forgotten all about it.

Now I'm sure they won't have forgotten it, they're just moving with the times, said Herr Cosimo, who sometimes came along. Besides, they have a lot on their minds.

Forgotten, all forgotten, said Grandfather, who was often

annoying now, and given to contradicting. Yes, after the beginning of the sound-film era, Grandfather became annoying! He didn't talk much, and then mainly to himself. Other than that he didn't do much.

Why do you leave us to do all the work, instead of at least occasionally lending a hand like other men, asked Mother, bending over her sewing-machine. She had to sew chemises. Won't you do anything to help us at all, she asked Grandfather, what about weeding the garden?

Whatting the garden, cried Grandfather.

Weeding.

No, said Grandfather, I don't want to weed the garden. And when Grandmother put her head round the door and asked him at least to carry the washing up. . . . Not now, he'd say, maybe later.

When Herr Cosimo went to the graveyard, he had to go past our door. He would be wearing black, and he had a tie on. I'm going to visit my wife. Are you coming, Hofmann, he called up from the street. He had a bunch of flowers that got smaller with each time, because 'money's tight, and no love lasts for ever, even for the dead.' We would always have been waiting for him and looking at the time. Grandfather went up to the window and called: Oh, it's you! What a nice surprise. We're on our way. And then he would push the end of his bread and marge between his 'teeth which were nearing the end of their useful lives' (Grandmother).

Just a minute, he called, something's just occurred to me.

What is it this time, Herr Cosimo called up.

Something philosophical, Grandfather called back. 'That freedom for me is the great outdoors'. Do you get the barb?

Who is it directed against this time?

Against human frailty in general, called Grandfather. Wait, I'll jot it down quickly, otherwise I'll forget it again. Then he wrote it down in his notebook. He said to me: Now let's get out of here, before I suffocate.

We walked past the oil lamp that hung in the landing. 'I couldn't possibly afford electric light in the stairwell on the kind of rent you pay.' (Herr Lange). We went down the hollowed-out steps, Grandfather first. I could see his boots.

These boots remind me, said Grandfather on our way to the graveyard, of that incomparable film *Crainquebille* (1923, with Maurice de Féraudy and Françoise Rosay). In that, the green-grocer had boots as tight as mine. One day he is accused of insulting a policeman.

Really, said Herr Cosimo, what did he say?

Nothing I can repeat in front of the child, said Grandfather. That greengrocer always went around barefoot, because, like mine, his were too tight for him. Other people may have a spare pair to get into, but not Crainquebille and myself.

I have two pairs, said Herr Cosimo, how about you?

Just the one, said Grandfather. At home, to allow his feet to recover, he would always take 'a few paces without'. Then he squeezed his feet back into them. Because, he said, I'm Cinderella's elder brother. When the doves see me, they too go: Roocoocoo, blood in your shoe! And now? he asked.

Herr Cosimo said: To the graveyard.

In Indian file, Grandfather first, we walked out of town. The debonair gait of my dream is impossible in these boots, explained Grandfather. I know how I ought to walk – through the Hoher Hain, through the whole of life – but I can't do it. At home I go around in my stockinged feet till I catch my next splinter. I don't wear slippers, he said, because they're incompatible with the sort of picture of a man that every woman carries in her heart. If my wife sees me in my socks, she says it's bad manners. She claims: Men have smelly feet! I say: Not me! He said: My boots were given to me for a song by the cobbler Lieblich. He made them himself.

They belonged to tax inspector Malz who lived on the Mittweida road in Oberfrohna. But he's dead now. When Frau Malz took them back to Herr Lieblich, they were still warm. Just like in *All Quiet on the Western Front* (1930, with Lew Ayres), said Grandfather. That little masterpiece, he told us, is about the soldier Paul Bäumer, Sergeant Himmelstoss and their company. One day they are moved up to the front line. One after another they die. Each time someone dies, his boots are taken off. They are passed on to the next man, who straightaway greases and polishes them and feels happy to own them, and proudly slides his feet into them until he dies and the boots are available again and go on to the next man. Finally they go to Paul Bäumer, who in turn greases and polishes them and is happy . . .

We had the town behind us now and the road to the graveyard ahead of us. The road was empty.

Am I walking too fast for you, or too slowly, asked Herr Cosimo.

Grandfather said: Just right. I'm walking in dead man's shoes, only no one besides ourselves knows it. Anyone seeing me in these shoes would quite naturally suppose they were mine. But they belong to Herr Malz. I must admit though: If I could have chosen a pair for myself, I would have picked them slightly bigger, said Grandfather. But there wasn't a pair in my size for that price, as no one in my size had lately died. These I'm wearing now are crippling me. Anyway it was while wearing these boots that Herr Malz walked under a locomotive in the goods station, said Grandfather. He was dead on the spot. But for them, I wouldn't have been able to go to work for years in bad weather!

You mean to the cinema?

Yes.

Then, said Herr Cosimo, you would have had to hang around at home all the time, drumming your fingers on the windowsill and asking: What's for lunch today?

Very likely, said Grandfather. Whether he walked under the locomotive on purpose or by accident, nobody knows, he said. When Frau Malz was asked, she just cried and said: Not on purpose! The police called it horrific. A train and a locomotive that size could not have been missed, even by the bespectacled Herr Malz. He walked into it. Unfortunately, said Grandfather, I'm superstitious. I'm sure that something frightful will happen to me because of wearing these shoes.

Herr Cosimo said: Let's get a move on!

Why not, said Grandfather. When the graveyard had been reached, he stopped and said to Herr Cosimo: You're going in here with your flowers, right? Would you mind if my grandson and I join you, so that we can see where she's lying?

Oh, said Herr Cosimo, you know perfectly well where.

Well, let's go and have a look at it again anyway.

Very well, said Herr Cosimo, they say you should never say no to experience.

If that's the way you want to put it, said Grandfather. I expect you'd like to be rid of your flowers too.

We didn't often go to the cemetery, Grandfather and I. He said: There'll be plenty of time for that later. In general, we give it a miss, today's an exception.

First came the cypresses, then the cemetery walls. They were studded with glass 'to stop anyone climbing in, if he's in too much of a hurry'. Then came the graves with he dead people. 'Some have been lying here for years, they don't count any more.' Others were recent.

The cemetery management distributes them over the whole terrain, Grandfather told us. We were preoccupied with our thoughts. At first we approached the graves, then we picked our way through them. Do you know who is lying all around, he asked me. Man and woman, young and old, great and small. So who?

Man and woman, young and old, great and small, I said.

Very good, said Grandfather. I have now, he said, come to a time in my life where nothing is taboo any more, not even dying, and not even in front of my grandson. I can permit myself the luxury of absolute truthfulness. I may speak on any and every subject. That's real freedom, which you only come to late on in life. And truth, he asked me, do you know what that is?

No.

Nor do I, said Grandfather. I have just realised, he said to Herr Cosimo, returning from his wife's grave without his flowers, something I wouldn't like to keep from you. I have realised that if I think about certain subjects while walking, I can move quite effortlessly, even when going uphill. It's as though I'd been lent wings. Among these subjects are my healthy heart, my art, my mortality, and the film actress Pola Negri playing the Arab maiden in *The Eyes of the Mummy Ma* (1918, with Pola Negri, Emil Jannings and Harry Liedtke), in that order. They are my wingbeats.

With me, said Herr Cosimo, it's the other way round. He wiped his hands.

Won't you put your handkerchief away, asked Grandfather.

Yes, said Herr Cosimo, in my trouser pocket. Then we walked a bit more. Those wingbeats you mentioned seem more to inhibit my strides. I don't have any art that might lend me wings. I wouldn't know what it would be.

I suppose not, said Grandfather. He held my hand. When he wanted me to pay attention to a particular word or sentence, he would squeeze it. That meant: Did you hear what I just said? Now he said: I have so many worries. The thought of Herr Theilhaber makes walking impossible for me. With every step I hear: Theil . . . haber, Theil . . . haber! When I think that at this very moment – he looked at his fob watch – he's squatting in the Apollo and watching that marvellous film *Variété* (1925, with Emil Jannings and Lya de Putti)! And even making money out of it! Whereas I'm

99

condemned to wander around in the countryside and .... In *Variété*, explained Grandfather, convict No. 28, who was once the owner of a booth in St Pauli, is telling the prison director his life story. He had fallen so deeply in love with an exotic girl that he leaves wife and child and joins the circus to be the catcher in a trapeze act, if you know what that is, he said to me. His partner's name is Artinelli. He is in love with the girl too, and No. 28 suffers terribly as a consequence, jealousy of course. One day No. 28 kills him by failing to catch him as he comes flying through the air. It's barely ten weeks, said Grandfather, and my name's no longer mentioned on the Helenenstrasse. It's as though I'd never appeared in the Apollo. Under the pretext that the silent film will shortly be nothing but a fading memory, Theilhaber is trying to take away my last two evenings as well. Cosimo, what shall I do?

We were on our way home by now, Grandfather going on ahead. He had picked a bunch of flowers for Grandmother, bell-flowers and dandelions.

Of course, he said, I'd sooner be in the Apollo, doing my duty, instead of killing time out here, but Theilhaber has stabbed me in the back.

But it wasn't just Theilhaber stabbing him in the back, it was the people of Limbach as well, staying away from his Tuesday and Thursday screenings, or going to them only to laugh at the silent films. By doing that, they were giving Herr Theilhaber an excuse to relieve him of his Tuesdays and maybe even his Thursdays.

And that, said Grandfather, is treachery.

Come, come, said Herr Cosimo. He was forced to stop a moment, on account of his heart. He would have liked something to lean against, but there was nothing there. Grandfather stopped, and then I stopped. We had no choice. Grandfather jabbed his walking stick into the ground. There was a pause. He thought about the silent film era, Herr Cosimo about his heart.

Now we must consider death, first his, then yours and last of all mine. In certain books – the inevitable distillation of certain lives – there is talk of life diminishing, disappearing, and of death. But strangely immersion into the void – first up to the chest, then the throat, finally up past the eyes – produces such a dynamic, the negative is so vividly presented, that these very books refresh one's jaded appreciation of life, if you understand what I'm saying, said Grandfather to me.

No.

Only in cognisance of death, said Grandfather, does everything become clear. What he meant to say was: There was a lot of death around. People pulled their socks off and dropped dead. They opened the window onto the garden, leaned out and died. They cried: Never! and died. Grandfather, in his late period, had made his observations. 'All will be snatched away!' Fräulein Fritsche for instance, without whom he claimed he couldn't live – but then it turned out he could – was killed by a disease of the liver. Once, she had been his mistress, sitting behind him in the Apollo and sucking peppermints. If she didn't come, she'd be standing by her window at home looking down the short straight section of the Kanalstrasse to see if he wasn't on his way to her, calling out: I love you, Fräulein Fritsche, I've thought things over! I'm getting a divorce. It's you I want. Sometimes on our walks when we were near the Kanalstrasse, Grandfather's breathing would get louder. He put his hand on his heart. Then he suddenly stopped, looked at his watch, and cried: Oh, is that the time already! Something's just occurred to me.

You need to see Fräulein Fritsche, don't you, I asked.

That's true, said Grandfather. How did you know?

You always need to see Fräulein Fritsche when we're around here, I said.

Yes, I sometimes have important things to tell her, he said. Then he tugged at my jacket, patted my hair, and said: Smarten you up a bit! She won't be home anyway, but we might as well try.

Oh, I said, she's bound to be at home!

What makes you so sure?

Because you picked some bell-flowers to give her, I said.

Fräulein Fritsche saw Grandfather at least twice a week. In the intervals she drank a bit. Grandmother said: All that waiting around will kill her. Then he'll have not just one woman, but two on his conscience. She said this so quietly that Grandfather could only just hear it. But he didn't say anything. Apparently he started visiting Fräulein Fritsche when she was still slim and desirable. Now she wasn't so desirable any more, and his visits were 'not just a scandal for the entire neighbourhood, but frankly laughable' (Grandmother). Their first meetings were before my time. I imagine them to myself. It's early in the morning (or late at night) when Grandfather comes visiting, but that had to be, so that Grandmother was still (or already) asleep and Grandfather could slip out of the house and 'into freedom' unnoticed. Fräulein Fritsche had had a spare key made for him, which was left under the firewood in the shed. That way he could visit her any time. Sometimes he went to see her in the daytime, without a key. Then he would take me with him. We stood under her sitting room window, and Grandfather called out: Fräulein Fritsche, Fräulein Fritsche! He would keep his voice down, so that the neighbours wouldn't hear, but they knew anyway. Fräulein Fritsche bounded up to the window. Sometimes though she bounded in vain. She could hear him all the time, even when he wasn't standing outside. She was now almost forty, but she had 'a figure'. She also had quite a bit of hair, most of her own teeth and all of her commonsense. She loved Grandfather 'smartingly, hearteningly, beyond measure, her treasure, unable to leave him for years, if not forever'. All the time she heard his call, sometimes loud, sometimes soft. She was all alone in life, and needed to think of everything herself. Whatever she couldn't carry home herself, coal for instance, she had to have delivered. Sometimes Grandfather helped her by carrying something up the stairs for her. Then he would say to Grandmother: I'm just going over to that old spinster, I forget her name.

You mean Fräulein Fritsche, asked Grandmother.

Fritsche, hm, could be. She wants me to hump a few things up and downstairs for her. She's quite frail.

You mean that stout female you've been hanging around for years in the Apollo and the Kanalstrasse, asked Grandmother.

Anyway, said Grandfather, I'll be back soon.

Grandmother said: Happy humping. Mind you don't do yourself an injury. You're not as young as you think.

Fräulein Fritsche worked as a seamstress for the firm of Schaarschmidt in the Bismarckstrasse, and lived in the crooked little house of her father, master-hosier Fritsche. She had inherited it. Things in the house were always in need of cleaning because of the way Grandfather smoked. 'I'd rather he smoked in her place than mine, if he has to smoke at all' (Grandmother). Fräulein Fritsche was very busy, and never entertained silly notions. If she ever had any free time, Grandfather would bring along a stack of film programmes for her. Then she was busy again. When she saw or heard him coming, she came flying towards him cooing. When she saw that he'd brought me with him, she said: Oh! Oh, she said, you've brought the boy along!

I can't leave him on his own, whispered Grandfather. Where can I put him, without making her suspicious? Don't you think he's growing all the time?

Yes, she said, all the time!

Anyway, said Grandfather, I can't stay long. I just wanted to check if everything is still as I left it. And I've brought you a surprise.

Fräulein Fritsche was in her robe. She buttoned it up tightly at the top. She always ran to the door like that, even when it had just been 'her ears hoping', and she had just imagined it was

Grandfather. Grandmother said: Hope springs eternal and it's good for the glands!

On the stairs Fräulein Fritsche made little signs to Grandfather with her much-pricked index finger. They signified: I love you and won't ever leave you!

Well, replied Grandfather, who would have thought it. Another fine day.

Ah love, sighed Fräulein Fritsche.

Yes, he said, here we are again, and not empty-handed either. I have a great piece of news. Tomorrow we're showing the excellent film *Such is Life* (1929, with Vera Baranovskaya and Theodor Pistek). What do you say to that?

Oh, said Fräulein Fritsche again.

In this film, said Grandfather, a washerwoman tries to keep her family alive, because her husband, who was a coal-heaver, has lost his job. What a masterpiece!

Oh, said Fräulein Fritsche for the last time, who if she'd given up 'her adulterous relationship with a married grandfather' (Grandmother) could easily have become deputy director of the firm of J. P. Schaarschmidt, but Schaarschmidt didn't want her with a married grandfather in the background. 'The woman should finally realise the old man won't marry her, at least not in this life' (Mother). So the affair dragged on. Grandmother would 'never ever' forgive him, but that was all she could do. She had reconciled herself to the fact that he occasionally 'dropped in on Fräulein Fritsche and gave her a little bit of a shaking'.

Grandfather held his hat in his hands. He spread his arms. I stood behind him. If only he'd still been his old self, or at least a little bit younger! But unfortunately he wasn't, and he felt it all over. For instance he'd just climbed the stairs too quickly. But he couldn't let Fräulein Fritsche see that. We went into her living room. When I wasn't looking, he squeezed her thighs, but only very quickly. She said: My dear old buck! She had been born here, in this very room, but she wasn't going to die in it.

Not now, she said, pushing Grandfather's hand away.

The rooms, like all the rooms on the Kanalstrasse, had crooked walls. The floor was polished pine. On the walls were photographs of film actors and actresses that Grandfather had at some time given or lent her. We had the same ones hanging up at home. That didn't matter, though, because neither woman ever entered the other's flat. Only Grandfather and I knew both places. When she was expecting other visitors, Fräulein Fritsche took the photographs down. 'No one need know that we talk about the cinema so much.'

They know that anyway, said Grandfather, there's no law against it.

All the same, said Fräulein Fritsche, I'd rather take them down.

When she was expecting us, she got the photographs out of the cupboard and put them back up. In time, they had left pale patches on the walls, proof that something usually hung there. The photographs themselves had also lightened over the years.

When we first got to know each other, said Fräulein Fritsche once, they used to be darker.

Yes, said Grandfather, and so was I.

There were also less of them now, as Fräulein Fritsche gradually mislaid them. 'She's killing him off, bit by bit' (Grandmother). There was a picture of Grandfather on Fräulein Fritsche's sewing table. That way he was always close to her heart. It showed Grandfather with his walking stick in his hand. Someone had put their arm through his. But that someone, Grandmother of course, Fräulein Fritsche had simply cut off with her seamstress's scissors. Now he stood there all alone.

Grandfather must have come to this room many times in his younger days. She is said to have been quite enchanted by him, and to have said: Stay with me, if you like! Well, he hadn't stayed, but he did look in from time to time. Her little house had become a kind of second home to him. There were now two of a lot of things. Grandfather had a second pair of slippers parked under Fräulein Fritsche's sofa, a second hat – a present from her! – hanging on her hook. A second notebook lay in her cabinet in case inspiration should strike whilst he was with her. While Grandmother supposed he was up on the Hoher Hain, composing, the already-aged and sparse-haired Grandfather would be lying holding hands with Fräulein Fritsche on her double bed. They chatted about the most recent film they had seen, in the same showing but not side by side. Being long-sighted, she always sat ten rows behind him, that way she could keep an eye on the film and him as well. Sometimes, if the film was very dark and he happened to be looking round at her, she would kiss her hand to Grandfather, or rather a finger. No one else noticed that, only he. Afterwards she went home quietly by herself, and sat down at her machine. She was completely on his wavelength, and was able to continue his thoughts before he'd got to the end of them himself. Sometimes they opened their mouths at the same moment to say the same sentence. Then they laughed together. That was because they loved each other. If she knew he was coming, she would make him pancakes. When she saw that he'd brought me along, she said: Oh, you've got him with you! Well, she said, there's enough room! She helped first him, then me, out of our jackets, and said: There, now sit down! Then she made some rosehip tea and asked me what I wanted to be when I grew up. I had thought about it by now and said: A cinema owner! and she laughed. Grandfather, who had sat down as well, told her the story of *Such is Life* again, but this time the second half of it, where the washerwoman's daughter is suddenly expecting a baby. She loses her job as a manicurist because she slapped a customer who was pestering her. The washerwoman's husband has a mistress with whom he drinks away the rent money, and while the washerwoman is trying to rescue a child on the windowsill, she upsets her tub of washing, scalds herself and dies. (Luckily, having first saved the child's life.) Fräulein Fritsche who already knew the film, still hoped Grandfather would get a divorce and then marry her. It was high time! She worked to make herself indispensable to him. She waited for him to lose a button so that she could sew it back on for him. Sometimes she tore one off herself. Before he slunk off home at night or in the early hours – 'That's not your home at all, your home is here with me!' – they would listen to the church bells together.

Those are our wedding bells, she would say.

In his mind, every time he thought about her, he would just have entered the room. That was the best moment for both of them, they had everything still ahead of them then. They sat in the room that had the standard lamp with its flower-patterned shade. There was her Singer sewing-machine with the bottle of vermouth on it. Fräulein Fritsche had got it down from the cupboard for Grandfather after the rosehip tea.

No thank you, she didn't drink! Well, if he insisted, just a nip!

Her glass was bigger than the others, but Grandfather's was prettier. He was sweating after climbing the stairs. Or from excitement, or fear lest she suddenly 'make him a confession'. She was only waiting for me to get up and go over to the window and be out of earshot. (I did duly go over to the window, but I still heard everything.) Grandfather was now in his slippers. He was terribly worried that she might tell him – 'confess' to him – that she had someone else, someone younger. He knew anyway that she deceived him from time to time. He had told her about his fear and – for the moment! – she wanted to reassure him. I sat by the window, bored. I asked: Grandfather, what shall I do?

Grandfather said: Look at the cars!

There aren't any.

One will come along.

Yes, I said, but when?

They were now sitting at the table by themselves, and she whispered: By the way, if you want to know, I still love you, and have been faithful to you.

Grandfather drew a deep breath and said: So I have nothing to worry about? He tugged at his beard.

No, she whispered, nothing.

Nothing at all, asked Grandfather.

I just told you: Nothing.

Good, said Grandfather and mopped his brow, which might have had sweat on it, excellent.

Then, with that weight off his mind – 'you could practically hear the splash' Fräulein Fritsche once said – he looked at his watch again. Time, time, time pressing! A quick exchange of news. Grandfather had 'manufactured' a new poem, but didn't want to talk about it just yet. What about her? Though they lived in the same town, they saw and heard completely different things. It gave them a lot to talk about. First he would tell her what he had seen and heard, then, after a pause, it was her turn. It was often embarrassing what she said. For instance, Fräulein Fritsche, who was getting on, though in his eyes she still 'moved and felt like a twenty-year-old', asked him: Do you know I'm on my way to becoming an old woman? I'm getting grey hairs! I dye them a little bit so you don't notice them, but they're grey. Or she said: Death is doing the rounds of my old school friends, harvesting them, quite naturally. I suppose they are old enough.

My God, exclaimed Grandfather in alarm.

Fräulein Fritsche, who should have left him long ago, even before the Occupation of the Rhineland, only she lacked the courage and the opportunity at the time, said quietly: If I find someone who's willing to marry me and not just look in for five minutes at a time, with the lights off, I'll leave you, Karl. I don't want to wait any longer. Anyone who wants me can have me.

But I've got you, whispered Grandfather, giving her a look.

Oh, but not on the quick like that, that's not what I have in mind, whispered Fräulein Fritsche.

So you do have someone else?

Not yet, she whispered. Do you think I'll not manage to find anyone?

I hope not, said Grandfather very quietly. And he wondered to himself: How could I secure Fräulein Fritsche to myself for ever, without marrying her on the spot to keep her from running off? Because, having already lost his job he didn't want to lose her too. Fräulein Fritsche, though, was after something that would get her 'off the shelf, and all for herself'.

Can we go now, I asked, Grandmother's waiting. I was still looking out of the window, but there wasn't anything coming.

All right, said Grandfather, hold your horses. In a minute. Fräulein Fritsche has something important to tell me about a film she once saw.

I have such strong feelings within me, and you don't need them all, Fräulein Fritsche whispered to Grandfather.

I do, I do, growled Grandfather, I need them!

But Fräulein Fritsche didn't believe him. She began – she had drunk a glass after all, and Grandfather was having another now –to cry a little bit. A tear came out of each eye, and trickled down her nose. How maddening, I've walked so fast and even picked her some flowers, and now she's crying, I expect he was thinking. Should I just put Herr Malz's shoes back on and take the lad home? Or what shall I do?

Three weeks after the treacherous snapping off of his job – 'stealth, stealth is their way of doing things!' – Grandfather had a fit. It was summer again. We were in the countryside. Grandfather climbed over a stile and drank the milk from a cow.

I would have loved to be a farmer, he said, but it didn't work out.

Sometimes we would steal a young lettuce, wraps it up in Grandfather's handkerchief – he had an extra large one – and carefully take it home. If we ran into the farmer on the way, Grandfather would engage him in conversation. The farmer's eyes would be riveted to the lettuce, but he wouldn't say anything.

Ah yes, Grandfather said as we went on, town life and country life!

Since his fit he didn't talk much. He didn't even shave.

Grandmother leaned against the washing-up table and said: Running around like that!

Well, said Grandfather, that's the way God made me, with stubble!

You're never short of an excuse, are you!

All at once, after he'd been looking out of the window for a while, Grandfather decided he didn't want to live in Limbach any more. 'It's stifling me!' Ever since he couldn't go to the cinema any more, Limbach had been constricting. He wanted to sell up and leave, and take to the mountains by himself, to the hut where he had once unforgettably spent the night as a young man.

To Rübezahl eh, said Grandmother, well I never! The dwelling place of giants, that's the place for him! There he can live off mushrooms and berries, and whatever the kind villagers will supply him with.

And what will become of me, I asked.

But I needn't have worried, nothing came of the Riesengebirge. Instead, there was an enormous scene between Grandfather and Grandmother, which the whole of the Kreuzstrasse heard as far as the Apollo.

The Scene happened over dinner one Sunday, in November I would say. But it could equally well have been October or December. Anyway, fog had settled over the house. The Scene had settled too, and wouldn't go away. It went on into the night, and even then it wasn't finished. It was about Grandfather's 'willingness to work, or rather his art'. As Mother, in her tie-around apron, doled out the boiled meat from the slaughter-house, with potatoes and carrots and lovely gravy, Grandmother suddenly raised her hand. That meant she wanted to speak. She waited for us to be quiet, and then she said: It can't go on like this!

Of course we were all shocked by that. Even Grandfather looked up in alarm.

She knows a man, said Grandmother, who has a great talent, one with which he towers over everyone else, simply dwarfs them. You couldn't spot it right away, no, you had to wait a while for the talent to show itself. But when you'd observed it a while, with disbelief and amazement, you could see the full extent of this talent. It was a gift for avoiding all forms of work, and every other kind of exertion, and leaving everything to his wife, who had married him 'out of carelessness', and to the daughter this wife had borne him. Like most men, this man viewed himself as a higher being, who, out of the kindness of his heart consented to dwell among his mortal family. Of course he refused to lift a single finger to keep this family and to satisfy their bodily wants. Such people, she said, exist! Others might rack their brains and do everything in their power to try and stay afloat in these difficult times, only the man she knew – and once she had been happy to know him – did nothing whatsoever. Or he mooched off to the cinema, and 'prattled stuff that no one was interested in'. Or from time to time he wrote a little poem, so that posterity would know how he felt about the world. And he talked, if at all, well, what else? About his art, cried Grandmother. Now unfortunately the art in question didn't contribute so much as a penny piece to the running of the household. This art in fact only ran up bills, for writing-paper, for instance. But this man . . .

Talk all you want, I can't hear a word anyway, said

Grandfather. He was sitting on his chair. He pointed to his ear. Look, he said, I can't hear you! Not a syllable!

And this man, cried Grandmother, this artist . . . . She stirred her soup.

What's that, cried Grandfather, I can't hear!

This man . . .

I can't hear!

I was sitting between Grandmother who was talking so much, and Grandfather who could hear nothing. I was wearing my pale pullover with the red hearts on it. It was a present from someone I didn't know, but who knew me and who loved me very much. The pullover was 'cack-yellow, the man's favourite colour' (Mother). I had my felt slippers on and my long stockings, because it was getting near Christmas. Mother was still stirring the pan. I had a napkin on. It hung down to my knees. I was thinking of a different man. He had his glasses on so he could see the bones while he was eating, and not choke. He had taken off his jacket because he wanted to 'fill his boots', and rolled up his sleeves. His arms were hairy. This man was sitting on my right, and his breath came hard because he wasn't in the best of health any more, and was probably going to go to Heaven soon. Now he covered his eyes with his hand, he didn't want to see anything of the world any more. Of course the man in question was Grandfather. Who suddenly pushed his plate away, towards Grandmother. And no longer listened to her or replied to her questions, but acted as though she didn't exist, as though she was empty space and he could see right through her.

Mama, you haven't given Grandfather any meat yet, I said.

Grandfather held his hand, with the wedding ring, which was back at home just now, over his empty plate and cried: I want no meat! No thank you! And when Mother at least tried to give him some carrots and potatoes, he cried: No! I want no carrots and potatoes either! I decline!

Very well, said Mother, never one to force her good cooking on anyone. She put the lid back on the pan and took it back to the stove. We all took our spoons and started eating. Only Grandfather didn't eat. He just looked at us, especially our mouths. If he had spoken now, surely he would have said: How can you manage to eat at such a moment! Grandmother ate little, Mother ate slowly, I ate quite normally.

Artsy-fartsy, cried Grandmother suddenly, who on this particular Sunday didn't seem to want to eat, only to quarrel. She liked to quarrel, especially when there was no money in the house. She mostly quarrelled with Grandfather, but he never quarrelled back. Sometimes she quarrelled with Mother, some-times even with me. Today she cried: You and your art! and then she stopped, because she couldn't think of what to say about Grandfather's art. Your art, she cried, is nothing but a lie! Instead of doing a proper job like millions of other people . . .

A proper job, cried Grandfather, is of no value to me!

. . . and working hard at it, cried Grandmother. What is it that makes a grown man scuttle off to the cinema and invent stories? Shadow stories, she cried contemptuously, where shadow beings have shadow conversations and think shadow thoughts, of a kind that no one in real life would ever think, but which only exist on paper or flicker on the screen! Who wants to watch or read that kind of thing anyway, cried Grandmother.

I do, cried Grandfather, and pointed to his heart, I do!

A person, said Grandmother, would be far better off eating his soup and going for walks and being left in peace than wasting his time over things that have been cooked up and concocted . . .

These beings, cried Grandfather, breathe the pure air we call the truth!

But this man, cried Grandmother, is besotted with his air stories, claiming they are actually better than reality! As if anything could be better than reality!

Grandfather, having up till now stared at his plate, now stared at the ceiling. He said: In the delightful, though not exactly heavyweight film *Kohlhiesel's Daughters* (1920, with Henny Porten, Emil Jannings and Gustav von Wangenheim) two men are courting the daughter of a rich farmer. She has a sister, though, a disagreeable and quarrelsome person, and this sister . . .

Ha, cried Grandmother, there he goes again! Any minute now and he'll say the word art!

I forbid you to use that word so dismissively in my house, said Grandfather. In fact I forbid you to use that word at all!

Aha, and now here come the prohibitions!

What word, I asked.

You'd better stay out of this, said Mother.

Anyway, what do you mean *your house*, cried Grandmother, who had to raise the money for the rent at the beginning of each month by herself, because Grandfather kept forgetting to put any money aside. He would reach into his pocket and say: Oh dear, I haven't got a penny today! Besides, it wasn't a house, just a three-room rented flat.

You surely won't have a quarrel on a Sunday, said Mother. She was stirring her soup. She was keen to go on eating.

I won't allow it, Grandfather said again.

What word, I asked.

Now let's eat before we get back to quarrelling, said Grandmother calmly, and we ate.

After dinner, Grandmother and Mother cleared the table. Grandfather's unused plate went straight back to the cupboard. Grandmother said: It's time there were a few changes here! I want that man to pack his things and move out of my bedroom.

Where will he go then, I asked.

I don't care, said Grandmother, he can sleep anywhere he likes. I'm not having him in my bed any more!

And that selfsame evening, while Grandfather was taking a

114

turn round the block – he must know every pebble, said Grandmother – and got lost for hours somewhere by the sewage works, his coverlet and pillow were taken out and dragged into the corridor. Then she put the key on the inside of the bedroom door. When Grandfather got home that night, exhausted from his walk, and tried to get into the bedroom, he couldn't. He couldn't even knock, because then he would have woken everyone up. So he spent the rest of the night on the living room sofa.

Serves him right, Grandmother said the following morning.

Mother said: You are hard on him!

This next day Grandfather spent unshaven by the living room window, 'blackening the curtains with his smoking'. He didn't say a word to anyone, not even me. As the evening came on, he yawned a lot. When Mother or I asked him something, he didn't reply, just stared at whatever clouds happened to be in the sky.

The clouds moved first one way, then another. Once more, he didn't eat anything, at least not with us. But Grandmother had seen that coming, and hadn't cooked for him, but saved time and expense. Then he knew where he was.

Let him creep off to his other woman, or up to the attic, said Grandmother, he's not coming in my bed! Let him sleep with the hens, then at least I won't have to look at him.

And where will you sleep, I asked.

Where I always sleep, said Grandmother, and that night she locked herself and Mother in the bedroom. Mother had spread a cloth over Grandfather's mattress, to make it clear in the daytime as well that he'd been evicted. Since their quarrel, the flat looked completely different. Even the garden and the fence and the sky looked different, especially at night. When I got up to pee or have a drink of water, I climbed over Grandfather, very quietly so I didn't wake him. Once, when I wasn't quiet enough about it, I did wake him after all. He wasn't even wearing his nightshirt, his hair was completely dishevelled. He lay there in his day shirt, having

115

been asleep. He looked at me a long time. He didn't know where he was. He kept looking around, but he couldn't remember. Then he sat up and asked: Where am I? Is this my room?

This is the corridor.

What am I doing in the corridor?

Grandmother says you have to sleep here.

But it's so musty here, said Grandfather. Why did she do that? How am I supposed to breathe here when it's so musty?

I don't know! I can!

I have, said Grandfather, this great big family – actually Grandfather had quite a small family, with one child, but, as I now knew, two women – and no one to look after me. Couldn't you look after me just a little bit? Why do you treat me this way?

I don't know either!

Then the door opened, and out came Mother. She had heard us. She was wearing her purple dressing-gown, which was far too elegant. She leaned over Grandfather and asked: What's the matter with you now?

What is this place, said Grandfather, where have you put me?

Mother said he was in our flat.

Which is in the Kreuzstrasse in Limbach in Saxony, in Germany, in Europe, on Earth, in the Universe, I said.

You're in the corridor instead of the bedroom, said Mother. Don't you recognise the wall, she asked, stroking it with her hand.

After he'd looked at the wall for a while – Grandmother always said: scrutinised – and felt it, Grandfather said: Yes! Then he shut his eyes and again said: Yes! Yes, he said, now I recognise it. That's the wall.

Then Mother pointed out other bits of our flat which he might not have recognised either, the mirror, the coathooks and the door from the corridor. Grandfather recognised them all. Having recognised them, he asked: So is this my bed?

116

Yes, you're in your bed.

And why is my bed not in my room?

Then Mother explained to him why not.

Oh yes, now I remember, said Grandfather. And then he remembered that he was only allowed to explain one film per week and accompany it on the piano, and even that perhaps not for much longer. And then he grew very quiet. I was in the lav and could hear how quiet he was. Mother was quiet too. There wasn't a sound from outside either, or from the houses around us. Then Grandfather suddenly started to gulp and to groan and finally to sob. I could hear it all. I heard Mother quietly saying: Come on, pull yourself together! and: Haven't you got a handkerchief? Grandfather did have a handkerchief, but he went on sobbing. And yet Mother had been warning him for weeks and explaining to him that it was best for him to give up his job as a cinema narrator and piano player, because there wasn't any more demand for them now, at least not in Limbach. They're redundant now, said Mother, don't you understand? (Actually she should have said: You're redundant now, but what she said was: They!) And that he had to adapt himself, and quickly! But Grandfather didn't want to adapt, 'not at my age'.

But you must, you should do something using your hands, not just your mouth, said Mother that night, cheekily. And now don't think about it any more, go back to sleep, she said, and wanted to go back to her bed. But Grandfather wouldn't let her, he held onto her dressing-gown. He couldn't sleep, he had to keep thinking about the eighth scourge of mankind.

Remind me what that was, said Mother.

Unemployment, he said. Of course there had to be unemployment from time to time, the laws of economics demanded it, but not for such long periods! And Grandfather had to think about the many dying professions, and the many families that were dying with them. Although it was only just after midnight, he had

117

had enough sleep, he was too worried to sleep any more. He felt like getting up and preparing himself, but what for? To spend sleepless nights lying in the corridor was unbearable to him, the way the walls and the ceiling pressed down on top of him. And it was cold there too. Aren't you cold?

No.

I am.

So Mother took Grandfather's cover and pulled it into my room, because there was a little stove there that was on in the evening and still held a little heat.

The floor is warmer in here too, she said. Then she put me back in my bed, and laid Grandfather down on his mattress. She switched the light off and said: Go to sleep now! With that she left us. I couldn't see Grandfather any more, but I could hear him. I could hear him breathing and sighing and bashing his mattress at intervals.

Why are you doing that, I asked.

What am I doing?

Making a noise.

Oh, you mean that noise, said Grandfather, and thought about why he was making that noise. Each time I think of a new worry, I try and picture it. Then I punch it, he said.

Your worry?

Yes.

So you've just thought of another one?

Probably.

Can't you remember?

I forget them right away. There are so many of them.

What about now, I asked, because Grandfather had just made the noise again.

That one too.

Well, what was the last worry you can remember, I asked. But Grandfather didn't tell me. Nowadays he had to think for an awfully long time before he spoke. Even then, he often said nothing.

Can you see me, I asked later.

No, I can't see you.

But you can hear me?

Hear you, yes.

And sleep? Are you able to sleep?

No, I can't sleep either.

Then I asked Grandfather if he had just been having an important dream when I walked into him in the corridor.

Grandfather thought for a long time. Then he said: No, I don't have dreams any more.

Not even about the cinema?

No.

Why not?

At my age, you can't allow yourself to do that.

All you think about is work, isn't it, I asked, and knew what was coming. And Grandfather duly replied: Ever since I haven't had any, because they didn't need me any more, yes! I used to think, he said, that as an artist I was something special. But it isn't true. I'm on the street, same as millions of others, and all of us treading on each other. Soon I'll be reduced to begging, artist or not! It's not just that I don't bring any money into the house, I'm no longer the higher being I always believed I was. Strictly speaking, I shouldn't wear my artist's hat any more either. I've lost everything I ever had, said Grandfather, and he made the noise again.

I turned over, pulled my blankets up to my chin and went to sleep.


It was, as Grandmother put it, the time between the Sino-Japanese War and the Spanish Civil War. She put on her coat. It was fraying at the bottom. It was already quite old. Every

119

afternoon Grandfather took down his artist's hat and because he could stand it at home no longer, went to visit Fräulein Fritsche. Sometimes Grandmother pushed me out after him, crying: Quick, you go too! She'll be glad if you go! Fräulein Fritsche would be waiting for him, with a glass of vermouth already inside her. Sometimes I had to wait outside, sometimes I was allowed in. Grandfather never needed to knock, the door was always wide open. Fräulein Fritsche wore the red dress with the long sleeves. She was mostly cheerful. Grandfather, not so cheerful, sat down at the table and talked about his headaches. When one was coming on, he felt it first in his eyes. They would start to water. The inside of his head was bad too. He packed me off into the corner, where the pictures of film stars were hanging, because I wasn't to hear what they were talking about. I heard it anyway. At first Grandfather whispered: Am I mistaken, or are we destined to spend a little more time together?

Fräulein Fritsche raised her eyebrows and asked: Why do you say that?

Because it seems I will go on living a while yet.

Oh, she said, that's nice!

Yes, he said, and grow even older! Isn't it ghastly? Not really old, of course, for Heaven's sake, but old enough! What do you think, he asked Fräulein Fritsche, shall I go on living awhile yet?

At that Fräulein Fritsche, having poured them both a glass of vermouth, would laugh, and shake her head at such a question, which only Grandfather would ever have asked. Of course you should, she whispered.

Or else, if Grandfather's head was especially bad, he said: It's all up with me, I'm finished! Everything, he said, must come to an end! And when she asked: What's the matter now, he whispered back: We should say goodbye to one another, preferably here and now!

Ssh, she whispered, the boy can hear you.

Then, he whispered, I could face my coming death with more equanimity. I feel it coming, you know. And when Fräulein Fritsche was downcast and made no reply, he said: Or shall I get a bit older still? I know what you're thinking, he whispered. You're thinking: *Even* older, aren't you? It's strange, he said, actually I don't feel all that old! On the contrary, I feel . . . I feel like the clay man in *The Birth of the Golem* (1920, with Paul Wegener, Adolf Steinrück and Ernst Deutsch) whom they breathe life into, played by Paul Wegener. Do you remember?

No.

In that excellent film, Grandfather explained in his normal voice, the Emperor passed a decree that all the Jews have to leave Prague before the new moon. Then the rabbi Löwy kneads a statue out of clay. Out of the lump which has been lying in his washtub he fashions something in human shape, and people are curious and stand around it. I remember, said Grandfather, the way they put their hands behind their backs as they walk around it. That's to show how pensive they are. They step up to the new man and touch him. One man touches him on the arm, another on the neck, a third under the chin. Some even went so far as to lick him. The rabbi then imbues the artificial man with life, said Grandfather with me by now sitting on the sofa, eating a sweet, by means of a secret magic formula, so that he can follow orders. I remember how he saves the Emperor's life by holding up the collapsing ceiling of the palace long enough for him to . . . . Unfortunately he falls in love with the Princess. He tries to elope with her. He drags her by the hair through the city in an attempt to get away. Then everyone joins together and they drive the clay man up a tower from which he falls and meets his death.

Oh dear, said Fräulein Fritsche.

Yes, that's the way the film goes, said Grandfather, whose memory for details wasn't what it used to be. Previously, when he'd spent a couple of minutes on Fräulein Fritsche's chair and had taken a sip of vermouth, he had always pulled her off the sofa and 'dragged her off to bed, I know him!' (Grandmother). But Grandfather no longer functioned so quickly any more. Often he forgot all about giving her a shaking. When we were on our way home, he would ask me: Wasn't there something else I'd meant to do? Think, he said, think!

Weren't you going to talk to Fräulein Fritsche about Hans Albers?

No, that was last week. Never mind, he said, it'll come to me sooner or later! Oh yes, he said, as we passed the Apollo on our way home, where they were just showing *The Last Alarm* (1936, with Tom Keene and Karen Morley) – another sound-film, of course! – now I remember!

What was it?

Oh, said Grandfather, it wasn't important.

Sometimes he was even afraid of it. Or, to demonstrate his good will, he made Fräulein Fritsche take off her rayon chemise and show him her 'as they say in popular novels, small but firm breasts' (Grandmother). Maybe that helped, who knows! Either that or she – always drinking a little more than him, and therefore always a little more cheerful – without saying anything, would simply take his hand and pull him into her bedroom where she had her double bed. Grandfather would say to me: Now you stay here like a good boy and look at the picture book Fräulein Fritsche has bought you. It's very pretty and educational. I'm just going to pop in here for a minute, there's something important I need to do. No need for you to be afraid.

Will you be long, I asked.

Oh, five minutes at the most, said Grandfather. Then he went next door, where Fräulein Fritsche was already waiting. He locked the door. In the book Fräulein Fritsche had given me and that I was allowed to look at, a witch was being slaughtered. She lay in the straw quietly and submissively, with her eyes shut. First

122

they cut off one of her legs, then the other. I heard a noise from next door. But instead of the short, vigorous, brutal juddering and panting on the brass bed, making the springs jangle, there was now always a long silence. Then the bed gave a single creak, Grandfather groaned, Fräulein Fritsche emitted a whispered: Oh!, and that was that.

My life is ruined, said Fräulein Fritsche quietly. I should have married and had children!

What, exclaimed Grandfather, married another! And me, what about me? He had sat up again, he was probably putting his trousers back on. Fräulein Fritsche let slip another: Oh!, she couldn't think of anything else. Then she beat the bed with the flat of her hand and said: How long have I been sitting here, waiting? And how much longer will I have to wait? You say you love me! Fine, she said, I love you too! But I can't stand any more of what we have now! I want to be needed by someone, not just to be looked in on! I want him sitting in my house while I'm sewing or cooking or when I come home, she said at the time of the Olympic Games. I was often sitting next door, I could hear her easily. On my lap I had the witch book that I had to look at. I heard Grandfather too. He said quietly: Don't leave me! Then the door opened. Grandfather stood before me. His hair was all messed up, but he was dressed again. All except for his tie. He had his jacket in his hand. He looked at his watch.

Oh, he said, you're still here then! Did you have a nice look at the pictures?

Yes, I said, and what about you?

I, said Grandfather, do a lot of groaning. But it doesn't mean anything. It's just something I do. Then he put on his dreadful tie, and got into his jacket. It had a stain. Fräulein Fritsche had offered to remove it. But he didn't let her, because it wasn't her business, it was Grandmother's. Grandfather sighed once more. Then he put on his artist's hat. Suddenly he was in a tearing rush.

Something impelled him homewards. He went up to the bedroom door and knocked and called: Hallo, Fräulein Fritsche, are you still there? Won't you come out so we can say goodbye to you, the boy and I?

We heard Fräulein Fritsche sigh. She said: All right, I'm coming! She had her black shoes on. Her dress was buttoned up to the very top. Are you going, she said.

There's nothing else for it, said Grandfather. Did you wash your hands after your sweet, he asked me.

Yes.

Then say goodbye nicely to Fräulein Fritsche!

I said goodbye. Grandfather said: Well, what can I say? That's life, isn't it! Then he kissed Fräulein Fritsche the way they kissed in films, first on one cheek, then the other. He whispered something into her ear as well. It was either: Don't leave me! or: Don't believe me! or both.

Fräulein Fritsche, with in all likelihood a longer lifespan ahead of her than Grandfather, merely looked at him. Then she looked at the floor and shook her head. That signified either: Well, that's that then! or: Never again!

What with Grandmother's 'perpetual griping', Grandfather just couldn't stand it at home any more. Sometimes, when we were just arriving home, he heard her voice and turned on his heel and walked away again. I followed him. He said: Let's take another turn! There's nothing for me in the Kreuzstrasse, he said, nor anywhere else in the world for that matter.

Grandmother, who would have heard us coming, watched us going. She had an apron on, and was standing by the ironing board. She liked to refer to the fact that, for all his gifts, Grandfather brought no money into the house, while other men, far less gifted, 'have made a packet since Hitler took over. Some are just too lazy to look!' She would have liked to throw him out, just like that.

Nor was Grandfather any happier on the street outside. It was too narrow for him. He wouldn't sit on the bench in front of the Apollo, not until his 'employment situation was settled, one way or another'. The present one, I tell you, is unendurable, he said as we passed it.

He was still going 'to work', that is to the Apollo, once a week. Because he would have felt too lonely in there by himself, he usually took me with him. When he showed 'something silent', the whole place would be empty, and I could sit anywhere I liked. Often I moved around. Sometimes, instead of going to the cubbyhole to change, Grandfather sat down next to me in the empty cinema and closed his eyes. His head was slumped between his shoulders. He still had his artist's hat on, and was staring at the floor. He didn't greet anyone, not even Herr Cosimo and Herr Lange.

Grandfather, I said, you must get changed. The film is starting any minute.

Oh yes, he said, I'd quite forgotten. I'm going up the line.

Then he got his little tailcoat out of the cubbyhole, quickly slipped it on and showed us – all five of us, maybe – *Alraune* (1927, with Paul Wegener and Brigitte Helm), in which Professor ten Brinken works on the problem of artificial insemination for so long until he actually cracks it. Alraune is born, the daughter of a prostitute and a murderer who went to the scaffold, explained Grandfather. She brings misfortune to everyone, especially anyone who loves her. Therefore the Professor is compelled in the end to kill her and himself as well. A week later, he showed *The Last Man* (1924, with Emil Jannings). In that one, the porter of the big Hotel Atlantic commands universal respect until the day he is allegedly too old for the job, and is transferred to the lavatories. Of course he's in despair, and behaves in front of other people as though he were still the porter and not a lav cleaner. Until his daughter's wedding. Then he has to steal his old uniform, so that everyone respects him. But his theft is discovered, and he would have had to go to prison, had not . . . . The following week, there was *Madame Dubarry* (1919, again with Emil Jannings, Pola Negri and many others). The heroine starts her career in a fashion salon until the king's eye alights on her, and she becomes his mistress and the most powerful woman in the land. But then the revolution comes along, and she is going to be beheaded along with everyone else . . . . When Grandfather explained a film in the Apollo now, he did so much more slowly than before. 'He can no longer think of the words' (Grandmother). He left long pauses between sentences. He hoped something would come to him in the silences. Sometimes he closed his eyes too, as though he could talk in his sleep. It was to show that under such conditions his job no longer interested him. Besides, he wanted to show how unhappy he was. For long stretches he would say nothing at all, and merely pointed at the screen. And he would say: This is the film for which you have shelled out so much of your money. Now you must look at it yourselves. What's the point of my talking about it? From now on, I'm keeping my mouth shut! And that was all he would say.

He doesn't enjoy it any more, he has nothing left to say in him, said Grandmother, and wished he would stay at home.

Even fewer people now came to his showings, if that were possible. All of them would have preferred to see a talkie. Instead of being glad and clapping when Grandfather stepped up to the screen with his little stick, they were disappointed and said: Oh no! In the most exciting places, they laughed because there was no sound. Or they called out: What's going on, Hindenburg, tell us! No one any longer wanted 'something silent', no matter how outstanding. No wonder Grandfather lost heart, and ended up saying nothing beyond: The programme is beginning! Or: Just the scene with the dwarf now, and then it'll be all over. Then he tinkled away on the piano for a while and stopped. He just let the film take its course.

You didn't talk about the film today either, I said as we went home.

Grandfather said: Talk about the film!

And why not?

Because I've used up all the words I was given at my birth, he said.

And what will you do now?

From now on I'll keep my mouth shut, he said.

When Grandfather had a visitor, for example Herr Cosimo or our landlord, and the visitor knocked on the door and said: Grüss Gott! or: Heil Hitler!, Grandfather made no reply, or he said: Who are they!

Mother, coming in at the same time, said: Don't be put off by our hermit here! Come inside! There he is cowering in his corner, obstinate as a . . . I don't know!

I'm really not bothering him? asked the visitor.

How could you? He's not doing anything!

Grandfather sat in his corner. He had laid his hands on his knees, and didn't want to work any more. It was really embarrassing. When a visitor came, he did at least improve his posture and sit up straight, but he wouldn't speak and 'in his mind he'd be off somewhere else'. If they asked him: What's on your mind, Herr Hofmann, he wouldn't say. When he was alone with the visitor and me, each of us would sit in his own corner in silence. Sometimes Grandfather would lean forward and examine his fingernails. The visitor sat in the comfy chair, and hoped Grandfather would say something, it needn't be anything earth shattering. Just so long as he said something! And sometimes he really would say the odd word, such as: Dark! or: Cold! or: Nothing to say! Then he would be quiet again. The visitor would be just as silent as Grandfather himself. And so would I. When Herr Cosimo walked up to the Hoher Hain with us now, and talked about his heart, he had to do it all by himself. Grandfather wouldn't say anything.

127

Well, Hofmann, said Herr Cosimo, not saying anything today?

Nothing, said Grandfather.

You have been cutting yourself off of late! May one ask why?

Grandfather looked down at his boots, then up at his old friend. But he didn't say why.

# Six

The curtains parted and I saw two men fighting. Then the curtains closed again. Someone in the Apollo audience shouted: Look at them! and laughed. The men fought on, in front of the curtain now. They were wrestling each other. Then the curtain parted once more, and this time the feature began, over the top of the men. It was the sound-film, *The Old King and the Young King* (1934, with Emil Jannings and Werner Hinz), a historical drama. The young Crown Prince of Prussia, fed up with his strict upbringing, plans to run away with his friend von Katte . . . . My eyes had grown used to the dark. I could make out the two men. There was Theilhaber in his black coat and health sandals. His hat was rolling around on the floor. And beside him stood Grandfather in his little tails that he now wore just once a week. The film was projected onto them and . . . . The young Crown Prince, with Lieutenant von Katte, plans to run away from home, so the old King is forced to have von Katte arrested. Von Katte understands, and he puts up no resistance. He even allows them to tie a handkerchief over his eyes and shoot him. Once he's dead . . .

Grandfather and Herr Theilhaber hadn't exchanged a word for some weeks. They had nothing to say to one another. Now, in the darkness of the Apollo they set about one another.

Take your hands off me, Hofmann, whispered Herr Theilhaber.

You're trying to starve me into submission, whispered Grandfather.

You're hurting my hair, whispered Herr Theilhaber.

But I'm not going to let you, whispered Grandfather.

Let go of my hair, whispered Herr Theilhaber.

You're trying to starve me, wheezed Grandfather.

And with the film running on top of them they fought on. After the execution of von Katte, the young King changes in just the way the old King had always hoped, but never dared express. The lover of the arts and all-round weakling becomes a proper king who goes around in boots, and only comes to understand his father in the hour of his death and . . . . Grandfather and Herr Theilhaber were both red in the face. They panted for breath. They looked out into the Apollo, they looked at me. Then each tried to push the other off the stage. But the other fought back. In both their eyes you could read: He's gone mad, just look at him! Thank God, it was the matinée. There were only five people there. They were all watching the fight, not one of them was watching the film. Suddenly Herr Theilhaber got up on tiptoe and screamed something like: What do you think . . . you're doing, grabbing me . . . by the hair! Let go of my hair . . . at once, Hofmann, take your hands off . . . my hair and . . . . But Grandfather didn't let go of his hair. He thought: If I can free my arm, the performance will go on and I'll finally get my job as film explainer back! Whereas Herr Theilhaber wished the curtain would come down again, so he could have the film wound back and started all over again, once Grandfather had left his cinema. In the darkness, Herr Theilhaber looked small but solid, and he tried to tear Grandfather away from the curtain, until his sleeve, which Grandfather was tugging at, suddenly ripped, and Grandfather . . .

Grandfather, I cried. Everyone laughed.

Grandmother said afterwards that it was his fault, he'd had a 'relapse'. He had wanted to carry on as before, but films nowadays were doing their own talking. He had wanted to go up on stage and tell the people about *The Old King and the Young King*, whereas Herr Theilhaber wanted him away from the screen so that . . .

Herr Theilhaber kept shouting: Draw the curtain, Salzmann! But Salzmann didn't draw the curtain. Then there was the terrible, laughable thing – but, as Grandfather said later, 'they always go together: What is laughable is terrible, and the terrible is laughable!' The curtain, in its rail, pulled by Herr Theilhaber in one direction and by Grandfather in the opposite direction, came down on top of the two men. They both stood there, swathed in curtain up to their bellies, and . . .

Grandfather, I cried.

Grandfather wept on the way home, but he had a handkerchief. When he couldn't find it right away, there was always his sleeve. Sometimes he spoke too. He said: Oh God, why hast Thou forsaken me?

Come on, I said, let's go home!

I have no home, said Grandfather. He walked close beside me, so he wouldn't fall over. His hair was everywhere. Tears rolled down his cheeks, and dripped down onto his best shirt. Herr Theilhaber was said to have been crying as well, when his wife came running into the Apollo, into the room marked 'No Admission'. That's where they had taken him. She sat down beside him and spoke of 'consequences'. I took Grandfather home. He had scratches on his face, and grazed knuckles which Grandmother treated with pork fat. As for Herr Theilhaber, he was missing a whole handful of curls over his left ear, which Grandfather had never been too keen on, and which were found the following morning when the Apollo was cleaned.

These are yours aren't they, asked the cleaning woman.

Oh God, groaned Herr Theilhaber.

The cleaning woman wrapped them up in a sheet of newspaper. She pressed the package into Herr Theilhaber's hand. Grandmother told me about that when we were talking about it later.

The following weekend our womenfolk were discussing politics again. Another Pact had just been torn up. I lay in bed wondering: What for? I wasn't asleep yet. Then the front door opened. There stood Grandfather. He staggered inside. He couldn't find his chair. And yet the ceiling light was on, the flat was bright, the chair was right in front of him. Grandfather had already fallen down once. You could see that from his trousers.

That's all we needed, now the unhappy man has had a fall as well, Grandmother said to Mother. They put down their needles, Grandmother her knitting needles, Mother her sewing needle. Then they went over to Grandfather and helped him to sit down. They helped him out of his coat. A fall, said Grandmother again, and she shut the door of my room. I got up out of bed. I opened the door. Grandmother had her eyes closed. She was leaning against the cupboard. She felt 'sorry for the old fellow'. She decided to let him sleep in her bedroom again, so that it wouldn't happen a second time. This time it was him who didn't want to.

I'd rather lie on the floor, he whispered. I can die there too, if you like. He talked with such a bleached-out voice I could hardly understand him. He couldn't find the words he wanted right away. He just left spaces and said: Yes, that's what I mean! Sometimes he said things that didn't make sense, or that didn't even exist, like the word *endinsight*.

And what does that mean, I asked Mother. I was in the room with them by now.

Oh, said Mother, something or other, even if it's not given to us to understand it.

If someone sees him lying in the corridor, by tomorrow all of

Limbach will know that we're a broken family, said Grandmother.

He'll die on us there, said Mother, that's all we need!

And why did he lie down, I asked. I was standing in front of him now. His face was pale. He had shut his eyes. And it wasn't even that late.

If he walks around, he'll only have another fall, said Grandmother.

And yet Grandfather hadn't had anything to drink, which is what we had at first supposed. He hardly ever drank now, he couldn't afford it. When he got up off the bench outside the Apollo as it got dark, he had had an attack of vertigo, which had 'pushed him to the ground'. The Helenenstrasse, far from running smooth and flat, was waving up and down in front of Grandfather, as did every other street as well. And so Grandfather had collapsed. He had barely made it home.

I'm not long for this world, he said quietly.

Maybe you should eat something, I said.

He said: No, I want nothing more to eat. I've already eaten all I'm going to eat in this life.

Typical of him to break down just at the moment when he would normally have got up to explain a film, said Mother, taking her lovely vegetable broth back to the kitchen. Grandfather didn't want it.

If you're as pig-headed as he is, it's easy to collapse, in fact it's hardly surprising, said Grandmother. We had pulled his shoes off and laid him on the mattress.

I asked: When is he going to get up again?

That's for the doctor to say, said Mother.

The doctor was Dr Lantsch. He wasn't in the first flush of youth either, hadn't been for quite some time. He looked like a doctor. When he knocked, Grandmother let him in. He wasn't surprised to find Grandfather lying in the corridor. Nothing surprised him any more. Not even that Grandfather had his eyes shut, that he didn't say: Good evening, doctor! and was barely breathing. The doctor went up to him. How has he been, he asked Grandmother, did he lie down himself?

Yes.

Is he able to stand up?

He prefers lying down, said Grandmother.

Well, said Dr Lantsch, then let him lie! Now, Hofmann, he said, and bent over Grandfather, a little evening mishap, eh, the kind of thing that might happen to any one of us, especially at the great age all of us are so rapidly approaching, he said. So saying, he took Grandfather's hand and looked for the pulse. He found it too. Grandfather hadn't said a word, not even: Good evening! At least he opened his eyes, but otherwise he lay very still and passive. Dr Lantsch shone a torch into his eyes. But he didn't say anything. He preferred to comment on the fug in the corridor, and he pushed open the little window. That got his fingers dirty, and he wiped them on his handkerchief, which he quickly put away. Once, Dr Lantsch bent down over Grandfather's chest with his long stethoscope, and listened to his heart. Grandmother was off towards the window, but he said: Can't you keep still for a moment! Then he put his stethoscope away and made as if to speak. But for a long time he didn't say anything, he just collected his thoughts. And then he said: He's been lucky. He was *this* close to catastrophe. He ought really to go to the hospital in Chemnitz. But every last bed in it is occupied, and they wouldn't take him. Then he went over to his doctor's bag and opened it. I have other calls to make, he said, such is life. Onwards and upwards, eh! He looked round our living room. No sooner have I arrived, he said, than I'm already looking for the door! Then, once he'd found it, he looked at Grandfather again. He had shut his eyes again. Dr Lantsch took his prescription pad out of his doctor's bag, and said that Grandfather could stay in bed 'or wherever it is you've got

134

him now' and rest for as long as he liked, but he wasn't allowed to stoop.

And why may I not stoop, asked Grandfather suddenly. He had heard every word. He could even speak, if a little slowly.

The earth, said Dr Lantsch, pulls us down with its gravity anyway, so let's not do its work for it by stooping as well. Instead, take the tablets that I've prescribed for you with a little water, three times a day at regular intervals.

Grandfather, not wanting to speak aloud, beckoned Dr Lantsch nearer. Herr Doctor, he said, am I going to die?

We are, said Dr Lantsch, all of us are!

I mean: Now?

That depends what you mean by *now*, said Dr Lantsch. On a geological scale of time, you're already dead. But when you said *now*, I expect you had no particular moment in mind, but were thinking of some stretch of time. Well, how long is a piece of string? Because die you certainly will, sooner or later, like all the rest of us. But, he said, at least you'll be armed with my prescription against dying, which I've left on your cupboard. There, he added, next to the gas bill, which you probably haven't paid either. And with that he left.

That all happened on a weekend. Of course we were all glad that Grandfather had managed to give Death the slip, and was still with us. He slept a lot now. Grandmother was always fussing around him. She had knitted him a little bonnet so that his head didn't catch a chill. But Grandfather refused to wear it, because she had made it, and because it made him look 'like a senile baby'. In the daytime we saw him moving around, and at night we heard him snuffling. As we sat over breakfast in the kitchen, he lay looking up at us, watching us eat. Although he was thin and pale, he didn't want anything, and pushed everything Grandmother set before him a long way away.

I don't want any, he said.

Come on, said Grandmother, not even that little bit?

Nothing, he said.

It wasn't only his shirts and jackets and trousers that got too big for him, his skin started to hang off him as well. Even his artist's hat, which had always fitted him so well, got to be too big.

I'll have to stuff a newspaper into the lining if I'm to wear it again in this life, he said to me.

I asked: Why shouldn't you wear it again?

I won't be with you for much longer, he said.

When we were eating now, he looked first at our plates, then our mouths.

How can you manage to eat all the time, he cried, do you really need all that food? He himself could no longer eat, there was less and less of him. Sometimes he said: Come here! and showed me his belly. 'Look at it, I'm shrivelling away!'

In the immediate aftermath of his collapse, we had resolved always to be nice to him, far, far nicer than we used to be. Mother smiled a lot more. Grandmother no longer said: Aren't you going to work today either? He just went on and on being ill.

Isn't he ever going to get better, I asked.

As Grandfather lay ill in the corridor for such a long time, we gradually forgot our resolution always to be nice to him. The first to forget it was Grandmother, then Mother, and then finally me. Grandfather, if he had ever had such a resolution himself, forgot it too. 'He simply has no idea how much having a grown man lying in the corridor gets in the way of a busy housewife with her pots and pans' (Grandmother). Unable to go for walks, he was always sitting at home. Sometimes when he'd been staring into space and sighing for hours, he beckoned me to him and quietly said something. He said: I've got an errand for you, but ssh!

Shall I, I asked, go to the Apollo?

How did you know that?

Because I'm always going to the Apollo for you.

Now listen, he said, whatever you do, I don't want you to go inside! I don't want *him* to see you. I just want you to look and see what they're playing today. And who's appearing in it, Grandfather called after me, so that I have some idea of what's happening in the world. Hurry up, he cried, I'm waiting!

Off I went. I had to greet a lot of people and tell them all that Grandfather was *better*, if not yet *well*. When I got back, I called out to him from the stairs: It's *Traumulus*! With Emil Jannings.

And Hilde Weissner, asked Grandfather. He was sitting up on his mattress.

Yes, I cried. Emil Jannings plays a professor and she's his second wife. Arnold Paulson is the no-good son from his first marriage.

All right, said Grandfather, I know it. So I'm not missing much. I had an idea he might get that one out again. I wouldn't mind seeing it once more myself.

Grandfather got in the way and bothered all of us, especially Mother. And she with so much to do! She was always bent over the sewing-machine, stitching and hemming. But Grandfather didn't let her alone. He was always after something. Often Mother wouldn't even reply, she just went on with her sewing. Then Grandfather would call through the doorway: Why don't you answer? Aren't I worth an answer? Am I a leper sitting outside the door, who doesn't deserve an answer? What about showing a little politeness towards an old man who also happens to be your natural father?

Oh, Mother called back, I am polite. I just have so much to do.

Grandfather got on all of our nerves, because he kept wanting things. For example he wanted to know what we were having to eat: Boiled beef or pancakes or 'some nice soup'. Often the women themselves wouldn't know. Or they didn't want to talk about food the whole time. But Grandfather, when he asked a question, wanted a reply right away. Often he leaned against the wall and demanded to be 'entertained'.

Entertained, cried Mother from the next room. She was sewing. No one was entertaining her either.

Yes, cried Grandfather, entertained! Then he closed his eyes expectantly. But mostly nothing happened. Then he became impatient, got off his mattress and went 'walkabout'. First he went into his former bedroom, as he was fed up 'with having the same wallpaper to look at' the whole time. Then he returned to the corridor. Grandfather wanted to be bedded in such a way that he had a good view of all the film star photographs, especially the one of Asta Nielsen. He didn't like it to be hanging in darkness. The women suffered from his whims, outrageously, so they said. Mother often thought her life would be easier if Grandfather's 'brain fever' had put him to sleep once and for all. But of course she couldn't say so. If only he'd be quiet, she often said to Grandmother, but he wasn't. If it wasn't a piece of bread with onion, then it was a drink of water but 'it must have been running for at least five minutes'. And after that he had to be taken to the lav, but he wanted the door left open. As if he couldn't find it unaided, God knows the flat's not that big, said Mother. Or he cried: Where's my stick? and demanded to be taken to the window overlooking the yard – it was summer again by now – that was left open in summertime, 'for the consoling perspective'. There were trees to be seen. From here, he said, you can see straight into the sickly heart of nature! Because the flat was so dark, in other words because it had small windows, Grandfather wasn't able to read his *Faust* I and II or his Friedrich Gerstäcker in the corridor or the living room. The main light had to be on constantly. And the expense! But of course he couldn't just sit and think about 'what's in store for me' either.

What will be will be, Grandfather liked to say, after he'd been brooding. So at least a body should be allowed to look at the garden now and again, to see if it still exists.

In the afternoon, when he couldn't lie down any more 'on account of his soft bones', Grandmother and Mother sent me in to be with him. I was to 'entertain' him. Sometimes they said: Tell him a story, sometimes they just pushed me in there without any instructions at all. I had on – summertime! – my shorts with the suede straps. Sadly, they were much too tight for me now. I tugged at them a lot. I sat beside Grandfather in the corridor, and looked down at him. I said: I'm supposed to entertain you.

I see, said Grandfather, propping himself up in his bed, and how do you plan to do that?

I don't know.

I see, well, you're not exactly overflowing with ideas. It's not an easy matter, being born and growing up in a dump like this.

Where's a better place to be born?

Preferably not at all, said Grandfather. When I sat down on his mattress, I had him lying underneath me. Slowly it got dark.

Another day gone, said Grandfather, what's left now isn't much.

The photographs of the film stars he had gathered around him in his sickness – 'they will protect me from the worst, I hope!' –were barely identifiable in the darkness. But I knew them anyway: There was Pola Negri, there was Lil Dagover, there was Willy Fritsch with his topper. Heinrich George, who used to be there too, was now over at Fräulein Fritsche's. Grandfather loved them all. Grandmother, if she wasn't tending the onions in the garden, was sitting knitting by the stove. Mother had her apron on and was sitting in the other room. She had the door open, and was sewing away. Grandfather, because I was there, was waiting for something. He had propped himself up. He wasn't supposed to lie so much. In the laundry cupboard he kept a shoebox full of photos from bygone days. He loved looking at them. I always asked: Can I look too?

If your hands are clean, he said.

Grandfather had got up and was sitting in the smoking chair. He wasn't smoking, though. He had the photographs spread out in front of him, and pushed them this way and that. One after another, he held them up to his eyes, so he could see something of them in the gloom. They were the ones he hadn't been able to pin up on the wall, because there was no more room for them. But they were good too, just as good as all the others. Grandfather slowly pushed them across the table to me, one after the other. And he would tell me who they were of. Then he said where their films were set, and who else appeared in them. He said: Above all you should understand that that's the real world, the only one that will last! At least for a while, said Grandfather, until something new comes along. Finally he had them all spread out in front of him on the table. Twilight came through the blinds.

They need to be protected, he said suddenly.

What from?

From everything that's bad for them. Do you know what that is?

No.

The same things that are bad for us all: Fire, damp, heat, dust! He put them back in their box.

Such a dreamer, your Karl! If only he would open his mouth a bit more, so that one would know what's going on inside him, said Herr Cosimo. He was standing downstairs by the front door. He asked: So how's he doing?

Grandmother wrinkled her nose and said: So-so.

Herr Cosimo asked himself whether he should go in, but decided against and went away again. Grandmother said: You can take a horse to water, but you can't make him wash! and she shut the window again. Later on she went into town. She needed to buy matches. Mother shut the door. She wanted to get on with

140

her sewing. I was alone with Grandfather. His thighs, having been in the light, were now in darkness, and his belly had been vanquished by his illness. I thought: Unless you say something, he'll start talking to you.

Suddenly he said: There is nothing to be said about this world!

I said: Then talk about something else.

Grandfather, whose moustaches hadn't seen a moustache-trainer for a whole year, pondered. That took time. Then he talked about the old days, it was all he could think about. It was always the same. There he was lying on his mattress – would he ever carry it back into Grandmother's room? – talking about how every night he had stood in front of the 'most magnificent sheet in the world' at the Apollo, back in the 'time of the Carthaginian wars', and he had . . .

I said: Yes, I know!

Ah yes, said Grandfather, it's a long time ago! And when I asked him how long, he said: I can't get over it! He had explained fifty films a year, sometimes a hundred! The silence when he had called: And now pay attention! and begun to speak! It was another world, much more interesting than this one here, said Grand-father, knocking on the wall.

The flicks will drive him insane, said Grandmother. She was washing the potatoes now, for potato salad, if I was a good boy.

He misses the stimulus of some ordinary tuppenny-ha'penny job, cried Mother from her sewing-machine. And the exhaustion with which you fall into the sack afterwards. The way I do, she said. She sewed and sewed without end.

Yes, those days, said Grandfather. It might be blowing a gale outside, but our evenings together were always fine. And now they're betraying me!

What did you show them, I asked.

For instance, he said, and his eyes shone, *Fury* (1936, with Spencer Tracy and Sylvia Sidney). In that one, Spencer Tracy is arrested on the way to his fiancée. He has been mistaken, as often happens, for someone else. He's accused of kidnapping a child, and thrown into prison. No one will talk to him. They've all forgotten how nice he always was to them, and all the things he did for them before the sound-film came!

What things did he do for them?

Oh, what do you think he did, said Grandfather, you always ask too many questions! When I was your age, we never asked that many questions, we did what we were told! Anyway, they want to lynch him. They set fire to the prison they've put him in, but he manages to escape. Like me, just like me!

Were you in prison, then?

In prison? All the time!

And you escaped too?

I did!

What sort of prison was it?

There you go again with your questions! Didn't I just say you asked too many questions, cried Grandfather. He had slumped back again, onto the stain left by his head. Anyway Spencer Tracy doesn't perish in the flames, he hides in a laundry basket, and waits to see what will happen next. Only he sleeps badly, because he thinks too much.

Like you?

Yes, like me!

And then what happens?

What do you suppose happens, cried Grandfather, what always happens! Spencer Tracy is acquitted, gets married and lives happily ever after. But *Fury* was a feast for the eyes, as it said in the programme, and a . . . a . . . . An 'education for the soul' Grandfather had meant to say, but again the words wouldn't come. We sat and waited, but they didn't come, and so we talked about other things. Sometimes he spoke, sometimes I did. He liked talking about his profession best.

142

My profession, said Grandfather, and he still hadn't let me switch the light on, because 'it's easier talking without', is not like any other. It's dangerous!

I leaned back against the wall. Dangerous, I asked.

Fire, said Grandfather, pointing at the setting sun, which had now coloured the whole sky red. At any moment, I have to be prepared for the direst contingency!

Even in Limbach?

Even in Limbach!

I thought you no longer had a profession?

Yes, he said, that's true, I suppose! But if I did . . .

Yes?

There are the widely feared cinema fires, said Grandfather, the worst thing you can imagine in the world! That's why, when I'm showing a film, I mustn't ever just look at the screen. I must have eyes everywhere, and sniff hard as well, in case something's smouldering somewhere. And I need to look and listen out for the back of the cinema, in case Salzmann's crying for help.

For help?

In case fire has broken out in the projection booth! In the beginning, you weren't born then, we didn't even have cans for rewinding, said Grandfather. We wound the film back into a laundry basket. And with all the heat from the electric bulbs, it was apt to catch fire, and a whole reel could go up in flames. That's why we always kept a bucket of water and a box full of sand at the ready, we had to. On two occasions I myself had to empty a bucket over a burning film . . .

Which were they?

*Vanina Vanini* (1922, with Asta Nielsen and Paul Wegener), said my sick Grandfather from his darkness, I remember it as though it were only yesterday! Asta Nielsen in a silk nightie with lace trimmings of the kind you hardly ever see nowadays. She plays the daughter of a general who has fallen in love with a young revolutionary, and . . .

And what about the fire? What did you do?

Grandfather hitched himself up. He leaned against the wall. There was no more sun. There was just the afterglow, as though the whole sky was on fire. Grandfather talked about how he had poured water over one blazing film, sand over another. In both cases, he had managed to extinguish the fire, and saved many dozens, even hundreds of lives . . .

Were there so many people there?

Yes, believe it or not cleverclogs, a great many, said Grandfather. Terrible tragedies can occur in cinemas if you're not careful, the most terrible tragedies, and there . . . . So much talking had exhausted Grandfather. His head had dropped against the wall once more. Above it, in the dark, was the stain. It was caused by the back of his head, because that was a bit greasy. When Grandfather opened his eyes again, he pointed at it and called: That stain will outlive me!

What about me?

No, he said, not you.

Grandfather still had his dizzy spells, but apart from that he was feeling much better now. He would occasionally wash the top half of him. He paused when speaking. Then he started all over again. He yawned a lot.

Don't you put your hand in front of your mouth when you yawn, I asked.

Yes, he said, when there are flies around!

And when there aren't?

My day, he answered, is all but done!

Because Grandfather was going to sleep soon, he had already taken his socks off. They lay under the bed. Mother's door was shut. She was sewing and thinking about money. Grandmother was in the back yard. She could hardly see anything there now.

144

Grandfather yawned again. I could see his brown gums. He wasn't allowed to smoke now, so he chewed tobacco. I thought, he's going to say something, but I was mistaken. Grandfather didn't say anything.

Grandfather, I said, what's the matter? Grandfather, I said.

It was then that the Führer said: I've thought it over! I'm going to say farewell to politics and become a private citizen again. We were all sitting together. Herr Lange was sitting by the wall. He said: He can't do that to us! Mother said: Stuff and nonsense! Her door was wide open. Grandfather asked: When's supper? Grandmother: That's codswallop! And: Just coming!

Grandfather still wasn't speaking much. He looked up at the ceiling. Sometimes he opened his mouth. Then we could see his tongue, and his teeth, some of them false. And we thought: Now he's going to speak, but he didn't. He'd been sitting round almost a year since his dismissal. When I asked: What are you doing today, he said: No, thank you, and when I asked: What's on your mind, he said: No, thanks all the same! Or he made a grim face and said: That Theilhaber, what else? I went off to play. When I came back and asked: What are you thinking about now, he said: You ask too many questions! Sometimes he pulled himself together, and we went round the block together. Once we met Herr Theilhaber, just ran into him. We had been to see what film we were missing in the Apollo. It was *Amphitryon* (1935, with Willy Fritsch, Käthe Gold, Paul Kemp and Adele Sandrock). We were still standing in front of the poster, and Grandfather was just saying: That's a piece of nonsense, when Herr Theilhaber came towards us on the opposite side of the road. Everything about him was new: new coat, new shoes, new hair.

Do I have to say hello to him, I asked.

If you want me to rip your ear off, said Grandfather.

So we didn't say hello, and he didn't either. He looked at the pavement in front of him, while Grandfather looked straight into his face, whistling something to himself, I think it was: 'High up on the hill, under the twinkling stars . . .'

And what shall we do now, I asked.

We've settled his hash, said Grandfather, now we can go home again!

At home, we didn't talk about our encounter. Grandfather once more didn't speak. Grandmother was ironing again. She was brooding. When the rent fell due, she couldn't count on any help from Grandfather.

Grandfather, I said, say something!

But Grandfather didn't say anything.

Grandfather, I said, go on, talk!

But Grandfather didn't say anything.

I'm not surprised he doesn't talk, cried Mother from her machine. Other people have speech cells in their brains, but he's just got silence cells!

He's like all poets, said Grandmother, he can only think about his own unhappiness, the whole street's talking about his lack of sympathy, for example over my leg! You'd think he would say something about it, but he hasn't mentioned it!

It's as though he's wrapped in insulating tape, cried Mother from her room, nothing can touch him!

I thought there was something wrong with your arm, I said to Grandmother.

With both arms, said Grandmother.

Not wanting to talk to us any more, Grandfather now preferred to eat by himself. Breakfast, dinner, tea, all by himself! 'His mouth finds it less of a strain!' Often he paced up and down the room, and ate nothing at all. Or he ate something standing in the pantry when no one was watching, just so that he could say: No, I don't want anything, when he was called to table later. Sometimes he started eating a piece of bread when the table was

146

laid, and we thought, he'll be eating with us today. He'd waited long enough in his life, he wasn't going to wait any more! When Grandmother asked him what he'd waited for so long in his life, he said: For a change in my existence! After that he went over to his mattress corner and did three knee bends, so that 'he might recover his strength after so much work' and 'rejuvenate his lower extremities as well'. Then he put on his artist's hat and went out 'for a walk'.

Will you take me with you, I asked.

No, he said, I want to be by myself for a change! He slammed the door behind him.

There he goes, rowing and shouting and walking out again, said Mother, sewing.

He's going to that woman, to get something to eat from her!

It's common knowledge, said Grandmother. I hope she's made him something nice, so he'll be in a better mood when he gets back!

When we ate, Grandfather was 'over the hills and far away', at her place. Or he was back already, if they'd quarrelled. Then he would squat in his corner, with his back to us.

A handsome back has its attraction, said Mother.

Mooning around like that, said Grandmother, and bemoaned her lot 'with such a man, and in this nest, where they can't even speak proper German!' She reproached herself for having gone with him to Saxony – 'of all places, Saxony!' My God, cried Grandmother, when I think of the men I could have found. But instead she had followed Grandfather to this, 'the most dismal spot on the planet'. Now the scales had fallen from her eyes, 'a little late, but for good now'. He's so lazy, said Grandmother, I've lost track of how many years it is since he last worked properly, in other words 'with his hands'. All that nonsense about art when things are so straightforward. He's workshy, and that's all there is to it! Once, when Grandfather laughed for the first time in ages –

147

it must have been a mistake, Mother said – Grandmother suddenly got up and handed him his artist's hat and walking stick. Then she pushed him out of the door, forcefully. There, she said, if you're able to laugh again, that means you're feeling better. Go and get a job.

At first Grandfather didn't understand. He was sorry he'd laughed.

That's right, she said, get weaving! And she gave him instructions. He was to put in an appearance at the labour exchange after his long 'convalescence' before they forgot about him altogether. Perhaps they thought he was already fixed up. Tell them the truth! Don't say you're a scholar, or I'll disabuse them myself. Say: Because I was too indolent as a young man, I never learned a trade, and will take whatever you can offer me now. Grit your teeth, swallow your false pride, no beating about the bush, just tell it like it is! Tell them: I'm an unskilled labourer, and lazy with it! Tell them: I've stuck my oar in all over the place, but I'm not qualified for anything! Basically, I like hanging around cinemas, shooting my mouth off.

Of course Grandfather would have preferred to stay at home and sit down again, but Grandmother simply pushed him down the stairs. 'There, and now get lost!'

On the day Grandmother shut Grandfather out, there wasn't anything for unskilled labourers. Anyway, that's what he said. After half an hour, he was back, with his fine hat. He was waving it in the distance.

There isn't anything, he shouted up the Kreuzstrasse, nothing at all!

I'm not surprised, said Grandmother, he always waits around until everything's gone! What was striking was the impassive expression he still had. A head of concrete, said our landlord Lange, when he came to collect the rent. Grandfather didn't say anything.

His obstinacy, keeping his mouth shut for days, sitting there in dudgeon, said Grandmother. Mother didn't say anything. She had to sew slips.

Grandfather sat around in silence for weeks on end, getting his breath all over everything: the neighbours, the cupboards, the flowers. Or he stared at a point on the wall.

I'd like to know what he's staring at, said Mother. She pointed at the spot. Sometimes she passed her fingers over it.

Grandfather, I called, don't go to sleep!

But he didn't speak. When I asked: Why do you keep looking at the ceiling, he said: I'm looking for something I left in a previous life.

And what might that be, asked Mother.

Ah, he said, if only I knew!

But he did go for walks again now. Or rather: He ran off. We said something, he'd reach for his hat and be gone. 'He's sulking again!' (Mother). For example when the womenfolk made fun of 'the holiest thing left to him'. That holy was his death. His death was coming soon. Grandfather loved to talk about it, it made him very happy.

You'll see, I'll be dead and then you'll be sorry, he cried and was off.

He's gone for a walk again, said Mother.

I know where, I said.

Grandmother cracked four eggs and said: 'Him and die! If I know him, he'll never die. He's off to his bit on the side.

And why will he never die, I asked.

Because he goes for so many walks, said Grandmother, and then she had to think about cooking. Or she had to laugh. When I asked if he mightn't die *after all*, she said: Bah, he'll outlive us all!

Ha, cried Grandfather, who was already back and sitting in his corner.

Even me, I asked.

Now you've offended him, said Mother.

Sure, said Grandmother, even you.

Me and go on for ever, cried Grandfather, ha!

All of us, said Mother, will be dead and buried, and he'll be lying there looking out the window.

Me, and looking out the window, cried Grandfather, ha!

And me, I asked, will I be dead and buried too?

You, said Mother, you are going to live for ever too!

Now that's enough of this macabre conversation, cried Grandmother. What were we talking about?

Supper, I said.

After supper, Grandfather with hat and stick, – 'as long as I have my stick, no one will grind me down' – Grandfather walked up to the Apollo with me hurrying beside him. He grabbed my sleeve and said: In fact it's like this: As far as my own self is concerned, I don't believe in death. I will just go on and on.

So if you don't believe in death, what do you believe in?

Eternity, said Grandfather. As an artist, he said, and with his stick he scratched the word *Eternity* on the pavement, it is my duty to believe in eternity. It's like this, he said as we went on. I can only believe in what I can imagine to myself. Nothing else exists! I can't imagine my death. Therefore it doesn't exist!

And why can't you imagine your death, I asked, because I could very well imagine Grandfather's death.

Because while I'm imagining it to myself, I'm not dead, am I?

What about me? Could I be dead sometime?

It's different with you, said Grandfather. He stopped again. He took off his artist's hat, his head needed air to be able to think. I believe in other people's deaths. Everyone does, it's natural. Only my own isn't natural. And so I don't believe in it! And he shook his head again, and smiled his 'conceited superior smile' as Grandmother always called it. Dying for me is out of the question.

Of course I may refer to my death from time to time, it sort of slips out, but only to show people how preposterous it sounds. Or, he asked.

And now, I said, what shall we do now?

What do you think we're going to do, said Grandfather, we're going to the Apollo to have a look at the photos.

In the afternoon, when he stood by the window 'letting time run away', Grandfather saw Herr Cosimo walking up the street, just like before. He was on his way to the Hoher Hain.

Why don't you go with him, there's a vacancy next to him, said Grandmother, keen to be rid of him. Get some exercise!

But Grandfather didn't want any exercise. He preferred to wave Herr Cosimo upstairs. The two of them sat down in the living room. I thought they would talk again. But they didn't talk. It was a comfort to Grandfather that Herr Cosimo had been unemployed for so much longer than himself. He wanted to be told again and again. He rested one foot on top of the other and asked: How long did you say you've been out of work now, and when Herr Cosimo said, once again: Fourteen years, he said: As long as that! and was then quiet.

Grandfather liked being quiet by the window best. He looked out over the nearby houses. He had got his cane, but didn't rest on it. Sometimes he thought of his illness and how it had violently thrown him to the ground, to the ground of ultimate realities. No security wherever you looked, nothing solid! No wonder his head couldn't take it. Grandfather hadn't 'kicked off' yet, but it wouldn't be long. Until that time he kept diminishing, everyone was talking about it.

He said to me: Look at that jacket! And this poor shirt! How everything sags on me! He could hardly believe it himself. The Chemnitz painter Krogmann, who had once said: Everything that isn't art is worthless, came out to see us on his bicycle, and after looking Grandfather over a long time with his painter's eye, made him an offer. He wanted to paint him, for his 'wonderfully emaciated body' for a Descent from the Cross, everything but the face.

And what's the matter with his face, asked Grandmother, doesn't it fit?

I've already got someone, said Herr Krogmann, doing the face.

That way, just by standing still he could have earned fifteen marks in three days and he would have been exhibited in Chemnitz. Grandfather asked for time to think. Then he thought about it for a week and declined, because as Christ he would have to have been naked. Even the hospital in Chemnitz, which hadn't wanted him as a patient, suddenly wanted Grandfather. Because of his emaciation, he could have clarified some rare phenomenon for junior doctors. But again Grandfather refused, he was an artist, 'not a piece of meat to be prodded and poked around!' Medical science, I ask you! The pharmacist Stock, putting Grandfather on his scales, took Mother aside and asked: For Heaven's sake, what have you just brought me? What's the matter with him?

He's unhappy, said Mother.

Why's that?

Because he's not able to go to the pictures any more.

Oh I see, said Herr Stock.

Grandfather weighed less than ninety pounds at the time. Because of all that lying, everything has wasted away! Not a trace of fat anywhere. And the skin and sinews just hanging off you.

I know, said Grandfather, and that's not even the worst of it.

What is?

My arm is so sore! The one I used to point at the screen with.

Rubbish, arm, cried Dr Lantsch, you're a hypochondriac, Hofmann! You should think of all the bits of you that don't hurt instead of the other ones! What's the matter with your arm?

Herr Theilhaber tugged at it.

When?

A year and a half ago.

Bah, there's nothing wrong with your arm, even if someone does have a tweak at it now and again. It's your feelings that are hurt. If you insist, you can rub your arm with some of the alcohol I prescribed recently, and stop thinking about it. Don't drink the alcohol, mind. In your present condition, it could finish you off.

You mean I could die of it?

I wouldn't tempt fate if I were you, said Dr Lantsch. Think of something pleasant! A nice film.

Oh, said Grandfather, I never see any films now.

Mother said: He needs to get his mind on other things!

Cheerful things, said Grandmother, singing to herself. He wasn't to think about his future so much.

Grandfather came back from his 'stroll'. Grandmother chucked him under the chin. But whatever she tried to talk to him about, he always said: I don't know! And when she said: Say something, he said: Nothing to say! When, after days of silence, he did get into a conversation, he always came back to his lost job. Or the way everyone stared at him when he was walking. 'They can't wait for me to finally collapse!' Or he got onto his thinness, 'from his neck down to his little toes'. That's what the sound-film had done to him. Grandmother got him a blanket. She said: It's a difficult time for him!

On one particular day – Grandmother had made stuffed cabbage – Grandfather had suddenly had enough of 'all the blah, with sound and without'. When someone said the word *cinema*, he blocked his ears. Or he asked: Excuse me, what does that mean?, but didn't wait to hear the answer. The arm that Herr Theilhaber had pulled was still sore.

See how stiff it is when I'm trying to smoke, he said to me, letting it drop.

He's doing that deliberately, letting it dangle like that, said Grandmother, it's so he doesn't have to lend a hand.

Finally, after being so mute and so light already, Grandfather shrank even further. When he went out to buy rolls with me, he no longer needed to bend his head going into the shop. He had 'queer sensations'.

He's hoping he's becoming an eccentric. He doesn't even move like a human being any more, never mind an artist, Grandmother said once.

No, I asked, so what does he move like?

Like a pariah, said Grandmother.

And he smells like one too, said Mother.

He smells like Herr Cosimo, I said.

He has bad breath, said Mother.

Because he doesn't clean his teeth, said Grandmother.

And when he opens his mouth he talks like a pariah too, said Herr Lange, and laughed. As though life was nothing to do with him any more. That's probably what he thinks too.

How would you know what he thinks, asked Grandmother.

The eyes, said Herr Lange, looking at Mother, are the windows of the soul. One just has to look at them carefully.

We ought to be thankful he says anything at all, never mind how much he opens his mouth, said Mother. She was about to yawn again. Then Herr Lange would go home, while Grandfather . . .

Grandmother said: He has a lot on his mind.


Following his 'return from the dead' and his silent period, Grandfather started going for walks again. Sometimes he went alone, sometimes he took me with him. Let's go for a totter round the block, he said.

When he was alone, he went to Fräulein Fritsche's. That took him an hour. Usually she would cook him something, some treat. Sometimes she made him buckwheat pancakes, sometimes potato dumplings with bacon. Grandfather would then smell of her bacon for weeks, especially his beard. When he took me with him, he held my hand.

Let go now, he cried, when he saw someone coming who he wanted to take his hat off to. He needed his hand. Once he'd passed, he said: There, now you can give me your hand back!

Herr Theilhaber had taken on a young man with one eye, 'because they cost less than someone with two' (Grandmother). At any rate, he was supposed to have a glass eye, but we weren't sure on which side. Sometimes Grandfather said it's the one on the right, sometimes, no it's the left. Or he said: It's not true! He hasn't any glass eye! In the garden it was autumn again. Like Grandfather or Herr Salzmann before him, the young cripple swept up the leaves from the entrance to the Apollo, to make it easier for people to go in. Using Grandfather's gluepot and brush, he stuck up posters: *I'm a Fugitive from a Chain Gang* (1932, with Paul Muni), *Morocco* (1930, with Marlene Dietrich, Gary Cooper and Adolphe Menjou), *Little Caesar* (1930, with Edward G. Robinson and Douglas Fairbanks, Jnr). Or *Hitlerjunge Quex* (1933, with Heinrich George and Berta Drews). They were all talkies.

The cinema's finished for me!, said Grandfather.

To comfort him, I said: And for me!

Every evening now we sat around at home, waiting for it to get dark. Then Grandfather would look at his fob watch and say: The Apollo's just starting now! Sometimes Mother got an apple, and cut it into four. Grandfather took his penknife and peeled his quarter. Mother gave me his peel and said: That's got all the goodness in it, only he won't believe it. I didn't eat it either.

After a while Grandfather looked at his watch again and said: Now they've got to the bit where he tries to kill her.

Who does he try to kill, I asked.

Who do you think? His wife, of course!

And, I asked, does he kill her?

No, said Grandfather, he lets her go on living. As punishment. I wonder how the audience today . . .

Grandmother fetched the cards. She said: Come on, let's have a game! To while away the time.

At about ten, when I'd won, the film at the Apollo would be over, and Grandfather said: There, they're going home now!

And then what will they do, I asked.

Then, Grandmother said, they'll take off their trousers and hit the sack!

And what about us, I asked, what will we do?

Every human being, said Grandfather, and therein lies the only difference between man and the other rodents, carries a cinema screen in his head.

Me too, I asked.

You too! And the name of that cinema screen is . . .

Let the boy go to bed, will you, cried Mother from the other room. She was sitting at her machine again. With luck, she said, he'll go to sleep!

Imagination, imagination, Grandfather hurriedly called after me, it's called his imagination!


So instead of Grandfather, it was the young cripple who now kept the key to the Apollo. He showed it to us occasionally. He asked: Do you remember this?

Yes, said Grandfather sadly, that used to be my key!

You can get in any time with that, said the young cripple. But why am I telling you?

Unlike Grandfather, he didn't keep the key in his trouser

pocket. He wore it on a string round his neck, so he didn't lose it. Sometimes the young cripple would be standing outside the Apollo, dangling the key over his belly and playing with it. He would say: Yes, yes! or: No, no! Grandfather and I stood next to him, eyeing the key. The young cripple talked. He lived all alone in a 'bedsitting hole, with no running water only bugs'. He spent his nights hunting. As he talked, he leaned against the Apollo wall, it was more comfortable than standing. He had just three fingers on his left hand, but he managed with them. Sometimes he held out his hand to me and said: There, have a good look at it!

But I didn't look. Then he pointed at me and said to Grandfather: You've got a sensitive grandson there! I disgust him.

It's because he's shy, Grandfather pleaded on my behalf.

He won't even touch my hand, just because I've got a couple of fingers missing!

Nonsense, said Grandfather, of course he'll touch it.

No, I cried, I won't touch it!

You see, cried the young cripple.

Then Grandfather stroked his beard, and once more apologised for me. Yes, he said, he's a sensitive plant. We spoil him. See what silky hair nature has given him! He's going to be a poet one day. He's already got the self-pity for it.

Sometimes, still being weak on his pins, Grandfather sat down in the mornings, when Herr Theilhaber wasn't around, with me on the bench outside the Apollo. Then the young cripple would show up and call: Hey, who gave you permission to sit on that bench? That's his bench! And he chased us away. Or he said nothing at all, but slowly limped up to us. He frowned at us with his one good eye, only we couldn't be sure which one it was. He even let us sit down again, and stood beside us. For a while we sat there, just breathing and not saying anything, until Grandfather felt that wasn't right, and he ought to say something.

I'm the foreign body here who was turfed out a while ago, he

157

introduced himself. Now I'm on the street, which is why I've got so much free time. My family comes from Turkey. I've been here some time, but the people of Limbach still haven't forgiven me for being a Turk. And that, said Grandfather pointing at me, is my grandson Kemal. The fortunate fellow doesn't know his father. He thinks he doesn't have one.

I'm a cripple, but you can see that for yourselves, replied the young cripple, raising his damaged hand. Here too, he said, and pointed to his eye, sometimes it was the right one, sometimes the left.

Yes, said Grandfather, I can see something's the matter with your hand.

The other one's crippled too, said the young cripple, and he held up his other hand. There was another pause.

I, said Grandfather once the pause was over, am his maternal grandfather. The little beggar hasn't a father. At least it's not known who he is, not locally anyway. I always warned my daughter not to bring a child into the house without its only begetter. But that's just what she did do.

I, replied the young cripple, was involved in a political brawl a couple of years ago in Berlin, where I lost a couple of fingers and an eye, but I never tell anyone which one. Now if war comes I don't have to be a soldier. I draw a pension of two hundred and eighty marks and ninety-seven pfennigs.

And I, replied Grandfather, have recently got over a long illness. I'm going on sixty, he lied. Can you believe that?

Yes.

Really, cried Grandfather, and there was another pause. My problem, he said, is I want to get away from here, back to Turkey. Unfortunately I can't walk that well any more. Do you go to the cinema a lot?

No.

Me neither, said Grandfather. Another pause.

Do you know, asked the young cripple, that you're sitting on a bench you're not strictly speaking allowed to sit on?

Is this not a public bench?

No, said the young cripple, it's in front of the Apollo! Then he said: Apparently I've got your old job, and am taking your wages every week.

No hard feelings!

What else could I do, said the young cripple. If I hadn't stolen your job, someone else would have stolen it. Theilhaber has been looking for someone to exploit for a long time. In the end he took me. So stop looking at me like that!

How do you want me to look at you?

A little more benignly, said the young cripple. Sometimes when we were sitting on the bench, he stood next to us and let Grandfather talk. Occasionally he went onto the little patch of grass and plucked out a few weeds. Go on talking, he said as he plucked, I can hear you!

Grandfather leaned back on the bench. He looked content. He didn't know what to say, so he just started anywhere. For instance that he'd once seen three films one after the other.

And? asked the young cripple.

That's all, said Grandfather. Or he looked straight into the eyes of the young cripple and said: I can do hypnosis!

What's that?

I take a rabbit, said Grandfather, out of its stall, put it on the table and hypnotise it. There is a power in my eyes, which I can use at will. Then it lets you stroke its ears! As the young cripple didn't say anything, Grandfather went on to say he'd also hypnotised our budgie. 'Unfortunately he plunged straight into a steaming pot of soup, laid its last egg, and departed this life.' Grandfather had also hypnotised the peacock on the Kellerwiese, and some kittens for Herr Lange to drown. That way they hadn't felt a thing. There are too many anyway.

What of?

Of everything! Grandfather could hypnotise each and every thing, so long as he kept his eye. Animals – people too – went to sleep, they would yawn if they could, but they can't even do that.

And what do you do in life besides that, asked the young cripple.

I try to hypnotise my wife, said Grandfather, but she won't let me.

I see, said the young cripple, and listened to the next story. Grandfather knew plenty, and he told them well. Then the young cripple suddenly called: Stop! Now, he said, you have to go! I can't allow you to go on sitting here. Herr Itzig doesn't permit it, and he might come at any moment! Do you know that he's brought a suit of malicious wounding against you?

Oh, that little incident, said Grandfather.

So what do you think?

I think we'd better go, said Grandfather, and took my hand. We all stood up.

See you, then, but preferably not too soon, said the young cripple, and he pushed us away from the bench. Or he said: You know – they had started calling each other 'Du' – what interests me? Why do you come here so often?

Force of habit, said Grandfather, I used to work here.

But you're not working here any more!

No, said Grandfather, but I'm still interested in films.

You see, said the young cripple, since I've started working for Itzig I've been getting threatening letters.

Then perhaps you shouldn't work for him any more, suggested Grandfather.

I wouldn't be able to find anything else!

Well, then I can't help you.

Anyway, you should be glad *you're* not still working for him, otherwise you'd be getting the anonymous letters, said the young cripple. There was another pause. Then he asked Grandfather if he knew anything about the anonymous letters.

No, said Grandfather.

The young cripple asked: And you don't know what's in them either?

No.

You don't write anonymous letters, asked the young cripple, and Grandfather shook his head and cried: No, I don't!

But all at once the young cripple no longer believed him. Maybe, he said, you get someone else to write them for you. So, say hello to them and tell them I don't work for Itzig out of choice, but because I couldn't get any other work. And tell them I'm a cripple as well! They should show some compassion!

But who am I to tell all that to, asked Grandfather, I told you, I don't know them!

At any rate, he said, tell them I'm on their side! I just stay out of it, because I don't want to lose my other eye.

But who am I to tell all that to?

The young cripple said: Your friends, of course, who else? You must have been carrying a swastika armband around in your pocket for ages. You're just waiting to put it on.

Nonsense, I've nothing in my pockets at all, said Grandfather, and he turned his pockets inside out. Of course, they were empty. But the young cripple didn't believe him. He said: If you talk to me like that, you'd better get out of here! You know I'm not supposed to let you sit here anyway! Shoo, shoo, he hissed, and he drove us away. Then he limped away himself, and went back to sweeping the path or putting up placards, to get at least a couple of people in. Sometimes the young cripple waited to hear whether Grandfather had anything further to say.

But make it quick, he said, looking at his watch, which ticked as loudly as an alarm clock.

And what am I to say so quickly, asked Grandfather. I stood close beside him.

Anything you like, said the young cripple, you've got three minutes.

Then, because it just happened to be going through his mind, Grandfather said: I won't have anything served up to me at table that reminds me of the animal as it was when it was alive! I eat fish only in pies and not whole, chicken in fricassees.

And why are you telling me that, asked the young cripple.

Grandfather gripped me firmly by the hand, so that no one could pull me away. Who needs chicken anyway, said Grandfather, now slowly walking home with me to our pot of soup. Or fish, he said. Give us soup any day.


There, said Dr Lantsch, round about this time to Grandfather, you're over the worst now. If your juices flow a little more calmly, you might live to be a hundred, if that's your intention.

When I think about life, said Grandfather, I don't think in terms of numbers.

So you're not satisfied with a hundred, said Dr Lantsch. And then, having examined Grandfather once more, in particular his heart and his head – he tapped it with a little rubber hammer – he said: You know what, Hofmann, you're a medical marvel? When I was called in to you – and I came very promptly – I wouldn't have given you another fortnight. Certainly, I have no idea what precipitated you into your condition, and what pulled you out of it again. You should thank the Almighty, or the power of nature, whatever your inclination happens to be!

# Seven

*Occupations and professions pursued by Grandfather in the course of his lifetime* (a selection).

Fencing tutor
Tanner
Cobbler
Plumber's assistant
Plumber
Air Raid Warden
Hosiery worker
Finisher
Circus handyman
Announcer, in German and French ('barker')
Under-stenographer
Stenographer
Stenography teacher
Sergeant, Staff Sergeant, Sergeant Major
Zither player
Piano player
'Film explainer'
Usher
Walker
Factory watchman

Prompter in the Stadttheater in Chemnitz, until during the dress rehearsal of F. Schiller's *Fiesco* he suddenly leapt out of his box, elbowed the director aside, and began giving the actors their instructions himself, with demonstrations. 'I couldn't stand another second of such stupidity.'

Barman

Standard bearer

Under constable

'Artist'

etc. etc.

# Eight

The first political meeting Grandfather went to must have been in September. It was getting to be autumn, anyway. Herr Lange was wearing a leather jacket. He said: Vienna's in the bag! It's the turn of Czechoslovakia next! He sat next to Mother and puffed away. Grandmother sat at the living room table. She couldn't stand Herr Lange any more. But she couldn't shut the door either, because then Mother would have been alone in the sewing room with Herr Lange, and she might have had to give him a kiss, and Grandmother didn't want that to happen. Nor did I, either. Grandfather, who didn't care about anything any more, sat silently in his corner. He had his dark glasses on. He had got out his shoebox of cinema pictures. Three times a week he sorted through them and said: This is all that's left of a beautiful epoch! But that's always the way of it! He would have been capable of working again now, 'but was still on the street'. In actual fact, he was still at home, dozing. Sometimes he hummed things to himself. He hummed:

> *At night*
> *A man don't like to be alone!*

or: *You're lucky with women,*
> *Bel ami!*

or: *We were anchored off of Madagascar,*
> *Flying the cholera flag!*

Often Grandfather crooned wrong things. Instead of:

*Take me*

*Far away, blond sailor boy!*

he hummed: *Take me on your roller skates*

*To Addis Abiba!*

He had forgotten the real words. 'Now he's really going downhill' (Grandmother). He forgot the greatest films and no longer remembered who had been in what, and in what role. He didn't want to know, either. When I asked: And who else was in it, he said: Oh, someone or other, Clark Gable, God knows! They're like pebbles on the beach! You try telling all the faces apart! Because we didn't go to the Apollo any more, we stuck to rumours. They came to us. Herr Theilhaber, we heard, was letting the Apollo go to seed. At any rate, he wasn't doing anything to prevent it. The seats, especially the ones at the back, needed repairing and painting. People slashed the padding. Or they unscrewed the armrests and tossed them into the aisle, for him to find the following morning. He picked them up and cried.

Does he really cry, I asked, with tears and everything?

Yes, said Grandmother, so they say! I heard it at the baker's.

Apparently Herr Theilhaber walked sadly through the empty rows of seats, tearing his hair at the sight of the vandalism. 'Why do they do this to me? Don't they know it costs money?'

Grandfather wanted to forget about Herr Theilhaber.

At mealtimes he tried to get by without using the name Theilhaber. Instead, he would say: The man I sometimes used to see earlier, or: The cause of all my misery! or: The fellow who once gave me candles. When I said: Do you mean Herr Theilhaber, he pursed his lips, and said nothing. After a while he would forget that he didn't want the name to pass his lips, and he said: That Theilhaber, the bastard who put me on the street! His piano too, people reported, got badly damaged during the darker sequences. 'I thank God I don't have to see this tragedy with my own eyes!' Herr Theilhaber walked down the rows of seats, calling out: Please not to touch the cushions! or: Kindly avoid doing needless damage to the costly seating! It is very expensive to replace!, but none of it was any use. At home he said to his wife: What sort of people are they! Tearing up my Apollo, turning everything to rack and ruin! His piano got the proper 'treatment'. First it was scratched, then the keys were ripped out, and then it was disembowelled. In the end, Herr Theilhaber had it taken back to his own flat on the Sandweg. There no one could get at it. 'There's a destructive streak in people that bodes no good at all' (Grandmother).

At supper, when everyone 'was wrapped up in his own thoughts', Grandfather was in his warm jacket again. The summer was over. Another one gone, he said and sniffed the air when we went outside. There's change on the way! I can smell it!

Then I remembered something. When are we going to the meeting, I asked.

Grandmother had said: Over my dead body!

Mother said: We're not going, and for a very good reason! She said such meetings are nothing if not fuggy and muggy.

Grandfather said: If people weren't so desperate, there wouldn't be so many meetings in the world! Every meeting is a kind of last straw that they try to clutch. Whatever, there was one every week in the annexe of the Deutsches Haus on the Helenenstrasse, on the ground floor, unless it was cancelled. Interest in meetings was not great in Limbach. There were always empty seats. The huge oak table from better days was pushed back against the wall, that made the poor attendance less noticeable.

And what do they do once they've sat down, I asked. Grandfather had put his hat on. Grandmother stretched her poor legs and with great difficulty put her feet up on the smoking-chair. That's what they do at meetings, she said, they're not the ones who have to clean up afterwards.

Men are pigs, and they do what they like, said Mother, thinking of Herr Lange, who never wiped his feet when he came to pay us a call. She herself had other worries than going to meetings. That's why she wasn't surprised that no one turned up.

I'd like to go, I said, may I?

Grandmother said: Not as long as I live!

On the evening we went to the meeting, Grandfather and I strolled through town.

A walk is good for all parts of the body, the head as much as the feet! Especially after this useless summer, which is best forgotten, said Grandfather, pinching his hat into shape. For months now he had been waiting for a summons for malicious wounding, but none came! Sometimes he went to meet the postman, calling out: Have you got my summons for malicious wounding today, but he never did.

There's no Theilhaber who can tell us not to walk about here, he said, and we walked back and forth in front of the Apollo. The street, said Grandfather, is a place of public resort, and is open to everyone who pays his taxes.

And why do we go for walks such a lot?

From sheer despair, said Grandfather, and we went down the Helenenstrasse, down the left-hand side first. Then we turned round, and walked back up the right.

And why, I asked, do we sometimes walk on one side of the road, and sometimes the other?

Because that shows us the diversity of the world! And because it improves our chances of finding a mark coin. You can't imagine how much money people lose.

Even in Limbach?

Everywhere, he said. Then he pulled out his watch and held it up in front of his eyes. Once more it was eight o'clock. The last of the Apollo cinemagoers went in past us.

Well, said Grandfather, it's not a stream, at least it's a trickle.

They all had their hands in their pockets, and were stepping out. None wanted to miss the beginning. Because they've grasped the notion that everything is contained in the beginning, said Grandfather. They're in luck today, he said, they're getting a treat. *Dr Mabuse the Gambler* (1922, with Paul Richter and Rudolf Klein-Rogge). That's one of the old ones, no one will be walking out of that one! It's spooky too. After all, the world is a spooky place.

Starring who?

With Paul Richter as the millionaire's son Hull, said Grandfather. Of course it's about Mabuse, who promises salvation to a struggling humankind. But he's lying. He's not a benefactor at all, but a cunning criminal. He gets a nude dancer to seduce the millionaire. That's how attorney von Wenk gets on to him.

And then?

The attorney gets to know Countess Told, but one night he finds himself sitting opposite Dr Mabuse at the tables. Von Wenk is able to fight off his attempt at hypnotising him. Naturally Mabuse wants to murder the attorney like so many others before him. Instead, he kills young Hull. His next victim is Count Told, whom he drives into alcoholism by his hypnotic gifts. Told kills himself. Thereupon von Wenk has Mabuse's house surrounded by his best people. Dr Mabuse makes his getaway down an underground passage which has been dug for him by blind men, working day and night . . .

And then?

Oh, you and your questions! Of course, Dr Mabuse evades earthly justice. He goes mad, what else, said Grandfather and at that moment he saw a bright red poster in the window of the photographer Wilhelm. It said on it: '*Is there a future?* With discussion'.

Grandfather stopped in front of the poster. He scratched at the paving stones with his stick. He said: The future is just so much bilge!

He was well over sixty now. 'Extraordinary, how much is suddenly behind you, and how little there is to go!' He looked his age too. For instance, he couldn't walk so well any more. After he'd been walking a while, he tended to drag his right leg a bit. He insisted it was getting shorter. He had to stop more often for a breather. His hair kept receding. 'I can picture him bald' (Grandmother). He had recovered from a fatal illness, if he had indeed recovered from it. He had lost thirty pounds, and he had no work. 'He has no future left, it's all behind him now' (Grandmother). He took his watch out of his pocket once more, and held it up to his ear. He let it tick a while, and then looked at it. He had one mark twenty-five pfennigs in his jacket. Enough for a beer for me and a lemonade for the lad, he maybe thought.

Oh, said Grandfather, let's go in and have a look!

In where, I said, hoping he would say *Dr Mabuse the Gambler*.

To the meeting, said Grandfather.


The Deutsches Haus was empty, but for its landlord Lampe, who was standing behind the bar, cleaning his fingernails with a penknife.

Evening, said Grandfather. And I said: Evening! as well.

If you want the meeting, said Herr Lampe, that's in the annexe across the courtyard, next to the Gents!

Grandfather took off his artist's hat. How do you know I want to go to the meeting, he said.

I can tell from looking at you.

Grandfather, who because of the vacuum in his life since his dismissal as a film explainer always yawned a lot, stepped up to the wall mirror. He looked at himself. He pulled down his eyelids, first one then the other.

How's the health, asked Herr Lampe.

All right so far as I can tell, said Grandfather, but then you never can tell! Yourself?

The wife's had to go for a lie down. She's not feeling too clever!

I'd sooner not talk about mine, said Grandfather. Been to the cinema at all lately?

No time for that kind of thing.

Then we said goodbye and went out again. We cut across the courtyard. In the annexe, Grandfather, a confirmed smoker, felt better right away.

It was even more cramped than the Apollo. There was a similar overhead light. It smelled like it did in the Apollo too. 'Floor wax and human sweat!' And why did they say 'on the ground floor', I said, there is only one!

Because it sounds better, said Grandfather. And now let's keep our eyes open, and take everything into our respective big and little skulls! Remind yourself this is like the whole of life: Whatever it turns out like, you can always learn something from it!

A few people turned up after all. Men, men, men! Grandfather had to look long and hard before he recognised anybody. There were Herr Götze and Herr Friedrich and . . . what was his name again? With many of them, he could only remember the faces, the names he had forgotten because of his illness. Some were persistent cinemagoers, whom he had often taken aside to whisper into their ears: I shouldn't really be telling you this, it's meant to be a surprise, but next week I'm expecting something very special, namely *Nju* (1924, with Elisabeth Bergner, Emil Jannings and Conrad Veidt). You remember, don't you? A young wife is so disappointed by her respectable husband, that she starts

171

an affair with a writer, but the new relationship soon goes the way of the old, and she's forced to leave the writer as well. When she sees that her husband has in the meantime found someone else, she kills herself. Well, what do you say? And if the cinemagoer said nothing, or merely shrugged his shoulders, Grandfather said: I see you're not saying anything, you want a bit of time to think about it first. Anyway, I hope you will honour us with your custom, he always said. He knew what was proper. He also knew what went down well with whom, and often said: This one's made to measure for you! Or: No, if I were you, I'd give this one a miss! Come back next week! And now they had all been unfaithful to him, and would only see sound-films. Of course they felt embarrassed about it, but they didn't let it show.

I'm a sceptic anyway where human nature is concerned, Grandfather said to me quietly, nodding and smiling at his one-time patrons. Sometimes one of them addressed him.

Fancy meeting you here!

I might say the same.

I've heard great things . . .

Me too. At the barber's.

Grandfather stroked his little grey beard. He had grown one again. They've not forgotten me, he thought, just betrayed me! Then he took me by the hand and led me through the meeting room. One speaker had come from Chemnitz by car, and had apparently parked it in front of the town hall to attract more attention. That speaker was the writer S. von Blasewitz, who had come with an armful of works to sell, all penned by himself, but which no one wanted to buy. 'The stuff comes pouring out of him, all he has to do is write it down' (Grandmother). He had his writings piled up in front of him, so that everyone would have a good view of them. They had titles like *The German Identity*, *Bread and Soil* and so on. Sometimes, lest they be forgotten, Herr von Blasewitz picked up one of his writings and brandished it about, sometimes he scratched his neck with one. Even so, no one bought one. We had no money for fripperies.

It felt airless and hot in the meeting, which was the idea. Grandfather held his artist's hat in his hand. We went over to the wall, where Herr Lampe's pictures were hanging. We took a look at them: *Native Soil* and *Happy Hunting*, both the work of E. Schulz, from Russdorf. Grandfather shook his head and said: Too much colour! Then we found a couple of chairs and sat down.

Before sitting down somewhere, it's as well to see where you'll be most comfortable, said Grandfather. This is the most comfortable spot, he said. Now don't fidget!

When Grandfather's beer arrived, he put it down on the old table between his fists, 'so it's nicely within reach.' Then he yawned and closed his eyes, but he didn't fall asleep. It was warm. I sipped my lemonade. I didn't fall asleep either, did I?

It was like this, Grandfather told Herr Cosimo a day or two later. They struck up the song 'Raise the flag, form up your ranks . . .' and we all got up and joined in. What are you grinning about?

Nothing, said Herr Cosimo, I was just trying to picture the scene! You, your grandson and your glass of beer . . .

Yes you did, I saw you grinning.

Grandfather hadn't actually joined in that day because he didn't know the words. But he had stood up anyway and done his best. He opened and shut his lips so that everyone might think he was singing. I opened and shut my lips too. Then we sat down again. After that we had a talk from Herr S. von Blasewitz: 'In a rational world we would all take to the skies and become a nation of aviators!' I drank my lemonade. Then the debate was joined, on subjects such as: Does Limbach need a swimming pool with a high diving board? and: What sort of constitution will bring about happiness?

An intervention from Grandfather, beer glass in hand: And what, pray, is happiness?

Reply from Herr Friedrich: Good question, Hofmann, which takes us deep into the realm of philosophy! But, as with everything, there is a simple answer to it.

And what might that be?

A steady job, food on the table and the children doing well, said Herr Friedrich.

A productive job, emended Herr Götze.

At the mention of the word 'job', a shudder went right through Grandfather from his eyes down to his feet. As if his artist's hat was too heavy for his knees, he set it down on the speaker's table. Everyone stared at us.

Now, Hofmann, was there anything else you wanted to say, asked Herr Götze, who had sat down in the chair vacated by the writer S. von Blasewitz. He had had another meeting to go to, and had driven off, taking his writings with him. Grandfather did want to say something else, and he shifted about on his chair. Sitting down made him even smaller. Then he got to his feet, but quickly sat down again. Then he said: I'm out of work myself! Silence, consternation followed. Herr Götze sipped from his glass.

So what are you trying to tell us, Hofmann, he asked.

I'm trying to tell you . . . . He gestured, but didn't get beyond that point.

The silence in the room deepened. Everyone stared straight ahead. A few scratched at the table. My lemonade was all gone.

I used to be at the Apollo. For a while I was still allowed to do one day a week, Tuesday, but since the argument I'm not even allowed that one day, Grandfather said quietly.

So I hear, said Herr Götze.

And as far as happiness goes, said Grandfather, and shook his head as if to say: That happiness business is just one of those things! And he returned to 'that concept of uncertain definition'.

You mean to say, asked Herr Götze.

Happiness, happiness, cried Grandfather and smacked the

table a bit. In addition to those already mentioned, he had a few more criteria to propose. Then he spoke about 'sensations of happiness' in himself, quoted a few films which took happiness or its opposite as a subject . . . . For example the Russian film *Happiness* (1934, with Pyotr Zinoviev and Yelena Yegorova) in which a poor peasant finds a bag of gold on his unproductive land and . . . . Grandfather scratched his ear a lot as he spoke. Sometimes he put his hand on the table in front of him, and slid it around. He said: So life just takes its course! He suggested for the next meeting – is he really coming back for more, I thought – a discussion of 'unemployment and unhappiness' and all their . . . . Then he was interrupted by Herr Reimann.

S. Reimann was the former swimming teacher in Hartmannsdorf. He had come on his bicycle. No one had ever been taught swimming by him because his pool was too dirty. 'He lets everyone piss in it!' (Grandfather). S. Reimann was wearing a white windcheater and plus twos, 'to show off his athletic calves' (Mother). His feet were in sweaty tennis shoes which had also once been white. He had once tried to gas himself, and even put money in the meter. But there hadn't been enough to kill Herr Reimann. His wife came home. Are you mad, you could blow up the whole house, she had screamed and dragged her husband over to a window. And so he was still among the living. He had been a gym teacher as well, and he said to Grandfather: What you say makes sense, but you draw it out so. Other people would like a word in edgeways. Anyway, there's no need to debate themes like yours. The answers are well known.

What themes do you mean, asked Grandfather.

All of them, said Herr Reimann. The Jews, and especially the business class, are to blame for . . . . Imagine, you come to this lovely town from Hartmannsdorf, and you go to a tobacconist's, and you want to buy yourself a cigarillo with your last mark piece. And you see that the name on the door . . .

175

*

At about ten o'clock Grandfather finally finished the beer he had been nursing all evening, and wanted to order another one on tick, but then, out of the blue, Herr Götze treated him instead.

I have to warn you, said Grandfather, I can't reciprocate. I'm broke.

Then it's time things started looking up, said Herr Götze. If you want another one after that, just order it. The bill goes to me.

Grandfather said: I'll do that! and he finally put his artist's hat down on the table. He felt so happy now in the Deutsches Haus he no longer thought about going home. And Grandfather wanted to talk too, he had so much to say. He was in such a rush to get it out, that the spit ran out of the corners of his mouth.

There's a film which I think . . .

Grandfather, I said quietly.

Yes?

I have to tell you something!

Do you need to be excused, asked Grandfather.

No.

So what is it?

It's something private. Then I moved closer to him, so I could speak quietly. I said: You're dribbling!

What?

You're getting wet. Your collar. I showed him where the spittle had wet his shirt.

Leave me alone, said Grandfather, and pushed me away. He just went on talking. There is, he said, an unforgettable film, I think it was . . . . I was sitting very close to him, so that no one could steal me. I wanted to go home. Grandfather looked at his watch and said: I have some business still to discuss. Then we'll go home. And he pushed me away again. It's strange, not having talked in such a long time, he said, and leaned across the table to the others, it's a feeling, I can't really explain it. Reminds me of

176

the film *Phantom* (1922, with Alfred Abel, Lya de Putti and Lil Dagover). There, the town scribe Lorenz secretly writes poems to Lubota until he's hit by a coach one day. That changes his life. He conceives a passionate love for the girl in the coach. But as she's the daughter of a wealthy merchant, she's unattainable for him. So instead he turns his love to a woman of easy virtue, just because she resembles her, and of course in this magnificent film she's played by the same actress. He robs his own aunt. In the end he even takes part in a burglary of her house, in the course of which the aunt is killed. Then, when he's about to go to prison . . .

What are you trying to tell us, asked Herr Friedrich.

I don't remember, I've been interrupted too often, said Grandfather. He was on to his third beer by now.

I said: Grandfather, I want to go!

The official part of the evening is concluded, said Herr Götze.

What part comes after that, asked Grandfather, looking about him curiously.

The human part, said Herr Götze.

Of late, said Grandfather, I have talked very little, you probably didn't notice because you didn't know me that well then. Of course I knew who you were, but I only ever saw you from a distance. I saw you on the street sometimes when I was going into the Apollo.

I saw you too.

I don't know, said Grandfather, why we never talked to each other. I would have liked to, only when the sound-film era began, I suddenly couldn't talk any more. I thought: There is no one left who is interested in your ideas. But now I'm talking again!

Keep going, Hofmann, keep going!

What with all his talking, Grandfather had completely forgotten about going home. When I tugged at his sleeve and said: Grandfather, come on, let's go, he said: Quiet there! or: Leave my jacket alone! And when I said: They're waiting for us at home, he said: Don't speak when there are grown-ups speaking, unless you're asked to! Listen, so you'll learn something!

Herr Friedrich said: We should save our debate for another day. Your laddie's bored.

Then go, if the society of grown-ups bores you and you want to go home, baby, said Grandfather to me, and pushed me away. He was in a temper because I was making a nuisance of myself.

Anyway, it must have been about midnight and I was long since in bed, when he got home. I heard his voice outside the door. Herr Götze and Herr Friedrich had 'dropped' him at the front door. 'Their fiddling around with the lock woke the whole street' (Mother on the following morning). Grandfather was talking about the cinema again. He was transformed, or at least his voice was. He had fresh courage, and was able to talk again. Like the earliest cinemagoers, whom he had told me about so often – full of curiosity they had gone into the cinema booths, and emerged from them stimulated, bewildered and enlarged – Grandfather was confused and enchanted when he came home from the meeting.

Hey, something's happened, he cried to Grandmother through the bedroom door. I could hear everything. He was still half in the corridor.

Yes, you've been drinking and I can smell it from here, Grandmother called back. Because of her neuralgia, she had put on his nightcap.

No, that's not what I mean!

What else? She could hear his stomach growling. What's that dreadful noise, she asked. On the night of his first meeting, he had drunk five beers and eaten just one piece of bread and dripping.

I'd go to a meeting like that every night if I could, so long as the Apollo doesn't want me. But I'd take care to eat something first.

I'm sure you'd love to spend the rest of your days in fuggy meeting rooms! Have you anything else to say to me?

No, said Grandfather, and shut the door again.

Mind you don't wake the women up, had been Herr Götze's parting words to Grandfather, and the three men all laughed together. Grandfather, because of all the beer he had drunk, held the hands of his two friends for far too long. Then the two of them had gone home to their respective wives. Grandfather apparently prowled around until five in the morning, pacing round his mattress in the corridor shaking his head, then when it got light he walked round the apple trees in the garden. Apparently he was talking to himself, playing various parts. Walking into the garden he said: Yes yes yes!, heading out of it: No no no! He had ended up getting his jacket snagged on the garden fence. Mother heard him too. She thought he had visitors, but it was just him talking to himself. After waking up, we put on clean shirts and socks. Then Grandfather put on his artist's hat, and we headed straight back to the Deutsches Haus. Grandfather said: At least there you can have a proper conversation! He wanted to propose the re-introduction of silent films in the context of national renewal, only he didn't get around to it, he kept looking at his watch and saying how many hours there were to go till the next meeting. Never did he walk up and down the Helenenstrasse with so much impatience, never did he buttonhole so many people. Where once we'd gone to the Apollo, we now went to the Deutsches Haus.

I'll say it today, he said. And: Can't you walk any faster, why are you dragging your feet? Get a move on, dammit! I'll say it today, he said. Then he tilted his artist's hat, and looked a bit more rakish. Finally, when we were standing in front of the Deutsches Haus, he suddenly wasn't so sure of himself, and said: What shall we do now?

Let's go in, I said.

Let's have a look from the outside first! We walked round the Deutsches Haus. It was all quiet. Grandfather said: Empty! Let's go home again!

I said: Are you scared?

Me, said Grandfather, what of? We went into the back courtyard to see if the meeting room was still standing. Grandfather said: It all looks fine. Unfortunately there's no one there.

I said: Well, let's go!

We can try again tomorrow, said Grandfather.

Once when we were peeping through the window of the meeting room we saw a shape, a shadow in uniform. The shadow hurried back and forth. Sometimes it was Herr Götze, sometimes Herr Friedrich, and sometimes we didn't know who it was. But we didn't want to disturb it. Sometimes we just imagined the shadow. And sometimes Grandfather drew a deep breath and said: Come on, let's say hello! and he lifted his hand to knock on the door. But then he let his hand drop again, and didn't knock after all. He said: Better not to be so pushy! They must have lots to do! and we went home again. At home, Grandfather sat down in the smokers' corner and said: It was a mistake! We should have put in an appearance! We're too well behaved.

Grandmother and Mother, whom he took to the next meeting, 'to give them a taste of what it's like', were disappointed. I'm not surprised, said Grandfather, in fact I would have predicted it. They don't have any patriotic feeling.

Being women, they got funny looks from many of the Limbach people at the meeting. Also the air was too poor for them, and the prevailing tone too coarse. That wasn't true just of the Deutsches Haus, it was true of everywhere. They only ever saw the bad side. They found it a bit brutal too.

In Grüna, in the Café Lichtblick, said Grandmother, they beat someone half to death with chair legs. It's a while ago now, but all the same. In Weidmannsdorf they came for the ex-Socialist Pietsch who called Herr Hitler 'a brushed-up monkey'. They drove him to the little Weidmannsdorf woods, and tied him to a tree. There they cut off one of his ears and sent it . . .

180

Why an ear, I asked.

Ha, said Mother, listening again!

When it was Grandfather's day to be critical, he suffered from doubts. He took Herr Götze or Herr Friedrich or both to one side to talk to them. He looked at them sternly. They put their hands on his shoulders and said: It's like this, Hofmann. These are all slanders that have been put into circulation. Never, not in a thousand years, would we ever cut off an opponent's ear, never! That's a slander. You shouldn't listen to such talk.

Grandfather inclined his head and said: But the man who told me had his own . . .

And *if*, I say *if* it's true that they cut his ear off, said Herr Friedrich, then it would make an impression. People need a good fright. They need something to be afraid of.

And why do they need that, asked Grandfather.

It's human nature.

Well, if that's what nature wants, said Grandfather, and tugged at his moustache a little. There is a film, he said, which has some bearing on this, I believe it's called *Shooting Stars* (1927, with Annette Benson and Brian Aherne). In that the young actress Mae is married to her colleague Julian, but has an affair with a comedian. When her husband finds out, she's afraid of a scandal that might put an end to her career. And so she decides to take the blank cartridge out of her lover's revolver and replace it with live . . .

After that talk, Grandfather once again relished the meetings. Happier than at home, where Grandmother after a lot of shillyshallying let him sleep in her bed in her bedroom again. 'He's quietened down'. He wasn't allowed to smoke in there any more. He didn't have much else. Mother said, because they won't have him in the cinema, he clings to the meetings like a bullrush in the sea, if they have bullrushes in the sea, she said.

# Nine

For all his lack of formal education – just six years of primary school – Grandfather was for a long time the embodiment of the unworldly scholar so highly respected in Saxony, thick-waisted from so much sitting, reading and beer drinking. 'You would think to look at him that he ate paper' (Grandmother). His beer glass and cigar he had put aside now, 'by force of adverse circumstance'. His eyes – the left especially – watered when he smoked. Seeing him in that state, Grandmother shook her head. She no longer said: He's been smoking again!, she said: He's been crying again! Being unemployed, he let his hair grow. It saved on the barber. It made him look like a hooligan or an old woman. Grey waves broke all over his head, which he called 'my little curls' and which gave him 'a Semitic aspect'.

I'm not, though, Grandfather told me, I'm much more heterogeneous.

And me, I asked.

After his illness, he looks almost intellectual because of all his worries, said Grandmother. If you didn't know any better, you might think he was a professor of mathematics, that's how thoughtful the geezer looks.

It's evident that in him you have a man who stands on his own feet, and thinks architectonically, said Herr Cosimo. I put my jacket on. We were going for a walk.

Grandmother said: Like a conman planning some new trick.

One might think him occupied day and night with the construction of a new natural philosophy, said Herr Cosimo. His searching glance seems capable of seeing through mere appearances . . .

The thirty-three-year-old carpenter Hermann S. has died in the Haftmeierstrasse in Rottluff, said Mother, who had just read it in the *Limbacher*. They had just remanded him when it happened. Wonder if he was a Communist?

Dear dear, said Herr Cosimo.

Then we heard some banging around in the bedroom. Are you ready then, called Grandfather, appearing in the doorway with his artist's hat and stick.

Ready, I said.


On our excursions Grandfather and Herr Cosimo walked in step. Sometimes one of them whistled softly to himself. If he lost the tune, the other would take it up. But they didn't walk so close together as before. Their sleeves didn't rub any more. Sometimes when the path narrowed, they did touch. Then Grandfather and Herr Cosimo both started and called: So sorry! or: My fault! But it happened less and less often, they had more space between them. They hadn't fallen out, they just weren't getting on so well. They know too much about each other, said Grandmother, they've lost their innocence. For instance, Grandfather knew that Herr Cosimo's character had 'many crudely materialistic traits', which his talk and civility had camouflaged up till now.

Over many years, and very adroitly, said Grandfather to me, that's how I failed to notice. Now, of course . . .


The trouble with Herr Cosimo was that he put all his trust in 'his own medium-sized person and his own enormous feet'. Being half Italian – if that was indeed the case – Herr Cosimo mostly talked about himself. If he talked about ideas, it was *his* ideas; if misfortune, *his* misfortune; a craving for bread and ham, *his* craving. Probably, Herr Cosimo would have been perfectly happy with his lot if he got enough macaroni with tomato sauce to eat, beer to drink, a cheap lodging, and a couple of magazines to browse through, a man of his type wanted nothing more. Artistically too, Herr Cosimo was a disappointment to Grandfather. When Grandfather spoke of a new idea or a particularly good film he just happened to remember, Herr Cosimo now simply turned his back on him and smiled. Also he lacked a sense of rhythm, 'and all that usually goes with it'. And that, Grandfather told me, is the most important thing in the world: everything, earthworm, bird or wave, has its own rhythm.

Me too, I asked.

Up to a point, said Grandfather.

And Grandfather had never liked the way Herr Cosimo was happy to be a drain on the public purse. He had just never said anything about it before. 'Sponging' he called it, and it went against his honour. It was anti-social. But Herr Cosimo wasn't bothered about honour. Whereas for Grandfather, honour was . . . . 'We're just completely different characters with completely different notions in our heads.' Grandfather walked too quickly for Herr Cosimo, and when they talked he was too idealistic and prone to take flight for lofty regions where his friend couldn't follow.

Because, said Herr Cosimo, those are regions where I have no business. I know my limitations.

You mean regions . . .

Elevations, said Herr Cosimo. Sometimes he now walked a step ahead.

When Grandfather had taken flight, he needed to be taken by the hand by Herr Cosimo, and 'gently, gently brought back down to earth and the world of hard facts', which was never without its disappointment. Plus 'the business of the two Cs, *cinema* and *culture*', which gradually got to be too much for Herr Cosimo. Typical of Grandfather that he usually began talking about the Cs in the Amselgrund, when we had a view out across beechwoods.

You never mention them while we're walking, said Herr Cosimo. It isn't until we get to the Amselgrund and have a break.

You could be right, said Grandfather, don't you wonder why that is?

Because the path there is straight, said Herr Cosimo, and you don't need to watch your legwork. When you stand there and rest and have some kind of landscape in front of you – anything, as long as it's fresh! – you start to enthuse. And that gets you onto your two Cs. Every time you open your mouth, you distance yourself from the human condition, cried Herr Cosimo, and we marched on. Occasionally a bird sang to us. The weather was always fine.

There is, Grandfather said, a wonderful film . . .

Ha, what did I tell you!

. . . in which the wife of a toy-maker . . .

Oh, said Herr Cosimo, can't we leave films out of it just once!

But there you have the whole of life! For me it's crystal clear, art can help us out of all sorts of difficulties . . .

By helping you to ignore reality, that's all!

Bah, 'reality'! Today it's one thing, tomorrow something else, said Grandfather, and we marched on.

Their relationship, Grandmother said in the kitchen that evening, has somewhat cooled.

Mother said: It'll turn to ice ere long.

Grandfather now preferred the company of Herr Götze and Herr Friedrich to that of Herr Cosimo. We were often made to wait for them a long time. Grandfather kept looking at his watch and tugging at his beard. He had 'expelled' the women. Now we stood beside the kitchen window, and gazed up the street.

185

No, said Grandfather, we won't chase after them! No, I won't let you either! You're to stay here and stand at my side and wait for them to show! And then we'll pretend to be surprised.

Why?

Because that's how it's done, said Grandfather. They don't need to know we've been waiting for them. That would just make them big-headed.

We went away from the window, so that they couldn't see us from below. They didn't come for a long time. Then there was a knock on the door, the bell was broken again. Grandfather slowly went over to the window and exclaimed: Oh, Herr Götze! Oh, Herr Friedrich! What a nice surprise! How unexpected!

We told you we were coming, said Herr Götze.

Yes, now I remember, said Grandfather, we'd just forgotten all about it.

We made them wait a while longer, then Grandfather said: There, that's enough! And we went down the stairs and set off. Grandfather was wearing a freshly laundered shirt, and I had a clean handkerchief. I had a little swastika banner too. Herr Götze had given it to me. He and Herr Friedrich were clean shaven. Their canes both had steel tips, Grandfather's didn't. Herr Götze and Herr Friedrich kept their caps on in all weathers. They took Grandfather between them, so he couldn't get out. Because the pavement wasn't wide enough for all of us, I had to run along behind them. And so we walked up the Kreuzstrasse. It was now called the Franz Seldte Strasse, Grandfather didn't know why. 'I'm afraid I don't know any Franz Seldte. I've never had the pleasure.'

Herr Götze had once been the manager of an artificial gut factory in Mittweida. That had gone bust. Now he was looking for work, but couldn't find anything. Sometimes he got onto his rattletrap of a bicycle and looked as far afield as Clausewitz, but he never had any luck. He was a familiar figure everywhere, and people waved to him from a distance, calling out: Turn back, Herr Götze! There are no vacancies here! Now Herr Götze told them at home that he was looking for work, while in fact he was going out for walks with Herr Friedrich. Soon he would start drawing his pension anyway.

Do you ever go to the cinema, asked Grandfather.

Herr Götze said: You've already asked me that once.

You see, said Grandfather, you don't. Otherwise we would have met before now.

Herr Friedrich was an unskilled worker. I don't want to compare myself with him, said Grandfather, we come from such completely different worlds! Herr Friedrich liked to talk as well. He had a way with words, 'in Saxon and in German too' (Grandmother). He had a loud voice and a signet ring he claimed was gold. 'Of course it's fake, I can tell that at a glance' (Grandfather). He could also play the zither, Herr Friedrich could, but no one had heard him as yet.

But what about the cinema, asked Grandfather, do you go to the cinema?

Rarely, said Herr Friedrich.

You see, said Grandfather, as I suspected.

Herr Götze and Herr Friedrich wore brown shirts. Both were Party members and wore 'a raspberry sweet over their hearts' (Grandmother). If they wanted to trick someone who didn't know them, and get him to incriminate himself, they hid it under their lapels. Then he would say whatever it was, and they had him.

The Party is there for everyone, no one can be too good for it or too bad! Including you, Hofmann, they said to Grandfather, who would much rather have gone on talking about the cinema. The woods were ahead of us now. Grandfather looked at them happily. He nodded and said: I know!

Then they slapped him on the back, one on the right, the other on the left. You too, sonny boy, when you're a bit bigger, they said to me. The Party had no objection to writers and intellectuals like Grandfather who wrote poems. The Party had its own introspective moods. That's why so many artists belonged to it, and more were joining all the time. Herr Cosimo couldn't understand it. He found Herr Götze and Herr Friedrich rather repulsive. So did I really. When they came to our flat, they made everything dirty. They wore leather jackets the whole time, and leather belts which had no buckles, which they just knotted. They wore riding breeches and knee-socks that slipped when they walked. Then one of them would stop to pull his up. In the meantime the other went striding on, crying: On, on! The world won't wait! Then after a while he would be obliged to stop and pull his up, while the first cried: On, on! They were shod in rough walking boots, that they wanted to march to the end of the world in. Do you know where that is, Herr Friedrich asked me.

No.

It's a long way, said Herr Friedrich, but we'll get there!

Everyone who marches as much should have boots like that, said Grandfather, only a little bigger, and he told them the story of Herr Malz. They hadn't heard it before. Grandfather's boots were anything but new now.

Herr Friedrich asked: What shoe size did you say you were, Hofmann? and three days later he brought Grandfather a pair of solid marching boots, not brand new, but in which Grandfather was able to march much better. It was love at first sight with those boots. Ideally, Grandfather wouldn't have taken them off at all, not even to go to bed. He greased them three times a day and squandered that expensive shoe polish like nobody's business. His womenfolk shook their heads, but didn't say anything. Grandfather was too difficult. Since he'd been banned from the Apollo and lost 'his work and his pleasure in one fell swoop' it hadn't been much of a life for him. So he needed something. So he took what Herr Götze and Herr Friedrich had to offer.

With their leather shoulders and their little heads, they look so alike, from a distance one might think they were twins, Mother said at home.

Nothing up top except their forage caps, said Grandmother. She couldn't stand the pair of them, and used to wonder which of them was worse. Now she said: Friedrich is worse! And now: No, Götze is!

Even so, it's better for him to go stomping about with them, than hang around at home, feeling the cares of the world on his shoulders, said Mother. He needs to be kept busy!

Yes, but what with?

A real man, Grandmother said, keeps himself busy.

When Grandfather came home each time, he asked whether anything had been delivered for him, he was very nervous. When Grandmother asked: Where from, he cried: Where do you think? From the court!

No, she said, not yet! Tomorrow maybe.

Sometimes after a long march – Herr Friedrich said: This is how we crossed Flanders! – they would talk about HIM. Both Herr Götze and Herr Friedrich had met HIM. Herr Friedrich, the smaller of the two, but with the louder voice, had clapped eyes on HIM in Munich, on the corner of Ludwigstrasse and Theresienstrasse, just as HE and HIS closest entourage were emerging from the public urinals. Herr Friedrich had recognised HIM at once. He had saluted smartly, but received no acknowledgement. HE had a fresh parting in his hair. On HIS feet HE wore walking boots, topped by knee-socks and a raincoat, because in Munich you never know with the weather! HIS aspect had so overwhelmed Herr Friedrich that he hadn't been able to use the urinal, but had spent the next few hours, until well after dark, running around, thinking only of HIM. He couldn't even say how he had finally . . .

That's just like Adele Sandrock in *Hypocritical Morality* (1921, with Adele Sandrock and Eugene Klöpfer), said Grandfather suddenly. In that, two young people who are destined for one another grow up under close supervision, but then suddenly the young servant girl Anna is expecting a baby from the young man, and Adele Sandrock has to intervene and break them up. She decides to marry off the girl to the coffin-maker Torgeir, that way she'd be rid of her. So she steals the baby, whereupon Anna becomes gravely ill . . .

Yes, yes, said Herr Friedrich, such things happen, I . . .

When the young man finally marries his intended, said Grandfather, Torgeir appears uninvited with a coffin for a wedding present. Inside the coffin, are you listening now, said Grandfather, is Anna's body.

And then, asked Herr Götze.

Of course the young man strangles Adele Sandrock, who has suddenly aged terribly overnight, what did you suppose, said Grandfather.

Herr Götze, walking on the right, nodded. He too was familiar with such cases. He too had seen HIM, and been just as overwhelmed, once in Berlin and once in Cottbus. In Berlin HE was just leaving the circus. There was still an animal smell about HIM. HE carried his felt hat in HIS hand, and was wearing a folkloric jacket. HE had talked so rousingly that HE was barely still able to stand. Herr Götze, who had long wanted to touch HIM, had pushed his way through to HIM, but then HIS adjutant Brückner had come along and pushed him away. What do you want with HIM, Brückner had yelled, can't you see THE MAN is exhausted, you bloody idiot! So Herr Götze hadn't been able to touch HIM, only nearly. The second time, in Cottbus . . . . Later on, in the Hoher Hain, there was sniffing of young trees.

*

Before the restitution of the Sudetenland, a 'half-dead martyr' was found lying in the dawn in the Franz Seldte Strasse. Apparently, said Grandfather, who didn't much care for trees because they didn't talk, he was lying on the pavement under an alder or some other non-flowering specimen. Herr Lange had shouted it up to the window, just as Grandfather was looking to see what the weather was like.

A dead man, shouted Herr Lange.

Aha, Grandfather shouted back, a martyr, I suppose!

Probably, said Herr Lange. The corpse was male, mid thirties maybe, with dark hair. He was in his shirt and trousers.

Fine, said Grandfather, I'm on my way. Then he shut the window. If, he explained to us, he's only wearing a shirt and trousers, it probably means he's from the garment factory. They go around in just shirt and trousers because they sweat so much at work. Even without having seen him, Grandfather could imagine him very clearly. He wanted to go and take a look at him, but not on an empty stomach; after breakfast, if he was still lying there, and with me. That kind of thing, he said, you don't get to see every day! But it's no good on an empty stomach. In the film *Money! Money! Money!* (1928, with Brigitte Helm and Alfred Abel), when the speculator Aristide Saccard has been driven to the brink of ruin by his great rival Gundermann . . .

It'll be a finisher, said Mother, I've no doubt on that score! She hadn't seen him either, and didn't even want to. She preferred to read about it in the paper the next day.

Or an unemployed man, said Grandmother, wanting to make an end. She poured out the coffee. In life, she said, there comes a point, which once reached . . .

No, no, it's a martyr, said Grandfather.

A what, I asked.

Martyr, cried Grandfather, a martyr!

And what is a martyr?

A martyr is a martyr, he said, and drank up his coffee. He got his hat and stick. He looked out of the window onto the street. An ordinary sort of day, he said, it's we who are out of kilter! We've got the martyr on our minds, no question. All ready, he said. In two shakes we were out of the house and on the street.

We've forgotten to wash, but you at least have combed your hair, he said. Well, we've got a lot on! First we should go and see if there's already a queue at the dole office. If there is, we'll see how long it is. You've got your green summer shirt and your wooden sandals that make such a racket. Everyone will think we've gone for a walk, but in fact we're just going to see if the dole has arrived.

And then?

Then we'll go back and take a look at the martyr!

The town hall was already open. We weren't the first. A lot of people were standing around, mostly in a queue. Some had already been to see the martyr. But they weren't talking about him. Others hadn't stopped, but walked on by. Others again hadn't even noticed him. And yet the martyr was clearly visible. We went up to him. He had a head injury, and was lying in the gutter. His eyes were shut.

Dear dear, said Grandfather, dear dear!

And why is he lying in the gutter, I asked.

Because that's where they laid him, said Grandfather.

Who laid him there?

If only we knew!

The martyr was lying on the Franz Seldte Strasse, formerly Kreuzstrasse, quite a long way up. Too far for him to be visible from our kitchen window, anyway. The martyr was of average build, and he lay very still. First we walked up and down in front of him, then we walked all round him, like the others.

He must have been lying here for a while, at least that's what it looks like to me, said Grandfather. He held my hand. But how long the martyr had been lying there he wasn't able to say. Nor did Grandfather know how he'd got there, 'except it wasn't under his own steam'. When we stood in front of him again, Grandfather looked at his watch. It was a quarter past eight. There were people still standing round him. They had their hands in their pockets and looked at him, as we did. A few were smoking too. The martyr's shirt was cut across his chest.

And in the form of a cross, see that, said Grandfather, I wonder if that signifies anything?

What do you think it signifies?

Well, could it be a sign?

The flesh under the shirt of the martyr had been cut too, or deeply scratched. The shirt was sodden with blood. Grandfather stood beside me. He studied the man. Perhaps he was thinking of a film in which someone is found lying in the street, about to die. Perhaps he'd just forgotten the title. He held my hand.

I don't know whether I should let you look at him or not, said Grandfather, and for a while he was undecided. Sometimes: This is nothing for a child, and at others: Have a good look, it'll teach you something about life! That's what you want to know, isn't it, he asked.

Yes.

Then have a good look!

Grandfather held me by the hand. We walked around the martyr. We looked at him from every side. Grandfather asked me: Do you suppose he got this treatment right here, or was it done somewhere else and then he was driven over to us on the Kreuzstrasse, or the Franz Seldte Strasse, and then dropped, what do you think? But I didn't know either. The martyr was lying next to the hydrant, and people were asking: Do you know the man? Do you? Do you? But no one seemed to know him.

Well, said Grandfather when we had returned home and had fully briefed Grandmother and Mother, and wanted to set off again to brief Herr Götze and Herr Friedrich, well, well! But they weren't at home. They had gone to the market to buy green onions. We went back to the Kreuzstrasse alone, and ran into lots of people. Grandfather kept having to take his hat off. Everyone said what lovely weather it was, and how the tomatoes were doing, and how there was a body lying in the Kreuzstrasse, probably dead.

Anyway, said Grandfather, it's now coming up to nine o'clock. The sun, having shone on the roofs, was now shining on the street. When we went up to him again, there was some blood on his hand. He's bitten his lips as well, poor chap, said Grandfather. He said: Something's just occurred to me! I wonder if his name might not be Willi!

Why should it be Willi?

Well, I don't know, but I'm just going to call him that, said Grandfather, when we were back in the flat.

And where does he come from, I asked.

Maybe Mittweida, called Mother from her room. She sat there and sewed. I think he's from Mittweida!

Maybe, said Grandfather.

Or Zwickau, I said.

Yes, perhaps he's from Zwickau!

Is his name really Willi, I asked.

It's no use asking me that, called Grandmother, you have to make up your own minds! Anything's possible!

It had to happen, didn't it, cried Mother, who still hadn't been to see him, from her sewing-machine. She had no time for that sort of thing, she had to sew and sew! But even if she had been able to go and look at him, she didn't know whether she should. Sometimes she said to herself: I'm going to go and have a look! and sometimes: No, I'm going to let him lie! Now she was sitting at her machine, crying: Now, when we could really use someone, no one comes to lend a hand!

Shall I lend a hand?

For Heaven's sake keep away, she cried.

Then can I go and have another look at him, I asked.

What, she cried, again? Well, if you must, but keep it short! And you're not to touch him, she said.

When we went up to him again, someone was just turning him over. Now he was resting on his side. His head lay on the paving stones, where people usually put their boots. Blood came out of one ear. Old Frau Sippel from the Steinstrasse thought he was dead. She leaned on her garden fence and told everyone so at the top of her voice. Later on, the martyr was turned onto his other side by Herr Müller, who had first spent a long time walking round him. He said: He'll be more comfortable this way! We had a better view of him too. Grandfather – 'as an artist, I'm attracted by anything unusual' – went up even closer, right up to him.

No, you're not to, he said to me, when I wanted to go closer as well, you don't need to have such a good view of him! There, go look at the houses!

But I know them already!

The clouds, then, they're always new! What'll it be, then?

The houses!

The houses were right and left of us, and they looked very near. Limbach, Grandfather was fond of saying, is too small for them. Some houses had benches in front of them, others didn't. Grandfather pulled me across the road, so that I couldn't see 'the invalid' any more. 'And don't look so glum about it!'

The whole of Limbach seemed transformed because of the martyr. The houses were gloomier. Even the sky looked different, the clouds, the air. Winter, said Grandfather as we went home, gives people like me who tiptoe carefully through the year, the *coup de grâce*! In here, he said, and pointed to his chest, through the heart! And winter's coming, I can feel it, he said once we were home again. He went into the kitchen, helped himself to a piece of bread and sprinkled salt on it. There, he said, nothing tastes better. Our town, he said, is crumbling! The houses are crumbling, the pavements are subsiding, everything is in need of repair, but no one can afford it. The guttering hangs off the roofs, so the rainwater flows anywhere. Then they carry the pipes up to the Kellerwiese where that crook Herr Kraft sells them again. We are being undermined, Rats, rats, he cried. Just stick your finger down a rathole, cried Grandfather, they're just waiting to bite it off! Soon enough, he said, we'll all be gobbled up anyway.

And what are we going to do now, I asked.

We're going to have another look at the martyr, what did you think!

Finally, finally, the police car arrived. They pushed us aside. We formed a circle round them so we could all see. Grandfather took off his artist's hat, in case the man was already dead. You see what they do, Grandfather said quietly. They arrive late on purpose, so we can all see what happens to those who . . . . Grandfather told the policemen who he was, and who I was. 'We live over there!' But the police didn't want to hear. They went over to the martyr and shook him. They they looked in his pockets. They were empty though. Then a man from Grüna suddenly said the martyr wasn't a martyr at all, but an 'escaped political prisoner' who had met his end while on the run from his rightful punishment. As to whether he was still alive . . . . The police held a mirror in front of his mouth. He was still breathing!

No, said Grandfather, don't look! The less you see in such cases, the better!

The police went into their car and came out with a stretcher. They unrolled the stretcher. Then they laid the escaped prisoner on it. Then we all picked up the stretcher.

Didn't I tell you not to look, said Grandfather. I looked anyway. I saw his hands, the back of his legs, his head. Where are we taking him, I asked. Then Grandfather gave me a strange answer which I didn't understand, but couldn't forget either.

They're taking him to the Jahnstrasse in Chemnitz, and putting him in the window, said Grandfather.

And when I asked: What, like a shop window?, he said: To make an example of him! So that everyone sees him, with his shirt and his skull and his nose! And is duly warned!

What about?

But that Grandfather didn't know or wouldn't tell me. Then it was time. We took the man, who now wasn't a martyr at all, and who kept groaning and opening his eyes – blue, they were – to the long, open, chrome-gleaming ambulance. Everyone wanted to carry a bit of him. Some held the head, others a leg, some just a hand. Grandfather led the way with his stick and didn't carry anything. Everything he might have carried was already in other people's possession. Only one bit was still free, and that was a forearm. Then Grandfather took that and carried it. I would have liked to carry something too, but Grandfather wouldn't let me. He kept pushing me away. I kept trying to help with the forearm, but Grandfather kept calling out: Yuck, don't touch that! There, look the other way! Look at the houses and the windows and the trees! Yuck, he cried, don't touch that!

On our walks, Herr Götze and Herr Friedrich moved in step. They were used to it. They harangued Grandfather, one from the left, the other from the right. Whenever one of them stopped because he couldn't think of what else to say, the other carried on. He would take Grandfather's arm and carry on from where the other had stopped, because both of them had exactly the same thoughts. Grandfather smiled the whole time and thought about a film. But he was polite and kept nodding. He was a wonderful talker, but he was good at listening too. He took every sentence on board. He didn't speak much. Then Herr Götze or Herr

Friedrich would ask Grandfather to stop nodding, and to say something himself, for instance about his wartime experiences.

There is, said Grandfather, a wonderful bit in the film *All Quiet on the Western Front*, about marching, and there . . .

We'd rather you didn't mention that production, said Herr Friedrich.

Oh I see, said Grandfather. He was still smiling. He took deep breaths, in and out.

Didn't you do anything in the war, Herr Götze asked severely.

Yes, I was wounded, said Grandfather. And he explained how he had come by his wound. 'It still bleeds sometimes.' He didn't say: When I scratch it. He stopped, untucked his shirt, and slowly undid the buttons. Then he showed us his shrunken belly with the scar. He said: A bullet, from here to here! You can touch it, he said, it's not bleeding today!

Does it usually bleed, then, asked Herr Friedrich.

Yes, said Grandfather, most of the time.

Then Herr Friedrich and Herr Götze moved even closer and said: Aha! Look! And with their fingertips they carefully brushed Grandfather's wound. Yes, they said, we can feel it!

All right, said Grandfather, and he put the wound away again. Then he said: This is as far as I can go with you today. I have to go to see my solicitor.

Really, said Herr Götze, what about?

My case is coming up, said Grandfather, I've been charged with malicious wounding.

Really, said Herr Friedrich, you must tell us about that!

In fact, said Herr Götze, why don't we accompany you.

Herr Lampadius, the solicitor we were going to see because he was defending Grandfather, was leaning back in his swivel chair in his office on the Badergraben. A sunbeam played on his round, broad skull. Grandfather had brought us all along. The office was almost full. Herr Lampadius said: If I succeed, my dear Hofmann, in defusing the accusation and getting you off with a fine . . . . Your little chap doesn't miss a thing, does he, he said, pointing at me. But it would be wrong to trivialise the matter! In the teeth of fourteen witnesses, we can't very well claim your twelve rounds with Itzig was just a disagreement between friends. I know you're not the first one who bristles at the sight of him. By the way, the bunch of hair you tore out will be exhibit No. 1 on the court table. He would hardly have torn it out all by himself, they will argue, someone else, i.e. you, would have had to give it a little tug . . . . Well, little chap, are you following all this too? What would you say to a sweetie? No? Just as well, I haven't got one anyway! Enough, said Herr Lampadius, I could easily produce a list of people who have been accused of similar offences and got off with a small fine, a trifle . . . Herr Lampadius pointed to a stack of files, and said: actual bodily harm, teeth knocked out, crushed larynx, fractured leg, broken noses, all sorts! Many of them going back years. Well, justice takes its course, slowly and not in the least surely, as I like to say, said Herr Lampadius. S by the way is short for Samuel not Siegfried, as we thought. The wife's name is Sarah, the children . . . Forget the children! Your case is a trifle, small and ugly. But I've taken you on so that's that. What I have here are common assaults just from Limbach and the outlying areas! There's no room in my files for any more. Just the local injuries. The whole of Saxony has gone to the dogs and cats, as I once put it. A man beats his neighbour to a pulp, another after umpteen years of marriage suddenly can't stand the sight of his wife any more, so he rearranges her features for her, yet another is crippled because of something he said in the presence of someone who took exception . . . . By Jove your grandson is a good listener! If he carries on like this, he'll get ass's ears! These cases, said Herr Lampadius, are springing up all over the place, and like the world in general, the law is no longer capable of keeping them in check.

At any rate, said Herr Lampadius, at any rate .... Theilhaber banning you from the premises is ridiculous! The Apollo's almost had it anyway! Ha, he's still listening! How would you like to pay an eventual fine? With such a trifling sum, it should be possible for you to pay cash, and keep the paperwork. ... No? You want to pay in instalments? Fine, let's draw up our application! Monthly payments ... say twenty marks? No? Well how much could you manage?

Grandfather sighed. With his fingers he signalled that he would only be able to pay very little. In the splendid film *Les Deux Timides* (1928, by René Clair) he said, a man is taken to court because he hadn't spoken to his wife for weeks. That was supposed to be emotional cruelty. But at the hearing it all turned out very differently. A mouse loose in the courtroom completely confuses his counsel. He gets tied up in knots, and gets his own client put away. It's very funny, said Grandfather a little desperately, as no one laughed.

I looked at him and smiled. He sat there, all spick and span. He had his better collar on, he was just a bit thin. He looked across to me and winked. Herr Götze and Herr Friedrich were looking here and looking there. They weren't smiling. Herr Lampadius sighed. Then he stood up and went to his filing cabinet, because he was obliged ...

Each time someone greeted Herr Götze and Herr Friedrich, they greeted back as one. Their fingers touched, 'look, they're holding hands!' (Grandmother). They did a lot of things together. If one of them sang, it was never long before the other joined in. One of them read aloud from the newspaper, and the other nodded in agreement. They spoke in unison: Our task is to bring new members into the Party. But each of them had to do that on his own. I asked: How many this week, Herr Götze, and he said: Two!

Grandfather said: Congratulations!

What about you, Herr Friedrich, I asked, and Herr Friedrich adjusted his belt and said: I've got three!

Gracious, said Grandfather and we went on.

A couple of weeks later I asked again: And how many have you got today?

Herr Götze said: A half.

And again Grandfather cried: Gracious!

But how do you do that, get half a member, I asked.

Then Grandfather banged his stick into the ground and cried: Don't ask so many questions! How do you think they do it? They just do it, don't you, Götze?

Herr Götze said: Let him ask. That way he'll learn something! And then, to me: Actually I haven't got anyone yet. I'm still looking. He was wearing his spectacles so he could see better. His breast pocket was full of forms. Next to them were some pencil stubs. If he ran into anyone who wasn't a member yet, but was interested, he would undo his breast pocket, then he could produce his pencil stubs faster. Then he would take the man who was maybe interested by the arm and say: Come on! We're going for a little walk! and he took him up to the Hoher Hain. After a while he would think: There, now you can ask him, and he popped the question: Well, how about it? Wouldn't you like to join? Wouldn't you like to try it out? Some said: I'm not meschugge! Some agonised and said: Maybe later! And some: Yes, I would! and they signed there and then. And so Herr Götze would have another one.

Grandfather was sixty-four now. 'Though I know nobody would believe it.' Herr Götze was younger, but didn't look it. When he walked through the Amselgrund with Grandfather and me and Herr Friedrich, maybe with some song on his lips, he always had the application forms on him. He liked to scribble away at them. And he would talk about the 'situation'. 'And so time passes, as it must, that's all it ever does' (Grandmother). Soon we were up in the Hoher Hain, tramping it down variously under our feet. Grandfather had his mushroom sack and knife with him. We crept into the undergrowth. Grandfather knew every single pine needle here. He crawled on ahead. He crawled 'slowly, but surely'.

I'm over here, he cried from time to time, and parted the branches so they didn't scratch our faces.

There aren't any mushrooms, cried Herr Götze, panting away in the undergrowth. He would have liked to go back to the clearing so he wouldn't have to stoop. We looked for ten minutes more, maybe fifteen. Grandfather said: There aren't any mushrooms, not here anyway! We need to go deeper in, deeper! Herr Götze cried: Even deeper? He didn't like mushrooms, he thought they were all poisonous.

When Herr Götze and Grandfather and I emerged from the undergrowth, we noticed it was raining. The boughs kept off the first few drops, but soon they were saturated. Grandfather stopped. He wasn't thinking about Party membership any more, or at least seemed not to be. He tipped his round head back and looked up at the sky. He said: I think we're in for a storm, and a bad one at that! He put his collar up. Then he said: Seek ye the beech tree! and put his mushroom knife in his jacket pocket. Lest the mushrooms see it and take fright, he said, winking at me. In the wonderful film *Homunculus* (1916, with the Danish actor Olaf Fønss), he said, the world famous Professor Hansen manufactures something in his lab during just such a storm, but what? Whatever, it develops into a so-called 'manikin'. When this manikin learns of his origins, he feels like a pariah among real people, and begins to long for . . . Well, what do you think? For love, of course, said Grandfather. He travels to distant lands where no one knows who he is, but whenever he tries to conquer a human heart, people shy away from him and cry: Yuck, a monster! Only one creature loves him: his dog! When the dog is poisoned, the homunculus despises people. Later he comes to hate them: they take away the best things in life! He dresses up as a worker and foments discontent. In the end, he starts rebellions. Finally a war breaks out, and it takes a bolt of lightning . . .

Grandfather, Herr Götze and I were standing under a tree. The rain came down even harder! Herr Götze had buttoned up his combat jacket. He buckled on his chinstrap so that the wind didn't blow away his cap. With his cap on and his collar up, he looked very soldierly. He sang something into the teeth of the gale. He was probably thinking, if I don't get my membership forms out of the pocket of my leather jacket and ask old Hofmann to sign, it probably won't happen today either, and he reached into his jacket and pulled out . . . . How it rained – we said: It's teeming – at that moment! No let up! No let up! No let up!

When it wasn't raining, we went past the Apollo to the Big Pond. There were dragonflies there. 'If one stings you, you're dead' (Mother). Herr Götze had a knotty stick. When the path narrowed, and we had to walk in single file, he said: Let me go first! When he walked too fast, he would lose us. He would shout: The way is clear! You can come! Herr Friedrich had got his wife to make up two batches of sandwiches which were in his knapsack. Of course Grandfather suggested to Grandmother that she might make him some as well, but Grandmother said: Once I start making you sandwiches, you'll never come home. And when he said: When have you ever wrapped a sandwich in greaseproof paper for me, she said: How am I supposed to pay for greaseproof paper! Today we were able to share with Herr Friedrich, because he had two batches. One batch was with liverwurst, the other had ham. Herr Friedrich kept fondling them both. Sometimes he sniffed at them too. Now he would sniff at the liverwurst, now at the ham. He asked: How about attacking one of these?

Herr Götze said: Yes, let's put them to the sword!

Grandfather, walking between the two of them, said: In the wonderful American picture *The Wedding March* (1928, with Erich von Stroheim), a father has arranged a money match for his son. He is to marry the lame daughter of the wealthy industrialist Featherstone, but then . . .

But Herr Götze and Herr Friedrich just walked on. To make sure, Grandfather said to me, fanning himself, we have a good view for our picnic spot. In the Hoher Hain we sat down on the grass. We put the sandwiches to the sword. They all took liverwurst ones, I took a ham one. Then the bottle of beer was passed around. Grandfather didn't mind drinking from the same bottle as Herr Friedrich. He didn't even wipe the neck. Then Herr Götze suddenly said: I suggest we call you *Du*! Herr Friedrich and Herr Götze already did that among themselves. But they'd known each other for some time. What do you say, Hofmann, Herr Götze asked Grandfather, would you mind being *Du*?

Grandfather thought about it. Then he said: We haven't known each other that long!

But we used *Du* when we were at the Front, said Herr Götze.

Grandfather said: But we're not at the Front now!

Yes we are, said Herr Friedrich, the Front is everywhere! Don't you read the papers?

I prefer the cinema, said Grandfather. But if you say so!

After the picnic we marched back. Grandfather did most of the talking. The cinema, he said, gives us a breathing space. For which, cinema, we thank you.

Herr Friedrich hadn't been paying attention, and said: If you say so! He had his pipe in his mouth. He had stuffed it with something he called 'his mixture'. He drew on it and coughed a lot.

We walked back to Limbach through the pinewood.

This pinewood, said Grandfather, is so thick at this point that from the road you can only see the first two or three rows of trees. But that's only the beginning. Nature equipped it with tops.

What do you mean: equipped, asked Herr Friedrich.

Stuck them on, said Grandfather, looking for his last cigar end. Like in the film *Macbeth* by William Shakespeare, where the wood suddenly starts to move and . . .

Aha, said Herr Götze, very true!

At the edge of town, the pinewood bordered the cemetery for a while. There wasn't so much talking there. I wasn't allowed to touch the wall because of the poison from all the dead bodies. Then hurriedly back into town! We had to do a lot of greeting. Mostly people greeted Herr Friedrich, then Herr Götze. But even Grandfather was greeted a lot. Sometimes he was the one to greet first. In the Kanalstrasse Grandfather looked up at Fräulein Fritsche's window. He hoped he might see her, but he didn't. Maybe she was hunched over her machine, sewing. Or she'd just nipped into town to buy something to drink. Later on, we were greeted by women who had put their chairs out on the pavement. The 'three musketeers' (Herr Friedrich) greeted back, one after the other.

What about you, Grandfather said to me, don't you greet people?

It was the first time since his serious illness that he had walked so far. It had done him good. His eyes looked fresh. Instead of looking slight and pale and shrunken, he looked slight and animated. 'Doesn't he look as good as new?' (Grandmother). Even his voice was different, from all his talking, and it would stay like that until his death – his decease, he said. He didn't even notice he had a new voice, he thought it was still his old one. Herr Götze had to point it out to him.

So I talk differently from how I used to, Grandfather asked.

Yes, they cried, like new!

And then when Grandfather had listened to himself talking for a while, he thought: It's true, I do sound different! No longer weak and hesitant, much firmer and more decisive. Sing, he cried, and we sang. We sang all the way home.

# Ten

At that time Grandfather waited impatiently for the man with the piece of paper to come. When he did come he wore a raincoat and was carrying a briefcase. He stood in front of the house to shout up to Grandfather. Grandfather was sitting on the lav. He cried: Go and see what that idiot wants!

Grandmother went up to the window and called down: What do you want?

The man said: He's to go and see Herr Lampadius, that's what it says here on my piece of paper. And he put it back in his briefcase.

Grandmother went up to the lav door and cried: He says he needs to talk to you. Lampadius has sent him!

All right, cried Grandfather from behind the door, I'm coming! He didn't have any shoes on, but still went up to the window, and the man with the piece of paper gave him the message.

All right, I'm on my way, said Grandfather, and the man went away.

What about me, I asked, can I come too?

Grandfather slipped into his shoes and jacket. Then he put his artist's hat on.

What about me, I cried after him.

He didn't say anything about you, cried Grandfather and he disappeared. I watched him for a long time. He stayed gone until after dark. You could hardly make out the trees any more.

He won't have lost his way will he, said Grandmother, who didn't put anything past him. But after his talk with Herr Lampadius, Grandfather had just gone for a beer in the Rüdesheimer, and then come straight home. Slowly, a little breathlessly, he shuffled up the stairs. Then, instead of telling us what Herr Lampadius had had to say, he went to the kitchen cupboard and made himself some bread and dripping.

How did it go, asked Mother.

Oh, said Grandfather, how do you think? He held his sandwich up in the air and said: That tastes so good! Then, forgetting to wash his hands, he sat down in the poetry corner. He said: Now please show a little consideration for an old man, who does nothing but work, work, work all day!

Grandmother hung her apron up on the wall, and said: Be nice and quiet now, Grandfather wants to write a poem. Who can say, maybe one will come to him!

And if one doesn't come to him, I asked.

That's no great matter either, said Grandmother. There might be one tomorrow!

Grandfather took off his boots, shielded his eyes with his hand, and reflected for a long time. He looked into one corner, then he looked into another. At times, when something had occurred to him, he smiled and shook his head tenderly, as though in surprise. Then he quickly wrote it down, so that it wouldn't go away again. Or he beckoned to me with one finger and whispered: A great day! I hardly even have to try today, it's coming all by itself! I had it on my chest a long time, now it wants to get out. Then he gave me a little smack and packed me off again.

And now, I asked him, when he snapped his notebook shut and put it in his pocket.

Now the little opus is finished, said Grandfather contentedly, not completely finished of course, no poem ever is. But for now any well-disposed person can be pleased with it!

207

Will you now tell us what Herr Lampadius said to you, I asked.

Another time, said Grandfather, I've just written a poem and I'm tired!

The man with the piece of paper called twice more. Both times he called up from the street: Is the old man at home?

Who does he mean, cried Grandfather. He was sitting in the smoking-chair.

I have no idea, said Grandmother.

He's to go and see him, your old fellow, sharpish, shouted the man.

But Grandfather, stepping up to the window, wouldn't be ordered about like that. He claimed he had a lot to do. He cried: Is it really so urgent?

Urgent, shouted the man with the piece of paper.

Then Grandfather sighed and said: This man will be the death of me, and he went off with him again. The last time, Herr Lampadius came round in person to take Grandfather for a stroll. Grandfather said: I won't bust a gut for him either! and he let him wait. He carefully rubbed cream into his beard with a fingertip and said: Always take your time when the great men of the world come to rush you. It's a matter of self-esteem! Herr Lampadius, who liked to hold onto your sleeve when he was talking to you, so that you couldn't run off, took Grandfather three times round our block. He had a lot to say to him. Sometimes he had to tug Grandfather when he threatened to put down roots. After the last time round, Grandfather came back on his own. He saw me standing by the window, and waved up to me. He cried: Now I'll be able to sleep at night again! And breathe, he cried, look! And standing directly under our window, he took a couple of deep breaths, in and out. The little rattle in his throat wouldn't, as he'd feared, be the death of him. Nor did the case Herr Theilhaber was trying to bring against him, proceed. 'No court case, nothing, nothing whatever.'

That is surprising, said Grandmother and shook her head.

Yes, said Grandfather, one crow washes the other.

Then he took me by the hand, and we went to the ice-cream parlour where, in celebration, I was allowed two scoops. First I wanted raspberry lemon, but in the end I had raspberry nut. So that if I ever die, you'll be able to say: I know what nut tastes like, my Grandfather, when he was still alive, once treated me to it, he said. Now I know, said Grandfather, that there is such a thing as justice in the world! At least I know where my place is once more.

In the cinema?

Grandfather laughed. You're right, I can begin thinking about the cinema again, without suffering palpitations. I'll be able to go again, if there's any money in the house.

What about me, can I go again as well?

You too, said Grandfather. The Apollo, he said, will once more be our place of refuge, accommodating all our troubled and difficult souls without batting an eyelid. And transporting us to another world, where we may breathe more freely than in this one. I wouldn't be surprised if in view of the different circumstances, they were to consider re-hiring me, even if only as an usher, seeing as the other thing no longer exists.

We were standing in front of the Apollo again. Grandfather gave me a nod. He took off his artist's hat and tried the door, but it was locked.

Hello, he said and looked at his watch, is today Monday?

No, Wednesday, I said.

Strange, it's locked, said Grandfather. It was coming up for seven o'clock. We went up to the window of the Apollo, where for so long we hadn't been allowed to show our faces. All was as before. Then we looked inside. It was dark and deserted. It was obvious they were playing *Closed*.

That was in summer still. It was hot once more. Because the

209

Apollo was closed – people said *it had to* – Grandfather went for lots of walks with me.

And where are we going, I asked.

Best not too far, so that we'll be at hand if they have second thoughts and open up again after all, said Grandfather.

And if they don't have second thoughts?

You mustn't always expect the worst in life, he said, it comes to pass anyway!

Anyone who now saw Grandfather on the street, under his artist's hat, with which 'he shields his thick skull from others' ideas' (Grandmother) no longer said: Hello, Herr Hofmann! He said: Heil Hitler! or: Another scorcher! When he then stopped and asked Grandfather what was happening with him and the Apollo, he would scratch the pavement with his cane, as though to draw something. But he wasn't drawing anything. He smiled and cleared his throat and waited to see if he'd think of something to say. Then he might say something cheeky, like: The Apollo and I are both alive and well and taking plenty of deep breaths! Or something philosophical, like: Everything as far as the eye can see follows its own predetermined course, which it is not given us to know. And if someone was very direct and asked him whether the Apollo would be opening its doors very soon, and whether he wouldn't be standing by the screen again in his little tails, he said: The tails are no more! They've gone the way of all tails! The irresistible process which we call age and decay, or in some cases progress, and which doesn't make an exception of us either, he said, winking at me.

So we won't get to see you standing by the screen?

Grandfather said: Cometh the hour, cometh the screen! Then he took me by the hand and said: For me the Apollo is of the utmost importance! I don't believe anything could be found in this world to replace it. What do you think, he asked me, in your experience? There isn't anything, is there, for men of the imagination like ourselves?

What if Herr Theilhaber comes back and catches you, I said. Don't worry, said Grandfather, he won't be back!

In that year Grandfather went up to the Hoher Hain with Herr Cosimo for the last time to talk about the cinema. It was early in the week, hot. We could hear the mice scampering outside the house. I wanted to feed them with bread, but wasn't allowed to. Herr Cosimo knotted the corners of a check handkerchief and wore it on his head to ward off the sun. While Grandfather . . . the artist's hat, obviously! He had it pulled down low over his eyes. He didn't want the veins at his temples to show. 'My worries', he called them.

You're not very talkative, said Grandfather, can't you think of anything to say?

There are moments in a man's life, said Herr Cosimo, when everything has already been said, and anything further would be merely repetition. Drilling holes in thick boards is . . .

Are you saying we've reached that point?

Why else, asked Herr Cosimo, have we only been talking about ourselves of late?

Because the cinema's still closed, said Grandfather, and we walked on. We were going, where else, to the Hoher Hain. It was very dry. We passed the old hut, it was a bit crooked now. Then through the brambles! The smell of dry leaves in our nostrils. I plucked at Grandfather's sleeve and said: Can I have a lemonade today?

Grandfather thought a while and then said: No!

Do you still have the feeling, asked Herr Cosimo, that you're getting smaller all the time?

Yes, said Grandfather decisively. Then we went on a little bit further. Headache, he said.

Learn to complain without suffering, said Herr Cosimo.

Do you not believe me, asked Grandfather. Ever since the cinema's been closed, my nerves have been shot.

If I were you, said Herr Cosimo, I'd rather be me! Let me guess what you're thinking about, he said after we'd walked a bit more. You're thinking about a film! Starring Greta Garbo?

No.

With Lil Dagover?

No.

Then with Shirley Temple?

Wrong again. I was thinking about the film *Shoe Palace Pinkus* (1916, with Ernst Lubitsch, Else Kenter and Guido Herzfeld), where Schmul Pinkus fails at school because of his consuming interest in the opposite sex. He finds work in a shoe shop and gets to know the dancer Melissa, who pays for him to have his own shoe shop, and whom he later . . .

Excuse me for butting in, said Herr Cosimo, but the dancer's name wasn't Melissa, but Melitta. And as I remember the hero is not, as you say, Schmul, but Solly.

Grandfather stopped still. He looked hard at Herr Cosimo, he said: His name is Schmul Pinkus. And the dancer's name is Melissa. And the film is called *Shoe Palace Pinkus*.

I'm not denying that the film is called *Shoe Palace Pinkus*. All I'm saying is that the hero isn't Schmul Pinkus but Solly Pinkus, and the dancer . . .

Do you want an argument?

Not at all! I'm only saying that the man is called Solly Pinkus, and the dancer . . .

So you're sticking to your story. . . ?

But it's the truth!

In that case . . . . Give me your hand, said Grandfather to me. I can't breathe in this atmosphere! Then he turned me round. Come on, he said, we're going. And so we left Herr Cosimo, who by now was standing with one foot in an anthill – 'he always was a rootler!' – left him standing there and went back to town. Herr Cosimo called after us: Hofmann, what's got into you? Where are you going?

Grandfather didn't even reply. What a louse, he said. How his hands shook when we got home!

Calm yourself, said Grandmother, what's got into you?

Oh, said Grandfather, that fellow made an assertion. That night, out of sheer disgust, he didn't swallow so much as a mouthful of soup. 'I couldn't get a single spoonful down!' Then he said: Ha, Solly Pinkus! Solly Pinkus, ha! By the end of the week, he was shouting: That knacker! I'll not say his name . . .

His name is Cosimo, I called.

I couldn't care less, said Grandfather.

To see him sitting surrounded by pictures of Emil Jannings, Pola Negri, Grandmother, Henny Porten, Charlie Chaplin and many others, with an empty stomach, crouched in a corner of the room, brooding! 'No, I can't eat!' He now regretted every thought he had confided to Cosimo over the years! There was gratitude for you! That that had to happen to him! 'Why does it happen to me, why always me?'

In the evening we still went to the Apollo, but because it was closed and 'Limbach was staggering on without a cinema', we couldn't get inside. We walked up and down outside so that everyone saw us. Then after a quarter of an hour, Grandfather would say: There, that'll do! Now they'll have seen us, at least those that want to! Those that don't want to, the malicious ones, we can't do anything about anyway! Or we stood outside the closed Apollo door, but without fiddling with the handle. I was only in shirt and trousers, 'so that the nice sun can roast my little nigger boy' (Mother). A shame that Grandfather was so shrunken! 'Now that he's showing himself in public once more, it wouldn't hurt if he put on a bit of weight.' (Grandmother).

Herr Theilhaber hadn't been seen, not for weeks, or even longer. 'He's over the hills and far away!' He had left everything, it just stood around in his house. We didn't know whether the

Apollo would be reopened or, like the Capitol in Russdorf, turned into a bowling-alley or something even worse which, Grandmother said, also involved knocking. Herr Theilhaber's shop was closed as well.

And where is he gone, I asked.

He's vanished, said Grandfather.

But where to?

Where do you think, said Grandfather, where does a man vanish? Into thin air of course.

Won't he come back?

I hardly think so.

Not even to say goodbye?

No, he's got nothing more to say! And now no more questions, I want you to take deep breaths to make your chest expand, the way mine does! Do you think you'll manage that, my little Grandfather asked.

There were a lot of changes happening now. Without exception things were becoming more presentable, more luxurious, Grandfather said to me. One fine day the Apollo and the delicatessen were 'sold'. They were now owned by one F. L. Kunze from Zwickau, 'who in the end will buy up the lot of us, but isn't that always the way of it. Some build everything up, and they're the unlucky ones, the lucky ones just own it' (Grandmother). F. L. Kunze was short, and if you looked closely, you saw that he had a limp as well. But he had a good nose. That's why he sniffed such a lot. He had a handkerchief that went most of the way in. 'And so the span of man's earthly life passes' (Grandmother). Whichever way you looked, left or right, you saw something that belonged to F. L. Kunze.

There's no need to worry about him overreaching himself, Grandmother said to me, he gets it all cheap. Because Herr Theilhaber had been in such a hurry to get out, he let him have the shop for next to nothing, and the Apollo too. F. L. Kunze took

214

it all over, and paid next to nothing. 'He should be ashamed of himself' (Grandmother). It was the talk of the town for weeks, albeit in whispers. Grandfather got to hear about it in the Deutsches Haus, where he still sometimes drank a glass of beer, Grandmother while doing her shopping, and Mother in the clothing firm where she took her sewing and was given more. The Apollo was going to reopen its gates too. Only F. L. Kunze wanted to have it redecorated first, to get rid of 'the smell of Theilhaber, the stink of the dead past.' He had it sprayed with lysol, to make it smell human again. Then he had it painted green. He had new seats fitted too, with stuffing. It was now forbidden to drink beer in the Apollo because that left stains. The old bedsheets – which had seen so much action! – were torn down by F. L. Kunze, and replaced by a proper cinema screen which 'smelled as fresh as a draper's shop' (Grandfather). Because it was bigger than the old one, you could fit more onto it, 'so people got better value for money' (Grandfather). Even the Apollo's façade was cleaned and painted yellow. 'People are more likely to go in then, than somewhere grey and drab looking.' One morning there was a new display case for 'still photographs of current and forthcoming features'. Herr Kunze had it cemented in place.

After we had looked at the case together, Grandfather said: Go on, touch it, it'll last for ever! But don't pull at it, or it'll fall on top of you and squash your feet! The new display case told you at a glance what was on and who was appearing in it. And we were permitted to 'drink in' the pictures again, while taking our ease on the bench outside, we were allowed to do everything! When Herr Lange came by and said to Grandfather: Well, we can see the cinema is starting up again, but what's happening about you?, Grandfather said: I'm just going to bide my time!

And then Herr Lange asked: How will you know if it's come?

By this, said Grandfather, lifting his hand up in the air. My little finger will tell me!

Well well, said Herr Lange, but I won't hold my breath.

The first time we were able to go inside the Apollo, and not just round the outside, my green suit no longer fitted me. I was wearing an anorak and it was autumn again.

Can you smell that, asked Grandfather, something's ending!

We went round the freshly painted Apollo. We went in the back way. It all smelled new. I wanted Grandfather to go in first, but he pushed me in ahead of him. Although the cinema was practically new, it was still half empty. Herr Lange was there, of course, and Herr Cosimo. He had taken a seat in the back row, so he didn't need to nod to us.

There's enough room at least, said Grandfather, spreading his legs.

I wanted to sit like that too, but I couldn't do it as well. Grandfather hadn't been inside a cinema for over two years. 'It feels quite strange.' It was the first time he wasn't there as film explainer and piano player. He was now 'prospective usher, that's the name of the longed-for, ill-paid job he's got his beady eye on now' (Grandmother). It depended on who was doing the box office, whether we paid anything or not. Herr Martin, who ushered for a time until he was replaced by the far more dynamic Grandfather, let him in half price, in other words for a child's ticket. I didn't have to pay.

Don't shout it from the rooftops, Hofmann, said Herr Martin, otherwise I'll get complaints from people who pay the full price. And then I'll get it in the neck.

The first film we saw after Grandfather's dismissal was *The White Hell of Pitz Palu* (1935, with Leni Riefenstahl, Gustav Diesel and the airman Ernst Udet). It shows how Dr Krafft, who lost his sweetheart during the ascent of Pitz Palu, makes a point of climbing the peak every year on the anniversary of her death. It's a compulsion. On one occasion he takes a young couple along with him. They are caught in an avalanche, and Dr Krafft magnanimously sacrifices himself for the two young people. They are rescued by an airman (Ernst Udet) who has watched the whole drama unfold from his cockpit. Dr Krafft is united in death with his mountain and his sweetheart.

Well, said Grandfather, dabbing his eyes as we went out into the dark street, what do you say? I understand, you need time to grapple with it. Well, you don't have to say anything! Just go on thinking about it.

If we felt like it, and if Herr Martin was in a good mood, we might be allowed to stay in our seats and watch the film a second time, to be sure we understood it properly. There were enough empty seats. Sometimes we went back the following day as well. *Three from the Filling Station* (1930, with Lilian Harvey and Willy Fritsch) we saw three times, the *Diary of a Lost Girl* (1929, with Franziska Kinz) four times. In that one, the girl Thymian is seduced. She gets a baby, and has to go to a home for fallen women, where she is tormented. She runs away from there. When she learns that her child has died, she wins fame as a courtesan, until finally someone marries her, and one day, as a member of a committee for rescuing young girls in peril, she revisits the home, where another girl just like herself in her younger days . . .

On the way home, Grandfather nodded a lot and said that was just what the world was like. On the other hand, he said, some young ladies were . . . .

Yes?

Delectable, said Grandfather and smacked his lips. Then they disappear from our lives. Just like the young cripple who replaced me disappeared too, to Bautzen, apparently.

And why Bautzen, I asked.

I suppose there was a vacancy for him there in the cosmic scheme of things, said Grandfather.

He always leaned back a long way while sitting down, that way he could breathe better. He was able to cross his legs again too, even if one was shorter than the other. Sometimes he waved it in front of him and called: There, suddenly it's this short! Then in case he found something 'that corresponded' in his pocket, he lit a cigar end and thought about his future.

Have you got one at all, I asked.

But it's only just beginning, cried Grandfather, and puffed – 'because he wants to die an excruciating death as soon as possible' (Grandmother) – at his cigar end. He smiled and was 'in a manner of speaking happy, as much as a man can be' (Grandmother). At least he was allowed back into the Apollo. Heinrich George and Berta Drews starred in *Hitlerjunge Quex* (1933), Paul Muni and Glenda Farrell in *I'm a Fugitive from a Chain Gang* (1932) and Willy Fritsch and Gerda Maurus in *Spies* (1928). As far as his re-hiring was concerned – 'with pension and death benefit' – F. L. Kunze remained undecided for a long time. He found Grandfather too talkative and a bit old too.

Well, he won't get any younger, said Grandmother, if he leaves him in suspense like that! People don't!

Once, when Kunze had given him a kindly nod, Grandfather thought: He'll take me on!, another time, when he frowned: No, he'll never do it! Every day Grandfather, 'who will probably still be unemployed when he goes to meet his Maker, that is, if He agrees to see him' (Grandmother), looked at the pictures of forthcoming attractions. Usually he took me along too. Then it was Sunday, another Sunday! After lunch – green dumplings with gravy, then vanilla pudding with raspberry syrup – there was the children's showing, which I was now able to go to once more. Grandfather, 'the old fop', put cream – 'it stinks!' – on his beard. Then, the only 'grown-up', he watched the picture with me. Not even Herr Lange, or, right at the back, Herr Cosimo were there. I was embarrassed: He was so old, and was probably going to die soon. I walked a little way behind him, and when he went over to

Herr Martin to ask if everything was running smoothly, I moved to a different seat. When he came back, he followed me to my new place.

You don't object, do you, he said.

Then he sat down next to me and perched his artist's hat on his knees. There were nothing but children in the cinema. They were all talking and making a noise, until it got too much for Grandfather. He stood up and shouted: Quiet, or I'll roll up my sleeves, and throw you all out! and he gestured towards the door. Then I'll have you banned from the cinema, and you won't get your money back either! Even though he was crumpled and on the street, Grandfather when he showed himself again was soon as famous as he'd been before. He went to see every film, especially the silent ones. 'He doesn't care if it's silent or not, in his dotage he'll goggle at anything that's put in front of him, so long as it flickers' (Grandmother). One day in the Helenenstrasse F. L. Kunze took him by the sleeve. Grandfather raised his hat. Herr Kunze said not to bother, he wanted a word with him. First they discussed film culture, which was going downhill in Limbach. Did he know of any explanation for it? Grandfather scratched the pavement with his cane and said: Well, like everything in the world, there's a reason for it! Then he took a deep breath and told Herr Kunze that he went to every film that was shown at his cinema because Herr Martin had no 'head for business', and let him and many others in for nothing, or for half price. That sort of generosity, said Grandfather, is expensive! In the long run, even the most flourishing enterprises can't go on like that!

I see, said F. L. Kunze, so he lets everyone in for nothing?

I thought you knew, said Grandfather.

After that there was a serious and concerned discussion between him and Herr Kunze about the future of the Apollo. The discussion was a lengthy one. Grandfather said to me: Look at the birds over there! Go play! and sent me away. My philosophy, Grandfather told Herr Kunze, is to let him learn about the world in his own way! Whatever one finds out for oneself is more educative! He cried: Look about you!

But the world that morning was the same as ever. Sometimes I looked – and listened – across to them. I heard how Grandfather gave it to understand that he would of course be a far better usher than Herr Martin, because he had so much experience already, and 'the cinema was in his blood'. Also, he would get many more people to come, because he was so well known. And he kept nodding. F. L. Kunze by contrast tended to shake his head, but he didn't say no. At the end they shook hands. Grandfather had been taken on again.

Placidly, his artist's hat on his ever-balding head, Grandfather pushed his way – it was another Sunday – through the crowd of waiting children, of us in other words, of us! We all, me included, greeted him. (As if I hadn't been with him all morning, and sat beside him at lunch!) A few whispers of: Here comes Hindenburg!, not behind his back, though, but to his face. Then he disappeared into his cubbyhole to change. But where were his little tails?

Gone the way of all tails, said Grandmother unfeelingly. Do you know where that is?

No.

It's where we all go when we're no longer in fit condition for this world. Into Hades, she said. Then she wondered what she should cook for supper. It was always eat, eat, eat with us! 'Oh, I've had it up to here with you!'

When Grandfather emerged from the cubbyhole, he wasn't wearing his tails. He had a cardigan on. It was a present from Grandmother on the occasion of his first day back at work. 'I hope you see lots of nice films, and never get bored again in your life!'

Grandfather walked up to the entrance. There he cast his eye over us. He heard us too and clenched his fist at us. That meant: Don't think you can make that sort of noise when I'm in charge! I stood next to him again, I could feel his breath. Then Fräulein Heiske appeared. She did the box office now. Really she was superfluous, Grandfather could have done it all perfectly well by himself. But Herr Kunze didn't want that. He liked to have a female presence there, for when he happened to look in. And in that respect Grandfather was no competition for Fräulein Heiske, however hard he worked. She just needed to wiggle her bottom, and he was at her feet. Whereas Grandfather could have wiggled his bottom till he was blue . . . . Fräulein Heiske was young, and 'she and Herr Kunze always seemed to have a lot to talk about together in the dark, I'm not suggesting anything' (Grandmother), whereas Grandfather could only hold out the ticket stubs to Herr Kunze and say: Only twelve today, Herr Kunze, but it's Hans Albers tomorrow, so there'll be a few more then.

Nonsense, said Herr Kunze, the last time we had Hans Albers, there were still only nineteen.

True, said Grandfather, but he was playing a Chinaman in that film, and who wants to see that. Sometimes Grandfather had to tell Herr Kunze: Fräulein Heiske isn't here yet, because she was often late. She would say: Sorry! and Grandfather could get on with opening the door. He had the key again. It was in his back pocket.

When Fräulein Heiske was late, Grandfather stood in the doorway and cried: What's keeping the woman? When she turned up, he growled: Well, not before time!

She said: Sorry, Herr Hofmann, I had to go to the chemist's for my mother who's unwell.

Well then, said Grandfather and looked at his watch. Then he shouted into the foyer: All right, those with tickets come forward! Not all at once please! And we all trickled in. Everyone held out his ticket to Grandfather, who tore it in two. I held out my free ticket, and Grandfather tore that as well. He winked at me as he did. Then came Leiser, the new projectionist, Herr Salzmann had been called up and was garrisoned somewhere in Silesia where he was awaiting the order to cut loose, 'it'll come, don't worry!' (Grandmother). When Grandfather had torn all the tickets, the foyer was empty. Sometimes there would be the odd latecomer, 'who maybe couldn't find his shoes in time' (Grandmother). Since the films had started talking, the queues had grown longer. 'People find it more interesting than some old man giving himself airs at the front' (Grandmother). Sometimes there wasn't room for everyone. Then Grandfather would remember the old days. He swiftly dragged a comb through his hair, went to the box office door and called: Stop selling, Fräulein Heiske, we've a full house! Then he went to the door, raised his arm, and called out: That's it for today! Those who hadn't got tickets were packed off home. Once the film was running he stood at the very back, where it was nice and dark. He stood with feet apart.

That's the way to stand if you've got a hernia. Grandfather did. God knows what I'm going to get next, Grandfather said.

I asked: What else can you get?

Grandfather shrugged his shoulders and said: I don't know yet, but I'm sure Nature will think of something! He was more often serious than before, 'because he takes himself so seriously' (Grandmother). He was a stern usher. You sit there!, he said. And he would look closely at everyone and wonder whether even to admit them or not. Sometimes he would say something: For instance: You wash your ears next time you want to come to my cinema! And if you replied: But I have washed them, he would straightaway come back with: When?, and if you replied: Yesterday, he would say: That's not good enough! Wash them more often! And Grandfather didn't even have much of an eye for ears. His sight was dimming.

When Grandfather had got Herr Leiser to switch off the house lights, – he brought his arm down twice, as though giving the signal for attack in the trenches – everything was quiet. Following his old habit, he leaned against the wall, the screen at an angle in front of him. Now he could have explained the film, but no one wanted to hear him any more. 'A lot of things could be done in the world, but there's no call for them!' From where he stood, he had a good view of the house, at least with one eye. With the other he enjoyed the film. By now he was standing in the place where he had previously always sat, overlooking 'his little paradise, now and always, as you write on postcards' (Grandmother). This was where his piano had stood. You could even make out Grandfather's fingerprints on the walls, if you looked very closely. Here Grandfather had always propped his back while talking. In the most moving bits he had been almost rigid. Now he leaned because he found standing difficult. He had written a new poem, something that had wanted to get out. He was in explanatory position, even though he had to keep his mouth shut. It was in that position that he met his end.

In April 1939 Grandfather was given a 'squitter-yellow meeting-jacket' for his birthday by Herr Götze. For weeks upon weeks he was never out of it. 'If he could, he'd wear it in bed' (Grandmother). The jacket was too big for him – what wasn't? – but he didn't let Grandmother 'get it in her clutches, there's no knowing what she'll do to something'. It was wearing that jacket that Grandfather took part as 'deputy flagwaver' in the Deutschlandtreffen of 1 May, in the Circus Krone in Berlin, a 'handpicked replacement' (Grandmother). He must have been one of the oldest there, being already completely grey. In that jacket, along with thirty others, he was driven in a tarted-up propaganda truck from Chemnitz to Berlin, 'like a beribboned ox to the gate' (Grandmother). He spent the night in a farmyard in

Zossen, where he stole a hen's egg. He meant to bring it back to me, but it was broken in the awful Berlin crush. When he got back there was a disgusting mess in his meeting-jacket, for which Grandmother never forgave him. A lot of things had gone wrong. Grandfather had had to make his own way to Chemnitz on foot from Limbach, carrying the flag, and back again afterwards, it was off the main route. He carried the flag now on his right shoulder, now on his left, sometimes he even had it tucked under his arm. On the Sunday night, he was taken back in the same truck, but by then none of the others were speaking to him. Something had happened in Berlin. They all sat together in a heap, giving 'spirited renditions of marching songs', but no one said a word to him. Grandfather didn't even hum. They dropped him and his flag in a sugar beet field outside Chemnitz and then drove on. 'They didn't even wish me Heil Hitler!' Grandfather had had to walk the last ten miles on his own as it grew light. No one else lived in the Limbach area, which historically has always been red. The walk was 'a martyrdom for his feet, it might have been devised specially.' And Grandfather had been so much looking forward to his 'excursion in uniform'. He got out so rarely.

And then?

It's twenty-five years, more or less, Grandfather explained when he was back at home, since I was last in a big city. Twenty-five years without crowds, without bright lights, without bustle. Without freedom, if you know what I mean, said Grandfather, winking at me. For decades I've only been able to see cities in my dreams. And now a chance to see Berlin again, which has become the most gigantic . . .

And then?

The rally began at seventeen hundred hours. You mean five o'clock, said Grandmother. Grandfather arrived having driven for eleven hours in which he'd not been able to stand or sit or move. 'And so I took a walk through Berlin!' He had three hours to go until he and 'four hundred other idiots had to be twitching their flags' (Grandmother). He will have said to himself, you should make the most of these three hours! Who knows how many more times you'll get to see Berlin in your life! He kept the flag with him. He was in his meeting-jacket. Apart from that, all his other gear was either borrowed or newly bought, for all the women's clucking. Or it formed no part of the uniform as such, and was 'merely improvised' (Grandmother). Grandfather decided that as he was in Berlin, he really ought to go and see a film. Flag in hand, he went to his colleagues and said: Can you look after this for me for a while, I have to go somewhere quickly, but I'll be right back! Then Grandfather passed the flag over to his comrades and was off. Hey, they all shouted after him, where do you think you're going? What are we going to do with your flag? I'll be back, cried Grandfather, and in his squitter-yellow jacket he plunged into the enormous city of Berlin, where none of them knew their way around. Where, for example, was there a cinema? But lo: He found one! In his fantasy uniform, plus egg and sans flag he turned the corner and walked slap into the Gloria Palais. When I tell you, Grandfather told me, what they were playing, you won't believe it!

What were they playing, then?

First things first, said Grandfather. The Gloria was empty. He bought a ticket and in his meeting-jacket went up to the usher. He shook his hand firmly, and told him who he was. He was in the business himself, he said, and had been around. Is that so, said the Berlin usher, but I've never seen you here before. No, and how could you have, said Grandfather, I've come up from Limbach, I run the Apollo there. But the usher had never heard of Limbach, or the Apollo either. Yes, not that many people know about us, said Grandfather, but that doesn't mean to say we don't exist. Then he wanted the usher to show him round the projection room, but the man said: No no, we don't let anyone in there! Oh well, suit yourself, said Grandfather and left him standing. And he went in to choose his seat. The whole of Berlin had to be at the rally, because the cinema was completely empty. The film hadn't begun yet, and Grandfather was able to try out various seats before he found the one with the best view. ('Every cinema has a seat like that, but not a lot of people know that!') And finally the film itself was the best of recent time, if not of all time. Grandfather sat down in his seat and took off his cap. He stretched his legs. He closed his eyes.

And then?

Then, before the film began – my first and last film in Berlin, said Grandfather – I played my life as a cinemagoer to my inner eye, beginning with my very first picture. Some went by quickly, some slowly, some completely stopped. Grandfather, 'fighting the good fight against the trouser creases', had gone into the Gloria Palais without collar and tie. He looked younger that way. He had a stack of bread and butter and a handful of pickled gherkins, that was what he lived on in Berlin then. In his clean brown shirt, with freshly polished black belt, the old man sat in the Gloria Palais in Berlin, all alone in the middle of the front row, and waited for it to begin, 'for it to wash over me' he said.

And then?

The film Grandfather saw and was to rave about until his death was of course *Gone with the Wind* (1939, with Vivien Leigh, Clark Gable, Leslie Howard and Olivia de Havilland). That he should be accorded that, and at his age! The film, which he was practically alone in seeing in Berlin at that time, took place in the Deep South during the American Civil War. The heroine's name was Scarlett O'Hara, and she hit Grandfather (as he said) 'like a bolt of lightning'. He talked about her for years. She was highly flirtatious. And, as her family came from Ireland, she had green eyes and a seventeen-inch waist. Later on, when she'd had a baby and it had gone up to eighteen, she wanted nothing more to do with her imbecile of a husband. The war widowed her, twice over. When she could, she stole the husbands of other women, even her own sister (Olivia de Havilland). But by the end of the film she was a changed woman because she had endured so much suffering. Of the three husbands she had had one after the other, the only one she really loved was the third, but it took her a long time to realise that. That man was Rhett Butler (Clark Gable). Only after he left her did she realise she loved him, but by then it was too late. She loved her daughter Bonnie too, especially, *especially* after she was dead. At four Bonnie took riding lessons, but when she jumped a fence on her pony, it fell. She had been too daring.

And then?

When the house lights came on again, it took Grandfather a long time to get his bearings back in the Gloria Palais. Yes, said the Berlin usher, and rolled his eyes: She's a tasty piece! Oh leave me alone, you fool, said Grandfather and stumbled past him into the street. He was a bit late already. He wasn't worried though. He thought they couldn't start without him, he had the flag! Or let's say: One of the flags, because there were hundreds of them, if not more! In the Circus Krone, where Grandfather as a veteran of all wars was to 'stand and gawp' beside the flag, there was a stage for HIM. Before that, the bands, the standard bearers, the flag wavers, the men with torches. I'll just call them the men with torches for now, Grandfather said, I'm sure they're called something else really!

And then?

At the entrances, said Grandfather, they were selling paper flags for a penny each. Everyone was talking about the Führer, thinking about the Führer, yelling: Führer, Führer, Führer! In the audience, I happened to notice, the majority of people had callings that were somehow *small*: small businessmen, small-holders, door-to-door smalls salesmen, sellers of space for small ads, all in uniform, said Grandfather, small people experiencing difficulties in their small lives, seven thousand of them in all! Suddenly from the stage there came the Badenweiler March, which Grandfather had always played in the Apollo when the film tore. Now he just needed to pee quickly, and then ... A wonderful atmosphere everywhere, even in the urinals. When Grandfather returned to his place at a quarter past five, his head full of Scarlett O'Hara, he found his flag had gone, along with his comrade from Hartmannsdorf. Where was it, where was his flag? Grandfather ran from one person to another, asking: Have you seen my flag, comrade? No! Then on to the next man: Have you seen my flag? ... Another no. And the rally was beginning! First the opening fanfare of trumpets and drums, and then, straight afterwards, a procession of heroes of yesteryear – heroes of political punch-ups, said Grandmother – were hauled onto the stage, men with mutilated limbs, bandaged eyes, without feet. They found it worked best, said Grandfather, when they allowed the martyrs up on stage with them.

And then?

Well, said Grandfather, the unfortunate thing was that they hadn't waited for me! Someone else had got hold of his flag, he didn't even know the man! Grandfather, in Herr Friedrich's boots greased and shined for him by Grandmother – 'I could have marched in them for days, if anyone had asked me' – had been unable to take his place in the procession of veterans. But he was still able to see a lot of what happened. He fell in with another group which wasn't even his. He wasn't standing right at the front, nor yet at the very back, he was where those people stood who didn't matter much in themselves, but who still had to be there, 'so that a vacuum doesn't appear' (Grandmother). Later on, Grandfather had gone somewhere else, where fewer people were standing. There he kicked his heels and told the others all about *Gone with the Wind*. They were all nice to him, and promised to go and see it themselves. From a certain distance, in certain light, Grandfather looked like Hindenburg again. And so, while he was thinking solidly about Scarlett O'Hara, they put a forage cap on his head, tucked the strap under his chin, and, while the people in front kept shouting: Quiet! and: Pipe down!, took his picture. One of them said he would send the pictures to Limbach for him to sign. Not as 'Hofmann, Karl, cinema usher' though, but as 'Hindenburg, von, Reichspresident'. Didn't I always say he was as bogus as Hell, cried Grandmother, when he told us about it . . .

And then?

On the day Grandfather was in Berlin, he had no flag. 'One man mucked up the whole rally' (Grandmother). The pole of the flag he was supposed to swing was metal. 'It was heavy, I can tell you!' Then all the flags were blessed. They were allowed to touch the bloodied banner from the Hall of Generals, all except Grandfather. In his place another man carried the flag he had lugged up from Limbach. With its tip, it touched the bloodstain of the 1923 uprising. They held Grandfather's flag there for so long that it caught, and then became just as sacred. Then everyone stood still.

And then?

There were many hundreds of drummers and flag-wavers, the big top was absolutely chock-a-block. Grandfather stood off to one side, thinking about Scarlett O'Hara. At the end of the rally, a few were allowed up on the rostrum to look at HIM. Some were unable to resist and even went up and touched HIM. The flag carrier from Hainichen touched HIM, the flag carrier from Hartmannsdorf touched HIM, the flag carrier from Wittgensdorf touched HIM. But the flag carrier from Hohenstein-Ernstthal called Grandfather a *bloody imbecile*. 'How can a grown man in a sober condition lose his flag, can you tell me that!' The flag carrier from Vogelsang had heard HIM speak many times. Each time HE spoke, HE lost seven pounds in HIS sweat. HIS underwear was always wringing wet afterwards. It was barely possible to see in

HIM the same man. But it was HIM. By the way, HE liked to improvise HIS speeches too, but not like Grandfather at the Apollo. And HE stood on a chest as well.

Grandfather was tired now. He drank his third beer. He said: It's impossible to describe the feeling that comes over one when Scarlett O'Hara takes Rhett Butler by the hand and tells him: Our Bonnie is dead! Then he took another drink and said: I would have liked to get a bit nearer during the speech, but they didn't let me! Then he took another drink and said: I was ready for that film, whereas even five years ago, I wouldn't have been! And Grandfather had admired HIS speech as well, even though he hadn't understood all of it. It was the fault of the acoustics in the Circus Krone. Just as Grandfather always tested the acoustics in the Apollo, so HE should . . .

And then?

# Eleven

At some stage Grandmother must have died, but I forget the date. When I left to go to school in the morning, she was still lying in bed. Her fingers plucked at the blanket.

Oh dear, she said, another day! Whoever ordered it!

Mother was at the factory. She was doing piecework sewing. I was on my own with Grandmother. She had Grandfather's photograph on the bedside table next to her, 'because he himself isn't there any more.' There was a glass of water next to it. Her door was ajar. Grandmother sat propped up in bed on two pillows, hers and his. Her breathing was regular. Sometimes she looked around to see if everything was still there. 'It could be something has disappeared overnight!' When I went out, she didn't say goodbye, but she gave me a nod. I don't remember what I said. Maybe: I have to go now! or: I'm off! or: Time I wasn't here! Or maybe I didn't say anything at all. In those days I was somewhere else. I lived in a world of my own. In the afternoon, when I came home after a 'heavy day' at school – I had started talking like Grandfather – Grandmother had 'passed away'. She had already been taken away, she was no longer at home. Her bed, from which she had commanded our little household, was empty. Herr Lange, who had seen me coming, called out: She slipped away, it was very sudden.

Right, I said.

Her 'flipflops' were still in the place where she had left them that morning, under Böcklin's *Isle of the Dead*. Her dressing-gown, her comb and her 'beauty cream' all lay on the dressing-table. How peculiar! When Mother came home, she made me a sandwich. There, she said, eat something! You need to keep your strength up!

Because the flat that day seemed so empty, I kept going into Grandmother's room and rearranging her bits and pieces. The last book she leafed through – her sight was poor now – was *Gone with the Wind* by M. Mitchell. She hadn't seen the film, and wanted to imagine what Grandfather had seen on that 1 May. She kept her curiosity to the end. Another photograph of him, with Party badge and Iron Cross, hung on the wall. I had painted over the Party badge with an ink pen when we were told: 'The Russians are coming!' That must have been in 1948, in the 'Zone', in the Ernst Thälmann Strasse as it was then called. In fact, I lived inside my head, as Grandmother did in hers. Only she couldn't afford to, she had 'too much burdening her'. In her last years she had only one wish, 'for that bitch Fritsche to snuff it before I do'. Stranger things had happened. The radio transmitter at Gleiwitz had been attacked, for example.

But we'll fight back, cried Grandfather from the corner where he used to sit after work every day. He was wearing his cardigan. Underneath it he had a woollen shirt that she washed once a week. 'We need to economise on soap' (Grandmother). Perhaps he economised too much himself. Anyway one thing led to another. In order to do her bit, Mother sewed shirts for soldiers. They lay in two piles on her sewing table. 'The ones on the left are done, the ones on the right are still to do!' Herr Lange was wearing health sandals, to help him climb steps better. He distributed ration cards. He didn't come round so often now. It hit Grandmother the hardest. She put on her 'begging jacket' and walked her feet bloody. Sometimes she took me with her. She reached for Grandfather's knotty stick, turned round in the doorway and said: Wish us luck, and ask God to send us some charitable soul!

Ask who, cried Grandfather from his corner.

Don't blaspheme, she said. Then we went round the farmyards. Grandmother peeped in at the windows to see if there was anyone home. I stood just behind her. Then she said: Come on, Marie! and knocked on the door. Either we were chased away or we were given a handful of dried peas, which Grandfather ground up in our coffee mill in the evening for us to make soup from. Or we walked to Mittweida. There Grandmother went into the shops and asked: Haven't you got a pair of shoes for my grandson here, God will repay you! But they didn't. Grandfather's hair had turned white 'from so much work'. He wasn't able to go to the cinema so often now, but he was once again important. When we fought back, in spite of his 'biblical age' – 'my womenfolk make me out to be older than I am and older than I feel!' – he was put in the munitions factory of Bleicher & Co. in the Herbert Norkus Strasse in Oberfrohna. He was given a mess tin. He was now employed not as an usher, but as a watchman. He would rather have been given field-grey to wear, but he was too old by now. And his sight was too poor, his hearing too bad, and he was too empty-headed, that kind of man's no use at the front, Grandmother said to me. Now Grandfather had to spend his whole long day inspecting the bags and pockets of the munitions workers, to check they hadn't lifted anything.

And even if it's an old floor rag, in times like these it's all theft and must be punished, he said.

Grandmother said: You mean off with their heads?

Grandfather: Examples are there to be made!

Grandmother: That's what I said, off with their heads!

Now and again Grandfather still went to the Apollo to work on the door, 'they don't need me any more often than that!' His place was taken by a woman with damaged limbs, who could serve no other function in the 'machinery of the world'. When she didn't feel up to it, Grandfather sometimes stood in for her. 'There he goes strutting up and down the Apollo, turning the whole place upside down' (Grandmother). Herr Kunze was away in France for the war, but just administration. He wrote Grandfather a field postcard, asking: Is my Apollo still standing? Grandfather, who had a lot on his mind just then, allowed a couple of weeks to pass before replying: At the time of writing, your Apollo is still standing, that's all the assurance I can provide! When he 'goes to work, as he calls it' (Grandmother), he now wore a security guard's uniform. It made him look much younger. Like Count Karamzin, the Russian émigré in *Foolish Women* (1921, with Erich von Stroheim), he got his medals out of his drawer and stuck them on his chest, so that everyone could see at a glance who he was. Grandmother said: His ironmongery! and refused to clean it for him. She wouldn't even fetch him the Brasso. When he got it out himself, and took too much, she cried: Merciful heavens, you're wasteful!

At Bleicher & Co. Grandfather was every bit as important as he had been at the Apollo. 'And at his age too!' The more young men 'were thrown to the front and butchered', the more important he became. A young corpse wasn't worth tuppence, whereas Grandfather for all his years . . . . Like the bar owner Kent in *Destry Rides Again* (1939, with James Stewart and Marlene Dietrich), he had a couple of revolvers in case things got really hot. One was a .34. It lived in a red leather holster from Morocco that Mother had given him for Christmas once. She might be getting a husband now after all, but she wasn't saying where from, only that they didn't grow on trees. 'Anyway, like the majority of men, he is called Hans, and he's far away from here now. He'd be a good father to you.' Grandfather slept with the revolver under his pillow. Sometimes it fell out during the night. Thank God it wasn't loaded. When Grandfather crawled out of bed in the morning – 'Yes, *crawled* is the word for it!' – he always trod on it. Of course he would have loved to have it loaded, but Grandmother had hidden the bullets. They were in a jelly-mould, but no one else knew that apart from me.

Grandfather had a lot to do at Bleicher's. He worked from morning till late at night, and barely remembered 'what the inside of a wood looked like'. Nothing would have functioned without him. Grandfather was responsible for all the side-rooms, the wardrobes, washrooms, toilets. Not that he belonged to the cleaning staff, they were merely his subordinates. When he gave an order and they failed to listen, he clapped his hands and shouted: Now listen to me, I don't want to have to say this again! If they went on talking, he shouted: I'm talking now, understood! So what did I just say? All three of the women would have forgotten and they would be quiet and downcast. Later Grandfather went to his desk. He got out a torch, and embarked on a tour of the buildings. He had to check everything. He checked whether the rooms had been properly cleaned. The three women were responsible for cleaning them. All three wore turbans on their heads, so they didn't have to do their hair. Grandfather kept going round the buildings, checking them. To save power, he didn't switch on the electric lights. He ran his fingers along the walls to see if they were clean. If his fingers picked up dirt, he held them under the noses of his staff and said: And what, might I ask, is this? Then they saw the dirt for themselves and cried: Oh! in chorus. With his old knotty stick, he went through all the side-rooms, crying: Halt, who goes there! Or: All right, out you come! and, if no one came out: Is there really no one there? He kicked open the last door, and pretended he was not alone, that others were following up behind him. He would have liked to do more shouting, but that was all he could think of. Ah well, he said, if there's no one there, then we might as well go!

In the evening, things quietened in the factory, and Grandfather could breathe more easily. He drank a cup of dishwater coffee. Then he got his old cinema pictures out of the filing cabinet and took them to the lavatory. If anyone knocked, he cried: Out of order! or: Closed! Meeting in progress! As soon as he'd sat down, Grandfather lit a cigar stub. He had his pictures on his lap. He looked at the gentlemen as well as the ladies. He drew no distinctions, loving them both equally. Sometimes he made a pile of actresses and put them on his left. Then he made a second pile of actors, and put them on his right. Sometimes he would pair off a lady with a man and say: Look at them! What a fine couple! Then he would put another man with the lady and say: But so are they! Then he looked first at one pair, and then at the other. He had a little smoke. Then he said: Oh, it would never have worked out! and he mixed them all up again. Of the ones he liked specially – 'my types', he said – he made a special pile which he kept in his jacket pocket. Then he stood up, flushed the lavatory, and went into the main washroom. There were always a couple of women sitting there smoking or drinking coffee. Grandfather got his special pile out of his pocket, showed it to the women and asked: Which is the one for you? They liked Clark Gable the best, especially as a Southern officer. Grandfather liked him too, and looked at him for a long time. But then he shook his head, said: Asta Nielsen! and put them all away again. Really, he loved only her.

Once Grandfather said: I've seen almost all the films there are. I can remember every one of them. They were the best thing about my life really. I've not got much to look forward to now.

He still wore the Party badge, but without conviction. When the air raid siren sounded he got his tin hat out of the wardrobe and popped it on his head. It made him look more soldierly right away. Because of the pressure of the helmet, he lost yet more of his hair, the bits growing over his ears. Thank God the whole thing couldn't go on much longer, no one nowadays could stand a long war. France and Belgium had long since been conquered, even Crete was occupied. In essence, everything was back to how it had been before, except there was nothing to eat. Grandfather no longer called on Fräulein Fritsche, and hadn't for a long time. As far as he was concerned, she was finished. Her house – 'his' house – was empty, her room was empty, her bed was empty, *for him*. That's it, *finito*, said Grandfather and grinned. When he saw her on the street, he looked away, preferably up at the sky. He and Herr Götze and maybe Herr Friedrich too, if his leg would allow, liked getting together and talking about 'wine, women and song'. That was on days when Bleicher & Co. could spare Grandfather. By now there were enough cripples and wrecks they could put in his place.

Strange, said Grandfather, but the war feels over to me, unless there's another bit to come. Only there were a lot of air raid warnings. Then we sat in the air raid shelter on the crate of potatoes which were all eaten now, while Grandmother and Mother stayed upstairs in the kitchen and at the sewing-machine. I went up the stairs a ways. I called: Won't you come down too?

No, Grandmother shouted back, we're fine up here!

But what if a bomb comes along?

Oh, said Grandmother, what difference does it make if it happens sooner or later? Then they went back to knitting or sewing. Grandfather got his tobacco pouch out of his pocket and crumbled cigarette ends into it. Then he rolled himself a cigarette, 'something to put hairs on your chest'. He liked talking about Fräulein Fritsche.

How could she leave me after all these years, he said to Herr Götze and shook his head.

Yes, said Herr Götze, she's had it now!

For me she has, said Grandfather.

She's waded into the beyond, said Herr Götze.

Why waded?

Or been washed away, said Herr Götze, on a flood of alcohol!

Like a fish, said Grandfather happily, a flat fish! He didn't seem to be at all sad any more. Then came the all clear. It settled on our roof, then on all the other roofs. Afterwards, I went up to the Hoher Hain with the two oldsters. We looked to see if anyone had parachuted down to spy on us. But they hadn't.

Whereas the pathetic remains are just a lie, said Grandfather.

What's that, asked Herr Götze.

I'm thinking about life, said Grandfather. A lie!

We weren't sure what he was trying to say, but it didn't matter anyway. 'Main thing, a man understands himself' (Grandmother). She called after him from the kitchen: Are you skiving off again, and leaving me with all the dishes? He's forever going out, the restless soul!

Stuff the dishes, Grandfather called back, swinging his walking stick.

Haven't you got enough on your plate with your meetings and your marches, your seven o'clock news and your special reports, she called after him. And the Apollo's got going again! Anyone would think that would suffice! All right then, Mariechen, she said to herself, get to work!

In his last years, when he took a quick turn up to the Hoher Hain with Herr Götze and me, Grandfather took his other pistol along with him, just in case. He said: You never know! This weapon was a pistol from the First World War, which he would have liked to use in fighting the French, only it had never come to that. Grandfather wasn't able to load that one either, his bullets didn't fit. It was in his right trouser pocket. We were all in terrible shoes, terrible socks, terrible trousers. Herr Götze didn't have his glasses any more, he had stepped on them once. I had to keep telling him he was about to tread in something if he didn't watch it. With our sticks in our fists, in case we were attacked – by any of the Poles or Russians who were then running away from our factories in droves – we crossed the Hoher Hain. That wasn't what it used to be either. People had cut down all the best trees, they needed firewood. I went on ahead, where else? I swiped at the tall weeds and trampled them under my feet. Soon Herr Götze was all in. We sat down on a bench, or what was left of it.

In the course of my life, said Grandfather, I've sat here many times.

Alone, asked Herr Götze, or in company?

Sometimes the former, sometimes the latter, said Grandfather discreetly.

With her then, asked Herr Götze.

Could be!

And what did you do?

We talked about everything as if it really existed: the world, God, our future!

How do you mean, as if it really existed, asked Herr Götze.

Yes, said Grandfather, so we did!

I got up. I went into the trees. I kicked at the ground. This was where he had pulled Fräulein Fritsche closer, and stroked her short, now greying hair. When he thought: He's not looking now, he had stuck his tongue in her ear. Sometimes he had said something too. Often he said: Stay with me, Fräulein Fritsche! But then Fräulein Fritsche would look at him hard, and shake her head, so that later he wouldn't be able to say it had come as a bolt from the blue. She had had enough. She said: I'd rather be dead!

Grandfather sighed and went: Oh!

What's the matter, asked Herr Götze.

Nothing, said Grandfather, nothing at all! and he thought: This bench is her grave now. He wasn't allowed to say it, but he had the sentence: She is dead! stuck in his head and in his throat. And then he stretched out his legs, as far as he could, and thought in how many ways she was now dead. Her body was dead, her soul was dead – if that woman who had continually deceived him had ever possessed one – her hands and her feet were dead. Even her long-legged strutting about, her pink cat's tongue, her eyes, her glances, her . . .

What are you thinking about, I cried through the Hoher Hain.

Nothing, said Grandfather, nothing at all!

Then what were you thinking about just now, I cried, hoping he'd been thinking about a film he would tell me about.

Just now, said Grandfather and pondered, just now I wasn't thinking about anything either!

If he was to write a poem now, or think of a film or a dream, then Fräulein Fritsche would no longer be sitting at his feet, kissing his knees. He had to do everything by himself. His next poem – about a local natural phenomenon, but really, like every poem, about far more – would come into being without her. He had to write it alone. No wonder that in his thoughts he spent so much time sitting on her grave, arms folded, with a cigar end. He breathed slowly in and out, 'to keep the whole thing on the rails'. He pulled his pencil stub out of his breast pocket, and wrote something down on the piece of paper he always carried around and called 'my work paper'. He wrote: ' "Arcadia", a poem by Karl Hofmann, age seventy'. That was as far as he'd got.

That was the time I used to sing a lot, like the rest of the family. (Except for Grandfather, who preferred to *think*.) Mother, to protect her skirt, had an apron on. Herr Lange, like Herr Cosimo, no longer came round. Mother opened the window, and let the fresh air in. Under her apron was her pleated skirt, which I used to like a lot. Now Mother stood next to me. She sighed and thought of the death in action of her Hans. She still believed she would find a husband, only now it would have to be someone else. Someone she hadn't met yet. 'And high time too' (Grandmother). While she folded up our clothes, Mother sang to herself. She sang:

*We're singing a song,*
*Our hats fly off.*
*We're singing a song,*
*Our beards fly off . . .*

Or:
*It's unique, it won't come back.*
*It's too beautiful to be true.*
*It happens just once in a lifetime . . .*

Or:
*The first time it hurts, you think*
*You'll never get over it.*
*But little by little, you get used to it . . .*

Or:
*So much can happen*
*In a night in May . . .*

Ever since the Fritsche business, Grandmother had worn black. When she went into town, she wore black, when she went to the baker's, black, black when she lay down on the sofa! Now she went out into the garden in black to pick a lettuce as 'fodder for her herd'. Grandfather was booted and spurred. He had volunteered today, he was going to the 'flicks'. He was going to put on *Ohm Krüger* (1941, with Emil Jannings, Gustav Gründgens and Ferdinand Marian), only he wasn't allowed to talk during it. Emil Jannings played Krüger. At first he's able to preserve the peace, but then the fighting breaks out again. At the beginning he and his Boers are on top, but then the tables are turned once the English Lord Kitchener (Franz Schafheitlin) resorts to the methods of terrorism, poisoning wells, and hauling women and children off to 'concentration camps', where they . . .

241

To avoid having to shave all the time, Grandfather had grown another beard. He had his moustache trainer on, and was muttering into it. I whistled or sang:

*Over the rooftops of the city*
*My song finds its way to you . . .*

Or:
*Sharing an umbrella,*
*You slip your arm in mine . . .*
*Sharing an umbrella,*
*You call me 'Du' for the very first time . . .*

Then the lettuce was ready, our 'rabbit fodder'. The bowl was passed around. I looked at the paper. I read out: 'From the sculptor's studio to the prosthesis workshop. From art to reality.'

That, said Grandmother, helping herself to salad, must be good!

What's a prosthesis?

Something artificial, she said, if you're missing an arm or a leg.

Why?

So we can keep crawling.

Let's eat now, said Mother, Grandfather has to go to work.

Grandmother said: He has to go to the pictures, more like.

# Twelve

On the afternoon of the 24 May 1944, a Sunday, there was a children's matinée performance at the Apollo of the Tobis sound-film *Operetta* (1940, with Willi Forst and Maria Holst). That information comes from an advertisement in the *Limbacher Zeitung* which Mother clipped and saved. I had already seen the film myself, on the Saturday, the 23rd. So what happened subsequently is partly my memory, partly imagined.

There wasn't a children's film on that day. *Operetta* started at half past three, following the newsreel and the patriotic cartoon 'Kohlenklau'. Sunday lunch was over, and the table cleared. *Operetta* was with sound. The lead was Willi Forst, 'the great heartbreaker of the German screen' whose photograph, among many others, was hanging up in Grandfather's collection. (To Grandfather, now seventy-plus, the art of seduction was something practised by actors on the screen.) In a tartan waistcoat, his right foot pushed forward, Willi Forst gazed cheekily out of his still photograph. 'It looks to me like he's singing' (Grandmother). His jacket had small, pointed, now unfashionable and ridiculous-looking lapels. He was good-looking, with a bit of a high forehead.

He looks too critical for me, said Grandmother. Where's his charm?

Well, that's the way God made him, said Grandfather. He

pinned him back on the wall. He was just off to the cinema, 'to his job'.

Outside, some indifferent, forgettable weather or other. Not sunny, not raining, not snowing.

I'll walk you some of the way, I said to Grandfather. I slipped into my shoes. He had his artist's hat on, his stick in his hand. 'So long as I've got that, I feel I can handle whatever . . .' He forgot the rest of it. We walked close together, not speaking. On the corner of the Apollo, without kissing him on the moustache – too often he smelled of onion – I said goodbye, and turned for home.

Wasn't there something else, asked Grandfather.

I said, no.

Well, at least you've had a bit of fresh air, he called after me.

Fresh air, I said, and went on with my own thoughts. I can't remember what they were. From time to time I met someone. Others were sitting in their upstairs windows, waiting for victory to happen. What comes next is made up, at least in part. It's such a long time ago, no one really knows any more. For instance whether Grandfather was already wearing his cardigan, or only got into it in the Apollo . . . . It was later taken off him, and taken to the cleaners. After that it came into my possession. It didn't suit me. Anyway, Grandfather was in his slippers, leather admittedly – 'fake', 'it doesn't matter so much in the afternoon!' In the absence of F. L. Kunze who was 'away defending the Fatherland with a sharpened pencil' (Grandmother), Grandfather was alone with Fräulein Heiske and Herr Leiser. All around him, the excited whispering of 'children aged ten or over', some of whom were only eight or nine, but had put on their brothers' long trousers, and said they were ten. Grandfather turned two blind eyes, 'if not all three'. A lot of noise always. When the noise got to be too much, he covered his ears and shouted: Quiet! or: That's enough of that!

The cinema wasn't full, but when was it ever? For that you

needed to go deep into the past, into an earlier age, said Grandmother. But the film began anyway, and straightaway everyone was completely engrossed by the sequence of events devised by the director W. Forst and his scriptwriter A. Eggebrecht, and represented by the actors Holst, Komar, Schellhammer, Hörbiger, Breuer, Waldau and others. 'Once upon a time, there was and there was not . . .' (F. Schiller). This time it was all about the operetta as such . . . 'For operettas have not always been with us, in fact they are barely a hundred years old' (the programme note). Nor did they fall from the sky either, as they say, Grandfather had explained that morning. He had read that in the programme too. What had contributed to their development had been: the people, actors and actresses, the composer, the lyricists, the male and female singers, and of course the conductor, who held everything together with a strong grip. The story, then, of the operetta conductor, who devised the operetta at a time when it hadn't yet existed, and who, by his art, brought it to immediate flowering. That conductor is Willi Forst, who in the film is called F. Jauner, after the historical original. As a poor musician, F. Jauner meets the famous singer and theatre owner Geistinger or Geislinger. When she asks him for an opinion of her singing, F. Jauner replies candidly: Madam, your singing is no good!

My singing is no good?

That's right! Your singing is no good!

Thereupon Geistinger or Geislinger, who would rather one truth than a hundred flatteries, signs him up for her theatre. The rise of the operetta has begun. Nor is the partnership F. Jauner and Geistinger/Geislinger confined to the artistic plane, rather it extends into the human and private. They fall in love. In spite of the fact that she's a difficult, capricious creature, with more moods and whims than a warthog has warts. And she's arrogant with it. When she leaves for America for four months to introduce the operetta over there in response to public demand, F. Jauner, who stays behind ostensibly to rehearse a new operetta, finds his luck has deserted him. Through his own negligence, the theatre catches fire and burns down. F. Jauner goes to prison for manslaughter of a fat, unlikeable, superfluous wastrel. The triumph of the operetta is under threat. It is only when Geistinger (Geislinger?) returns from America and learns what has happened, and goes to the Kaiser, who has spent many an enjoyable evening in her theatre, to get a pardon for him, that F. Jauner rediscovers his old form. With a brilliantly successful production of the operetta 'The Beggar Student' by K. Millöcker (C. Jürgens), he makes amends for everything he's previously done wrong. 'The players are the Vienna Philharmonic' (programme notes).

And that's about the size of it! Wouldn't you like to go, Grandfather asked Grandmother, having just put on his artist's hat, as he must have done, because no trace of it was ever found. Grandmother would not. She said: Load of rubbish. (As a former resident of Vienna, she also said: 'Farrago'.) And: I don't understand how someone who claims to be grown up can go running off to the cinema at such a time.

You can always go to the cinema, said Grandfather.

There's a few people have to work too, Grandmother had replied.

A man's will is his will, Grandfather had said, and he set off without her. In the film, as in novels and most other forms of lies, the sequence of action is presented in short, memorable chapters or scenes: F. Jauner in the café over an espresso, F. Jauner, lonely and bored, at the marble table in a bar – that was before he had got to know and to love Geistinger – F. Jauner chasing Geistinger down the Ringstrasse, waving a glove she'd dropped, F. Jauner on his knees before Geistinger, F. Jauner at the piano with Geistinger singing, F. Jauner and Geistinger, in tails and ball gown, arm in arm at the operetta ball. F. Jauner, who is on the point of folding her in his arms and kissing her, has a white rose in his buttonhole, Geistinger a red one in the décolletage of her lace dress. Then the actors Forst, Holst, Komar, Schellhammer, Hörbiger, Breuer, Jürgens and many others all take hands and dance and sing together in chorus:

*Oh oh oh, what a ball, this ball*
*Oh oh, what a ball*
*Oh oh oh, this is an operetta ball . . .*

At that point, more or less, the Apollo and everyone in it must have been blown to kingdom come.

# Thirteen

Excerpt from the parish register of the Evangelical-Lutheran Parish of Limbach/Saxony, Stadtkirche, year 1873, page 419, christening no. 164 : Karl Gustav, 5th child, 1st son, born on 23 April 1873 in Limbach, christened on 18 May 1873. Father: Gustav Adolf Hofmann, stocking worker and resident of Limbach. Mother: Anna Luise, née, Lange, from Limbach. Godparents: 1. Clemens Stülpner, Finisher and resident of Limbach, 2. Caroline wife of Leonhard Löbel, manufacturer in Limbach, 3. Otto Naumann, worker and resident of Limbach . . .

# Fourteen

Grandfather was taken to the Limbach cemetery in his packing-crate coffin. He was put in the ground by Pastor Someone-or-other and Grandmother, who, 'out of anger at such a stupid death', hadn't even changed or put on a hat. His grave was the eighth in the fourth row on the left as you go in. 'That's where they laid him, the bastards!' I wasn't there myself. I had a sore throat, an earache, a headache, and a temperature of at least a hundred and four. 'He won't be any better at coping with the world, he's ill again' (Mother). At the funeral, Grandmother was described as looking around in an absent-minded sort of way. She was so full of rage and anger she didn't even cry. She couldn't forgive Grandfather for having lured her away from Vienna, then deceived her over so many years, and finally leaving her so abruptly, without a word of apology for the 'apology of a life' he had afforded her.

I lay in my bed behind our broken window panes, mended with cardboard, surrounded by charred furniture, thinking of naked ladies. I thought about thighs and breasts, and passed the time. Because I wasn't at the funeral, I can't describe it for you. Hardly anyone today could. Oh, the squat and bullet-headed form of my Grandfather, rigid for half a century! Which will by now have turned into something most peculiar in the grave! Was he really, as he liked to think, in the world *for some special purpose*?

Along with the torn-off ticket stubs, the house-key – 'it will outlive all of us' – the Ulm pipe, and the lighter in his cardigan pocket, was the poem 'Arcadia', which he had written, embarrassing, so embarrassing! It starts like this:

> I am just a man
> Who came into the world,
> Wandered about it awhile,
> And will soon leave it, like you . . .
> . . .
> Old sky, old evening, old self . . .

Really I ought to take all the material about Grandfather and Grandmother and Mother and all the other dead people, put it all together and spread it out on a table and, this is what my sense of order tells me, give it some form, so that it amounts to something. I mean, you can't just pour it out unformed at people's feet! But as with all my other 'inventions' (my wife) and the other 'imperishables' (my ironic youngest daughter, Susi): lack of enthusiasm, lack of ideas, the depression of the summer months, the autumn months, the winter months, the hopelessly congested southbound motorway, making a quick getaway impossible, plus headaches, shortage of breath . . . . Grandfather at seventy said: In the beginning was the light. The light was switched off. I stood in front of the screen, all alone. I looked into the audience. There weren't many of them there. I gave the signal *Go!* He said: In all the films of that time, even if they played indoors, it rained. That was because the films had been damaged by the fingers of the projectionists. We lined the gate with black velvet to slow the film. Even that damaged it. Also, they got old and worn. Grandfather took me by the hand. He said: It wasn't the shaking projection that made everything tremble. Nor was it people's breathing. It was the heartbeat of the man who was supervising everything, the film explainer's, mine.